AND THE[illegible]

Deborah Grabien is the [illegible] y novels: *Eyes in the Fire*, *Fire Queen*, and *Plainsong*. She lives in San Francisco with her husband and daughter.

Also by Deborah Grabien in Pan Books

PLAINSONG

DEBORAH GRABIEN

And Then Put Out The Light

PAN BOOKS
LONDON, SYDNEY AND AUCKLAND

First published 1993 by Pan Books Limited

a division of Pan Macmillan Publishers Limited
Cavaye Place London SW10 9PG
and Basingstoke

Associated companies throughout the world

ISBN 0 330 32868 9

1 3 5 7 9 8 6 4 2

A CIP catalogue record for this book is available from the British Library

Phototypeset by Intype, London
Printed by Cox & Wyman Ltd, Reading, Berks

For Alice and Jean and both
Dees; and for Joanna,
the golden child

And for Elizabeth Barnett

All chapter heading quotations are from the works of Edna St Vincent Millay

CHAPTER ONE

Life must go on:
I forget just why.

(from 'Lament')

On a dull, damp Hallowe'en, Emily Moon-Bourne celebrated her thirty-eighth birthday and formally bid farewell to her thirteen-year marriage by acquiring a half a million dollars from the husband who had run off with another woman.

Emily, who was unused to noticing contrasts not directly related to her sculpting, would have been hard put to describe her own emotions. As it happened, there was no one left to question her. She was not willing, at this tricky point in her life, to identify the hurts too closely, especially to herself. Still, what reactions there were, were valid.

Anger, well hidden behind a mask of irony, was certainly present; it is neither flattering nor inspiriting to have your dull and unimaginative husband run off with a cuddly armful twenty years his junior. Nor could Emily deny a mixture of relief and disbelief at the sheer size of the settlement. Gareth Bourne had paid dearly for the privilege of indulging in his midlife aberration. But there were other things, some of them uncomplimentary and some of them actively bruising, that she was unprepared to admit even to herself. Spite, for instance. She couldn't remember the last time she had so enjoyed being spiteful.

Two things were definitely absent from this ill-defined emotional stew: grief and surprise. Within three years of marrying a rising corporate lawyer, Emily had been idly wondering why in hell they'd ever gotten married. For the past ten years, she had been wondering with increasing intensity why in hell they bothered to stay married.

Now, with the memory of her marriage rapidly fading and the pains and petty humiliations of the divorce fresh in her mind, she sat across the desk from a very respectful bank manager, listening with only half her mind to his explanation as to why five separate accounts would insure her money more completely than a single account could do. She had noticed that the bank, as befitted a public place on Hallowe'en, was bedecked in black and orange crêpe paper; peering myopically at her from a corner of the bank manager's desk was a jack-o'-lantern, carved with ragged teeth and holding an unlit candle in its scooped-out depths. The manager himself bore an uncanny resemblance to his vegetable companion, being short, round and possessed of spectacularly uneven teeth.

'. . . up to one hundred thousand dollars,' the living pumpkin face told her earnestly. 'That's per account, of course. You see, the law is designed . . .'

He droned on, his tone hovering between instructional and ingratiating. Emily smiled and nodded, keeping her hands folded in her lap. She disliked her hands, finding them even uglicr and more ungainly than the rest of her nearly six-foot frame. That they were spectacularly able translators of her talent did nothing to mitigate the fact that she privately considered them the hands of a large ape. They were strong and thick-boned, with hard knuckles and wide white crescents where nail met skin. Emily kept the thick nails short, as much to downplay them as because her work as a sculptress required it.

'. . . could draw on whatever funds you needed . . .'

'Yes,' Emily said, aware that the heavy black sweater she wore was in direct and uncomfortable conflict with the bank's central heating. The room seemed overly warm to her, and she felt a damp chilly sweat break out on her brow and beneath her breasts. 'Yes, yes.'

Claustrophobia swept over her, and she pushed it resolutely away. She longed passionately for a cigarette, but the no-smoking-please attitude in this corporate temple of Mammon, albeit unspoken, was almost tangible. She breathed deeply, willing the clammy chill away. 'I see, yes, thank you. I understand about FDIC insurance. Tell me, do you have banking partners in Europe?'

'Partners?' The little man stared at her, his lips closing momentarily over the nightmare teeth. 'I'm not sure I understand, Ms Moon-Bourne.'

'Well, correspondents, affiliates. I don't know the right word . . . banks that you do business with in other countries. I mean, if I wanted to arrange a transfer of funds to myself in, say, Rome or Athens or London, are there banks there where you could wire me my money, or open temporary accounts for me? Because I do know that you can only bring so much currency into a foreign country at one time.'

His face relaxed. 'Ah, I see. You're considering travel. Yes, we have correspondent banking organizations in every major city in Europe. Barclays Bank in England, the Crédit Lyonnaise in France. We deal with Asia, too, modern relations with the East being what they are. Our foreign exchange section would be glad to arrange one-off wire transfers, or we could open accounts in any city you'd like.'

Pompous little geek, isn't he?

She unfolded her hands, ignoring the voice in her head. The inner voice, her constant companion for as long as she could remember, was usually right. It was small and hard and usually without passion, but it had the uncomfortable habit of speaking at bad times. Shut up, she told it firmly. Pompous he may be, but he's doing his job and doing it well. Besides, I want the information.

When she gratefully escaped an hour later, she possessed four new accounts and a certificate showing her a sole owner of a hundred-thousand-dollar CD account, tax free until maturity, whatever that meant. She also had five thousand dollars' worth of traveller's cheques in drachmas.

As she exited the bank, hesitating about what to do next, she felt a tap on her shoulder from behind. Stepping out of the way, murmuring an awkward apology, she found herself staring at a beautiful female body, immaculate in a tailored white linen suit and a pair of black pumps. From one perfectly manicured hand dangled a leather briefcase. Surmounting this classic ensemble was the large head of a pig, tusked and bristling with tufts of stiff hair.

For a moment frozen in time, Emily stared into the hideous leering face. There was something about this encounter that was actively insulting; it was as if all the miseries of marriage and divorce had materialized before her, taunting and ugly. Bosch, she thought dizzily, and knew that she was an instant away from screaming. Bosch, or Dali. Surrealism. Nightmare time.

'I beg your pardon,' thc pig's hcad said politely, and strode off into the street, her briefcase swinging at her side. The little voice in Emily's mind spoke again, scathing but reassuring.

A mask, idiot. Only a mask. Now, isn't that a nice friendly way to start out on your magical mystery tour?

Emily remembered that today was Hallowe'en. She let

her breath out, lighting the longed for cigarette with fingers that shook. Well, she thought concretely, well. Happy birthday, Emily dearest. You need coffee. At the very least, you need coffee. After all, who deserves it more than you do?

How do you know when a marriage is in trouble?

There are any number of ways, for any number of people; a gnawing discontent suddenly ripening into virulence, a fad that becomes an obsession, finding your spouse in bed with someone or something else. For Emily, the first major indication had come not with a cataclysm but with a simple realization, a tiny warning of shoals to come.

Emily's studio was a small, one-roomed cottage that sat at the foot of the Bournes' garden. It was light, and airy, and just large enough for the soaring creatures she carved. Emily was not particularly tidy – a young college boy came in twice weekly and cleaned the house for her – but every so often, if her mood permitted, she would notice that the studio was knee-deep in wood chips, making it hard to breathe.

Cleaning out her studio one bleak winter day, she had come across a two-year-old woman's magazine, probably left there by her agent or one of her rare guests. Taking a cigarette break from her virtuous tidying, she had skimmed over the magazine, snorting at the clothes, raising her eyebrows at the inane articles ('Is your man anal compulsive?' 'What to do when the honey in your life is a chaser').

And then she had found the quiz.

It was a common enough thing, found in every magazine of the genre. 'Is the magic gone? Are you really meant for one another? Test your compatibility and see.' She scanned it, idly at first, then with an increasing curiosity to know how Gary would do on this bit of fluff. The Lord only knew, the questions were puerile enough to appeal to him. When she had finished sweeping up splinters and carefully rearranging her tools, she wandered up the garden path to the house with the magazine in her jacket pocket.

After dinner, as Gary was settling in for a long evening's work on a legal brief in his study, Emily followed him. This in itself was unusual; she rarely entered his study, disliking the dry masculine feel of it, uncomfortable with the shelves of legal tomes and the hunting prints. She had the magazine with her.

'Look at this thing, will you? I didn't know people actually got paid to write this stuff.'

He glanced at the quiz, his mouth tightening in a way that had become habitual with him. Gary was handsome in a rather pedestrian way, with clean features that, as he grudgingly climbed past his mid-forties, had begun their inevitable smudge into middle-aged puffiness. 'Oh, my God. You want me to take a quiz? Out of a woman's magazine? Emily, you're joking.'

Well, at least he'd brought it up. 'I'm curious, Gary. Let's take it. The results could be amusing.'

'Are you out of your mind? I've got to be in court with Dodie – Sue Dodieri – at one thirty tomorrow on the diet-food case, and I told her I'd have the brief ready. I've got a good twelve pages to do on it, and I don't have time for this childish crap.'

'Then make time.' She rarely spoke sharply; the cunning and energy necessary for argument with a lawyer were husbanded for times when she really wanted something from him. She did not stop to question herself as to why she had reacted so strongly; perhaps it was that casual

'Dodie' he had thrown out, or his even quicker correction of the name.

Her tone had its effect; Gary sighed, and laid down his casebook. 'All right, all right, anything for peace in the valley. How does the damned thing work?'

Restraining a sudden, inexplicable desire to hit him, she explained it patiently. 'We each take a piece of paper and a pencil. I read the questions, and we both put down an honest answer. Some of the questions are multiple choice, some aren't. There's a little summing-up thing that scores your compatibility factor when you've finished. Ready?'

They took the test, Gary with scarcely concealed impatience, Emily with a determination worthy of a greater endeavour. The questions rolled on, thirty of them. Are you afraid of showing your feelings? Are you a thinking or a feeling type? Is your attitude toward infidelity best described as *a*) tolerant, *b*) intolerant, or *c*) indifferent? Name the three traits you value most in a relationship.

They came to question nineteen, Gary by this time frankly hankering after his legal pad and only too obviously in a mounting rage. Emily looked down at the magazine, and read the question aloud.

'Nineteen,' she said. 'Write down a single word that best describes your partner's personality, emotional capacity or salient emotional characteristics.'

Tight-assed.

For a moment, completely appalled, Emily thought she had spoken aloud. Her pale pink-toned skin, legacy of her Swedish mother, flushed into vivid heat; the black eyes that had come from her Cherokee father widened into bottomless pits, olives with ebony centres.

Gary stared at her. 'What in hell's the matter with you, Emily? You see a ghost or something?'

Tight-assed.

It was true. There was no better word to describe him. She looked down at him, at the physique so carefully preserved by racquetball and saunas; it was showing the first signs of droop around the middle, and he spent half his time sucking in his gut to hide it. She looked at the manicured nails that were so much more shiny than her own. She looked at the stiff set of his shoulders, at his handsome empty face, at the tiny bald spot over which his hair was so carefully brushed. The strength and simplicity of the revelation was breathtaking.

She did not, this time, tell the little voice in her head to shut up. The little voice had answered the question with economy and brutal honesty, just as the magazine asked.

'Emily?' The pendulous, articulated lawyer's voice held an edge of sarcasm. 'Did you want to finish this idiocy, or can I get back to the real world?'

Tight-assed, tight-assed, tight-assed.

Without a word, she dropped the magazine in his lacquered wood wastebasket, picked up her pad and walked out of the room. When she had let herself out of the house and gained the safety of her studio, she sat down and tried to decide whether she wanted to laugh or cry.

After that, the end was inevitable. Emily, standing in court and acutely aware of her own humiliation, convinced herself that Gary had taken the first action only because she had been too lazy to do it herself.

It had not come at once, of course; such things never do. They had gone on, the handsome lawyer and the rawboned sculptress, for another six months. Gary spent most of his waking hours doing what he had always done, which involved practising law, driving his BMW and playing racquetball with others of his kind. The only apparent change came with the longer working hours, coming home from the office long after midnight.

Emily, during that static half-year, avoided thinking about the real world by immersing herself in her own work; she completed three carved and colour-washed statuettes, an amazing output in so short a time for one who hand carves from large blocks of wood. Two of them were birds in flight, a crow and an owl. These, done on commission from a state university, were technically perfect. While pleasing the customer, they were too harmless to please their creator.

The third statue was far less benign. It was a wasp, feral and evil, carved to the very edge of parody from a single piece of glossy koa wood. Its powerful wings arched upward for a kill; it bore a jutting stinger that was thick and brutal as a rapist's erection. It spoke to the senses, almost too powerfully, and Emily wondered what dark corner of her spirit had birthed it. Showing at a local gallery, the hideous creature had sold immediately to an anonymous buyer, despite its steep price.

On the fourth of July, when the placid neighbourhood was hideous with the shrieks of children and riddled with exploding fireworks, Gareth Bourne laid his barbecue tools down with a sudden air of decision and dropped his bomb.

Sitting in a Financial District coffee shop so many months later, Emily stubbed out her cigarette and stared at the menu. She had been doodling on it, a lifelong habit of hers. She had not carved, or even sketched, a human face since her seventeenth year, because pictures of the human face brought back pain. But she had sketched one now; Gary's face stared back at her from under her pencil, suspicious and self-satisfied. His body was a familiar wasp's body, complete with stinger.

Christ, she thought bleakly, my Freudian slip is showing with a vengeance. With that thought, the Independence Day barbecue came flooding back to her, in all its sickness and imbecility. It had been a perfect setting for the end of a marriage, silly, ritualistic, as ultimately American as the distorting mirrors at a carnival.

'Emily. I want to talk about something.'

'Sure.' He wore an apron that told the observer to kiss the cook, and two hamburger patties sizzled on the grill. In the next yard, the yuppies Emily had studiously avoided since their arrival were talking about boats. 'What's up?'

'I want to start a family.'

She stared at him. She had been wearing loose cotton pants and espadrilles, she remembered. In the long silence following Gary's announcement, several small things had declared themselves; a roman candle going off a few backyards away, the hiss and smell of the cooking meat, the whining conversation of the yuppies next door. Eventually she found her voice.

'You're joking.'

'I am not joking. I am perfectly serious.'

'*Serious?*' Emily unclenched her fists. 'Gary, get real. I know that's a lot to ask of a lawyer, but give it a shot, just this one time. The facts, Perry Mason, are these. You're in your mid-forties. I'm in my late thirties. When we got married, two or three life sentences ago, we agreed that neither of us wanted to be parents, period, finis, end of discussion. Remember?'

'Of course I remember.' There was a strange look on his face, a compound of obstinacy and something else that was less familiar. Emily, incredulous through her detachment, examined it closely and identified it as fear. Gary? The great lawyer, frightened of something? What in hell was going on here? 'I've changed my mind.'

The voices floated in from the next yard, an ironic counterpoint. 'And so I told the guy, if that cheap anchor can't be replaced, I'm demanding my money back under the lemon law . . .'

The conversation touched Emily's ears and died, ignored. She was staring at her husband in disbelief. 'Gary, what in hell's got into you? Do you really think I'm going to have a first child at nearly forty because you're on some macho ego thing and you want to see the famous Bourne birthmark genetically imprinted on a baby's ass?'

She almost, but not quite, regretted that taunting remark; Gary was highly touchy on the subject of the red birthmark that adorned his left buttock. For a split second she thought he was going to take a swing at her. His breathing shortened, his fists clenched; even his thinning hair seemed to bristle. She held her ground, watchful and amazed, feeling completely unreal. Anything was possible, she had to remember that. If he had gone so totally around the bend that he wanted to change diapers at his age, anything was possible.

As she watched, he got control of himself; it was apparently not done without difficulty. And the struggle for self-discipline had unleashed something, the naked rage on his face transmuting into something even more unpleasant. His mouth pursed into a vicious grin of triumph.

'And who said, my dear, that I was considering having a family with you?'

('I would have preferred a bigger engine, I mean it's a big boat, but the spars . . .')

There it was, as simple as that. She looked back over the past months, to the occasional casual mention of the young associate he worked with and his increased absences at night. Absurdly calm, she wondered at her own blindness.

You dumb bitch. Don't act surprised. You must have known something was up.

Stuff it, she told the little voice. Just stuff it. If you're so damned helpful, why didn't you pipe in with the info months ago? 'Ah. Sue Dodieri, I presume?'

'How did you know that?' His voice was a whiplash. 'Have you been spying on me, on us? Did you – did you hire a detective?'

'Why the hell should I tell you anything, you bastard?' The world was moving under her now, but her voice was calm, acidic, even amused. She felt as though it came from anywhere but inside her, so false a reality did it reflect. 'Sue Dodieri. The woman, so called, who actually prefers to be known as Dodie. Small and blond and cute as a button. Well, well. So she wants to have little Garys with you, does she, *Daddy*? She wants to see you taking Birthmark Junior to Little League games at age fifty-eight. Now, isn't that just too sweet? God, you're a moron, Gary. I mean, I always suspected it, but—'

'Stop it.' He was breathing heavily. 'Just stop it, Emily.'

'How old is the little idiot, anyway? Nineteen, twenty maybe?'

'She's twenty-six. And don't call her an idiot. She's twice the woman you are, even if she is half your age.'

'Not half my age, Gary,' she said immediately, and was reminded of a fencing match she had watched in college; parry, riposte, and lunge. 'Don't you mean half your age?'

('. . . and now the damned harbour master is being a jerk about me bringing the dog down there. He claims poor old Towser is crapping on the pier. I mean, just who pays for the dockage, anyway . . . ')

'Emily.' He was clutching the sides of the barbecue now, his hands wrapped tight around the wooden handles. *Kiss the cook, kiss the cook, kiss the cook*. 'If you don't contest it, let it go right through, I'll give you whatever you want, within reason. You can have the house, the car, I don't give a damn. But if you fight it . . .' His voice trailed off, understanding that he had betrayed himself.

'She's pregnant, isn't she?' The answer was plain on Gary's panic-stricken face, and Emily was very close to nausea now. 'Already has an itty-bitty bun baking in the oven, does she? Well, she may not be too bright, but she's fertile, apparently. Or maybe she's brighter than I gave her credit for.' She shook her head, amazed as much by her own rage as by her capacity for distant enjoyment of it. The rage was hot, and real, and it came from someplace valid. 'My God. A spiritual bankrupt in his forties and a female who calls herself Dodie. Two people less fit to reproduce I can hardly begin to imagine. This ought to be one spectacular little aborigine you two end up with. Where did you do it, Gary, you and Snow White? On your desk? In the judge's chambers? Or was it in my lady's chamber, no doubt complete with a canopy bed trimmed with lace and pictures of Bambi? Come on, honey, clue me in. Call it voyeurism, or just plain academic curiosity.'

'You gold-plated bitch!' He took a step towards her, but she flung a hand out and he stopped. There was a smile on her face, a smile that had never before sat there and of which she was unaware. He was immobile before its darkness and strength.

'I'm not gold-plated yet, but I will be when I'm done with you. Trust me for that, sweetie. And by the way, *Daddy*, your hamburger's burning. Maybe you ought to seriously think about flipping your damned meat.'

He turned the barbecue over, sending mesquite-flavoured charcoal and hamburger patties flying; they hit the flagstones with dull sounds and lay there. The conversation about boats ceased abruptly. Emily, still smiling, turned on her heel and walked down the garden path to her studio.

'Can I get you some more coffee?'

The past receded, taking the barbecue and the bank and the memory of Dodie and the smelly blue bundle of noise in her arms as they left the final hearing with it. Reality was a coffee shop with a fancy espresso machine behind the counter and a pile of fresh pastries under a plastic dome. Emily glanced up at the waitress, and from somewhere managed a smile.

'Yes, please. A *café au lait* this time, I'm splurging. Could you sprinkle some chocolate on it?'

'Cinnamon too, if you'd like. How about something to eat with that?'

'No, thank you.' It had been weeks, Emily suddenly realized, since she had really tasted anything. Food had become a distasteful necessity that she avoided whenever possible; all of her clothes had become loose, and her big-boned frame seemed larger and more ungainly than ever. 'I'm not hungry.'

'Well, if you're sure.' The waitress hesitated, looking down at her. Emily, forcing her fingers to relinquish the pencil in her hands, became aware that the girl had something to say to her. She lifted her head, actually noticing the girl's face, and was surprised by its liveliness; the child was barely twenty, but she had an air of self-containment that was pleasing and oddly comforting.

'Excuse me, but you look awfully familiar. Aren't you Emily Moon-Bourne, the sculptress? The woman who's famous for only carving things that fly?'

As a balm to the ego, nature could scarcely have delivered up anything better. Emily, who had never before been publicly recognized, felt a sting of tears behind her eyes; she stared up at the waitress, bemused and touched. 'Well, I don't know about famous, but I'm definitely Emily Moon-Bourne. How on earth . . . ?'

'It was that article,' the girl said eagerly. 'The one in *Western Arts* magazine about five months ago. I'm an art student, drawing and painting. I love sculpture, but I can't do it. I've got this weird sense of line, and I seem to see everything in colour. I went to your showing at the Carlson Gallery after I read the article. Amazing stuff. I loved the hummingbird and the hawks. I don't know about that wasp thing, though. To tell you the truth, it gave me the creeps.' Apparently feeling that Emily might find this less than flattering, she added hastily, 'Not that it wasn't amazing. It was just . . .'

Emily laughed. 'I know what you mean. It gave me the creeps, too. In fact, it was *supposed* to give you the creeps. That's its job.'

The waitress glanced down at the menu, catching sight of Emily's doodling, and her face changed. 'Oh, wow. Would you be an absolute sweetie and autograph this for me? I mean, if you didn't want to take it with you.'

'Not at all.' Gary glared up at her, his wasp's stinger seeming to quiver. Take it with her? Having just got rid of Gary for good, the last thing she wanted was to take it with her. 'This is just a spiteful little doodle, anyway. Are you sure you'd really like it?'

'You bet I would.' The waitress watched her sign her name to the menu, and then seemed to fully see what Emily had drawn. 'Jesus!'

'I warned you it was spiteful, didn't I? Definite shades of the wasp thing.' The cold constricting band around Emily's heart had eased; there is nothing like honest adulation to soothe the spirit. 'In fact, it's almost as spiteful as it is ugly. Are you sure you want this much concentrated malice flapping around your apartment at night?'

The girl, still staring at Gary with horrified fascination, gave a nervous giggle and began to move away. 'My God, isn't he nasty! And what a smug, self-satisfied little face he's got! He must have really pissed you off, whoever he is. Malice is the word, all right. But don't worry, he won't be doing any flapping. He'll be safely under glass, because as soon as I get out of here I'm taking him off to be framed.'

Emily grinned at her, the first untainted grin she had managed to produce since the meat patties hit the flagstones. She thought of Gary, imprisoned like a tiny homunculus and beating wildly against glass for eternity, his voice high and shrill and piping. 'Well, that's appropriate. I framed the original to the tune of half a million dollars. Maybe you ought to take this to the cleaners. Now, that would really match what I did.'

The girl, clutching the precious menu under one arm, turned back and gave Emily a brief look; it was amused, and conspiratorial, and completely female in the depths of its awareness. 'If the son of a bitch was half the creep he looks here, he had it coming. The coffee's on the house, by the way, I wouldn't dream of charging you.' She hesitated, then added rather shyly, 'Can I ask . . . are you working on anything new right now?'

'Yes,' Emily said immediately. Five minutes ago, wrestling with memory, she had had no idea of what happened next. But, with the girl's question, the pictures came strongly into her mind; an emptied-out studio, a house waiting to be sold to strangers, drachmas in the zippered compartment of her bag. She had procured that strangely named foreign money with no clear idea in mind, no plan, no special desire.

But the encounter with the waitress had pulled a trigger somewhere. Gary was gone, what pitiful human essence he possessed excised and imprisoned under glass in a student's apartment. He was out of Emily's life, reduced to a drawing on a menu, and Emily, for perhaps the first time in her life, was free. She spoke incisively.

'To tell you the truth, I'm working on spending that half-million I just mentioned. I think I'll start in Greece; after all, everything else seems to have started there. It's been really nice talking with you, you've done me a lot of good. And, by the way, I've changed my mind. I think I'm hungry after all. Could I have a cheese Danish and an egg-salad sandwich with that?'

CHAPTER TWO

Clutching at the wrist of Venture with a cold
Hand, aiming to fall in with him, companion
Of the old as of the new.

(from 'Few Come This Way')

After all the petty annoyances that accompany extended travel had been dealt with, it occurred to Emily that she had, after all, chosen Greece for a sensible reason. That the reason was subconscious made no odds; where else, after all, would a sculptor who had broken her life go but to the cradle, the womb, of art?

She arrived at Athens airport in a weeping downpour that suited her mood to perfection. The flight had been long, bumpy and boring, an uneasy mixture of mannerless small children running in the aisles and strange, indigestible plates of airline food.

The longer journeys of Emily's life had always been by way of American highways. Her sense of travel, therefore, was firmly rooted in memories of buses that slid easily past endless farms, cars that could be pulled into motel parking lots, legs that could be stretched and moved while cheerful waitresses prepared bacon and eggs. She had never before flown for so many hours, and this first attempt nearly convinced her that travel was a bad idea.

This was a new experience, one of claustrophohic misery and indigestion. Her senses were confused and battered and a brilliantly sunny day would have seemed in hideous taste at best and a personal affront at worst.

But Nikos, the proprietor of her taverna, was friendly and expansive. The poor lady, so tired from her journey, must have something to revive her. He rounded on his wife, who was tiny and silent, and burst into a sharp-sounding command. He then showed her to her room, which was bright and comfortable. As she lay stretched out on her bed, breathing deeply and wiggling her toes, Nikos' wife brought her a cup of hot tea, depositing it on the night stand with lowered eyes and a soft murmur. By sunset of that first night, the Athenian sky had cleared to supernatural radiance.

Cautiously, grudgingly, Emily began to believe that enjoyment might be possible. Coffee was available, good coffee, the kind that puts heart into whoever drinks it, and the food of Greece was a new joy. After she had stretched her neck upwards to see the Acropolis flaunting a corona of red-gold light, she decided that travel was broadening, and that planes were a necessary evil endurable for the sake of wonder. Greece would take her to its bosom, after all.

For the first week, Emily simply wallowed. She went to museums and to the Parthenon; she discovered feta cheese and souvlaki and rolled pastries that were meat and onions wrapped in flaky filo dough. She browsed in the shops and markets. Although Nikos assured her that the sun was a weak shadow of what it would be in summer, her pale face took what there was and darkened to a less fishlike tint.

And she saw things, things about which she had read and wondered since first laying hands to wood. She saw marble that had been given tendon and flesh, cold white smiles imprinted against the face of an eternity that could not touch them, carved feet that rose from blocks of dappled stone.. Everything, from the classical poses to the painted urns, had an odd familiarity.

All of this she saw, but little else. Sometimes the men in the streets, taxi drivers and workmen, would whistle or ogle at her; these episodes went unnoticed, and her lack of interest was so clear, even to those stallions of a warm climate, that the whistles would die half-way through in a kind of uneasy annoyance.

The weather was less brightly edged than she had expected of Greece, and colder as well. She had brought few clothes with her, sensibly planning to buy the bulk of them as she went along; what she had brought was designed for spring and summer. As a result, she was totally unequipped for cold weather, suffering from the delusion of all sedentary North Americans, that the islands where burning Sappho sang never dropped below eighty degrees. For a few days she dodged moving vehicles and took pictures of statuary with a streaming headcold. In the end, vaguely resentful, she bought a sheepskin jacket and some vitamins.

By the time the cold had subsided into a residual stuffy head, Emily had decided that she was tired of the ceaseless energy that was such a hallmark of Athens. She rented a car, an old Ford, and drove out of Athens, north-east towards Delphi and Helikon.

It was on this drive that she came out of her self-enforced abstraction long enough to admit something to herself. She had met with nothing but kindness, the people were helpful and hospitable and remarkably vital, but she was uneasy. As she dawdled along the roads, vaguely marvelling at the contrasts between the modern and ancient worlds, Emily came to realize that something about the so-called cradle of democracy was worrying her.

It took a long walk and a small incident in the hills above Delphi to reveal what the problem was.

She had gone out early, with bottled water and some goat cheese wrapped in muslin to eat. She had already eaten an amazing amount of fresh bread, pressed upon her by the wife of the hotel keeper, a weather-beaten woman who rarely raised her eyes. The morning was blue and gold, heartbreakingly clear, with the promise of glory to come. The paths were empty, and the hills were slightly speckled with rime.

She had not gone more than a half-mile before coming to the conclusion that she had worn absolutely the worst shoes she possessed for such a venture, a pair of slick-soled Italian leathers with a small heel. This conclusion was drastically confirmed when she put her foot down on a small rock, twisted her ankle, and felt the jerk of the heel parting company with the rest of the shoe. She sat down hard, feeling the dew soak with relentless immediacy into her skin.

'Damn.' The hills took her voice and echoed it back at her. Even distracted and discomfited, something about this endless repetition fascinated her; despite the sense of dislocation which had been her constant companion since the barbecue, she had already noticed that something in the Grecian air inclined people toward performance. Well, she thought, why not? I'm human, aren't I, and this is Greece, isn't it, even if I can't speak Greek? Encouraged by her complete solitude and the unlikelihood of anyone overhearing, she raised her voice to a strong, theatrical pitch. 'I said, *damn*!'

This time she was answered, not only by the echo but by the bleating of goats. Startled and resentful, she struggled to her feet and waited.

The goats came first, six of them; they were small and

lean and looked, to Emily's inexperienced eye, to be very frisky indeed. Christ, she thought, as she balanced precariously on her one good shoe, just what I need. Please don't let them frisk all over me.

'*Kyria*? You have hurt yourself?'

The man who followed the goats was of that particular Grecian variety, all dark eyes and crisp curling hair that seemed to stay black for ever; he might have been anything from twenty to seventy. Oh well, she thought grimly, at least he speaks some English. Feeling like an idiot, she gestured with her damaged shoe.

'I'm afraid so,' she said apologetically. 'I wore the wrong shoes for a mountain walk, and my shoe has . . . has . . .'

'Expired.' He gave her a broad smile, following it immediately with a sympathetic clucking. 'It is a shame about your shoe. But you have not hurt yourself? Your ankle, maybe?'

'Oh, no, I think my ankle's all right.' She flexed it gingerly. 'It's a bit sore, that's all, and I don't really think that I want to put my weight on it just yet. I think it'll be all right. But I don't know how I'm going to walk a half mile down the hill in these shoes.'

'It is a mountain, not a hill. As for walking down, nothing could be easier.' The dazzling smile flashed again; it was genuine, and beautiful, and for some reason almost unbearably annoying. Maybe it's because he's so blatantly virile, she thought. 'My wife makes shoes for the tourists, little cloth shoes with hemp bottoms. They sell them at the shoe places, in the town. She can provide you with a pair, and you will be able to walk wherever you choose.'

'Espadrilles?' Her mood lightened. 'Oh, perfect. Would she sell me a pair? Are they expensive? I'm – I'm afraid I didn't bring much money with me, but I could bring it up to you later.'

But this, it seemed, was unacceptable; he was genuinely appalled by the idea. The lady was in trouble, a visitor to their country, and what decent person would think of taking her money at such a time? And she must come back to his home and have a glass of lemon peppermint drink, while his wife found shoes that were of the correct size. It was very close by, and if she would just lean on his arm . . .

Emily did, not without another stab of irritation at his easy strength and a fleeting apprehension that she had, with her customary lousy luck, fallen lame and wounded into the clutches of the Boston Strangler of the Delphic oracle. But her fears were groundless; he had spoken true on all counts. The cottage was there, small and bright and immaculately clean. His wife opened the door, standing wordlessly aside so that Emily might enter. And Emily, easing into a wooden chair and offering thanks for a cold glass of something that tasted of the gods, looked into the woman's eyes and, with a pristine clarity of mind that was utterly alien to her, understood what had been worrying her about Greece.

It's your mother. Dear God in heaven, it's Mom.

It was simple, and true. Her mother's eyes peered back at her, set deeply into a tired face lined with premature age. The eyes were Grecian black instead of Swedish blue, it was true, and without any sign of the killing alcoholic haze that had put the milky blankness into those once-bright irises. But everything else that had marked her mother as a stereotypical wreck of a woman was there. There was defeat, and resignation, and a deep-rooted well of something that Emily, who had seen that look for too many years, immediately identified as the subservience of one too tired, too internally broken by life and by the vagaries of simple physical survival, to give battle.

Nikos' wife, Emily thought, the woman back at the

hotel in Delphi. This one. The same cloth, the same pattern, eyes that drop and fall and die away from you. Like my mother, my mother, my mother . . .

She rose abruptly from her chair.

'The shoes,' she said strongly, too loudly, forcing a smile that sat badly on her face. Her heart was beating strongly, irregularly; surely they must hear it pounding, these people. 'Really, it's so kind of you, but I would feel better if you would let me buy them. I was going to buy a few pairs in the town today, and they'd probably be ones you made anyway . . .'

The man opened his mouth to protest. Astonishingly, his wife interrupted him..

'Of course, *Kyria*.' She was staring into Emily's eyes with complete comprehension, understanding the revulsion if not the cause. She named a price only slightly lower than what was being charged by the shops. Her husband said something in Greek, his expressive face dark and angry, and the woman rounded on him.

'No,' she said coldly. 'Let her pay. The shoes will fit her better if she does what seems right to her.'

The espadrilles were well made and comfortable. Emily shook hands with the woman and said goodbye, aware that she was trembling and consumed by a desire to run. She heard her own thanks, and knew that her voice was unnaturally loud and her words effusive. The man, his hospitality spurned, stood in the centre of the room, averting his face from the women. His wife accompanied Emily to the door.

'Goodbye, *Kyria*,' she said and added, in a voice so soft that Emily had to strain to catch the words, 'Do not mind so much. It cannot touch you, after all. We must live with what we are, good or bad, for any other way is unknown to us. Our lives are as they have been since the sun first rose. That is the way of Greece.'

Then the door was quickly shut and the cottage had swallowed her. Emily went quickly back to the path, followed by birdsong and the bleating of the goats and a nightmarish sensation of complete helplessness in the face of a tradition that had become an ultimate reality. The hills towered above her, watchful and immortal, and if the walking gods saw her tears of memory they made no sign. Two hours later, she had checked out of her hotel and was driving, too quickly for safety, back towards Athens.

The next afternoon, after a mad scramble for tickets and currency exchange, she landed in Rome.

Memory.

Emily sat on a grassy slope on the Palatine Hill in a state of numb exhaustion eating, of all things, cold squid. She had no idea of what she ate, merely having asked the clerk at her pensione to pack her a breakfast basket. She munched her way steadily through the rubbery thing, needing the fuel it provided, not tasting it. She sat on a red-checked cloth, which kept the moisture in the grass from coming through to her; a very chilly night had become a lovely morning, a picture-book morning, soft clouds scudding across a Raphael sky. The city sparkled below her, the monuments tiny and perfect. It was not yet nine, and in the timeless distance at her feet Rome was waking up.

Emily saw none of this. She had lain nearly sleepless in her comfortable bed at the Pensione Marco, the ghastly treadmill of her thoughts irritatingly punctuated by pigeons and motorcycles and voices in the distance. Her thoughts were uncontrolled as only the thoughts of one who has avoided thinking for too long a time can be. The few realities of her own life that had come to her since the barbecue had been of the divorce, and those had been resolutely and violently pushed away.

Now, with a pair of tired black eyes and a lined face, she had been invaded, taken over, by a ghost. Try as she would, the door of memory would not close completely, and the insistent shadow slipped through to her, taking uncanny flesh in the darkness of a room in a strange city. There was nothing to do but cope with it. And she had a starting place, after all; the ghost had a name.

Kirstin Lindstrom Moon.

She had been a tiny woman, unusually small for pure Scandinavian stock, barely cresting five feet; wherever Emily's nearly six-foot height had come from, it had not been bequeathed to her by either parent. To Emily, a gangly teenager towering over her mother and topping her father by a good five inches, Kirstin had always looked light and insubstantial, a small blonde bird; she had seemed as frail and delicate as a china toy.

Define frail, why don't you? Would you really call her frail, I mean, considering everything?

'No.' Emily spoke softly into the night, answering the voice in her mind. Her mother had not, after all, been frail; it was true that she had given up the unequal struggle even before Emily's birth, joining her silent, embittered husband's personal hell by way of the bottle, but she had not, by any normal definition, been frail.

Lifeless is the word you want, sweetie. Lifeless as in having no life. Let's be realistic.

Emily turned on her pillows, staring at her window. She had left the curtains open, wanting at least the comfort of moonlight during what she had known with certainty would be a long, wretched progression of witching hours. Now she considered the definition. Lifeless, as in having no life? Yes, that much was true. But Kirstin had been a survivor, a physical survivor, as the spiritually or emotionally defeated so often are.

The ghost took shape, gaining substance, forcing Emily to look at it. A diminutive woman, bird-boned and quiet, with sad empty eyes and a meaningless smile and hands that trembled. A woman who would occasionally laugh at nothing, or at things known only to herself. A woman who, if she had never shown real affection or interest, had never shown cruelty or violence either.

Except once.

Emily's mind moved back, sketching the details with great clarity; it was astonishing, she thought bleakly, that good moments were often lost to her, buried under the weight of the occasional bad moment that could always be brought to mind with even its smallest details. And it had been a bad moment, unforgettable; what made it worse was the fact that her mother, drunk and exhausted and a million light-years away from any normal consideration of the normal world, had not meant to be cruel. She had merely said the first thing that had come into her head.

The cramped and dilapidated house, on the outskirts of Albuquerque. Emily, aged seventeen, sitting at the kitchen table. She was three days away from high school graduation, an event which she viewed with an intense and simple pleasure; no more teachers with their stodgy traditions that passed for ideas, no more giggling girls with boys on their minds, no more boys. Most of all, no more boys, boys who either mimicked her loping stride or ignored her entirely because she wasn't small and cute and cuddlesome. And there was something else to look forward to, as well; her father had promised to drive her to Three Rivers after school was done, to show her the thousands of ancient petroglyphs that dotted the hills along the road to Alamogordo.

She had been sketching that day, something she often

did. She sketched birds, insects, unicorns, angels, anything that had wings and could fly; she sketched on anything that lay to hand. This day her medium was a white disposable paper place-mat. And the sketch, for Emily, was unusual enough to catch the attention even of a mother who rarely cast so much as a glance at her daughter's work.

Emily had drawn a human face, a man's face. It was curving and long, but not to the point of parody; the mouth was humorous, merciless, and somehow wildly happy. A cloud of shoulder-length dark hair framed it, and the eyes held a promise beyond everyday vision. There was something indecently strong in it, something that the artist herself was too young and inexperienced to identify as the uncontrolled sexuality it represented.

For Emily, who never drew human faces, it was an incredible piece of work. What made it even more amazing was the fact that she had paid no attention at all as her hand moved across the place-mat; her mind was elsewhere, saying a glad farewell to the horrors of education.

Kirstin, faded and small in a blue print dress, had leaned against the sink. Her blue eyes, already clouded by her tenth or eleventh drink of the day, moved vaguely around the crowded, dirty kitchen. They rarely focused on any one thing; today, however, their sense was still open and her attention had fallen on Emily's drawing.

She had walked across the kitchen. Emily, to this day, could not remember her mother without remembering her walk; two or three tiny careful steps, stop, start again. It was as if the physical reality of movement had required the deepest concentration possible.

She had stood by Emily's shoulder, watching, saying nothing as her daughter absently finished the shading under the mobile jaw and set her pencil down. Emily had glanced up at her mother, noting the sudden intense awareness in the usually vacant face.

A tiny hand, blue-veined and tremulous, had reached out. It had taken the picture up, lifted it to eye-level, studied it deeply. For a moment, Kirstin's tiny tremulous fingers had clenched on the place-mat, crunching a corner of it. Then, carefully, Kirstin had dropped the picture, so that it floated around Emily's head momentarily before dropping, face down, on the dirty floor.

'It's very good,' Kirstin said, happily and simply and with no sense of complication at all. Her smile was wide and uncontrolled; for a moment, Emily saw the twin of the smile of the man in the drawing. 'He's very beautiful. And you're a whore.'

Emily swallowed the last of her squid and reached for the mineral water on the cloth beside her. She tilted it back, draining the bottle; it was cold and refreshing, and it took the edge off the exhaustion of a bad, sleepless night. When the bottle was empty, she drew up her knees and rested her chin on them. A sudden burp brought her back to reality, leaving the taste of the squid, pungent and nasty, at the back or her throat. My God, she thought, what in hell was I eating? A number two pencil, complete with eraser? Something stewed in indian ink?

Stop hedging.

'I'm not hedging.' She was alone on the hill, or as good as alone; the nearest person was a speck at the top of the path. There was no one to cast her equivocal looks, and it was safe to speak aloud. 'I can't be thinking all the time, can I?'

Why not? You can run all the time, run away, run from Mom and Daddy and humiliation and failure and . . .

'Shut up!' She raised a hand to her mouth to cover it; the words had come out in a shout. Maybe I'm losing my mind, she thought, and glanced frantically over her shoulder at the other human presence in this landscape. Go away, she thought wildly, don't come closer. Can't you see I'm in the middle of a mental breakdown?

The hilltop figure stopped and, to her own horror, Emily heard herself giggle. This would never do, she thought; she must take hold of herself, draw breath. Stop it, she thought firmly, just stop this. There is nothing wrong with you, you are merely exhausted from no sleep and a bit shaky from too many memories coming back at one time. She whispered into the palm of her hand, softly and clearly. 'I am not going nuts. I just want to be by myself. Please.'

The speck on the top of the hill had moved closer to her. It was a man, and he was watching her, but she was no longer conscious of him. For a moment he stood very still, as if considering. Then he shook his head, a tiny movement, as if to say, no, not now, not yet. A moment later he was gone.

Emily missed all of this; she was wrestling with reality and didn't turn around. Her chin rested on her knees once again, the light that had illuminated the work of painters from Titian to Tintoretto glinting off the bone-deep fold of skin where her wedding ring had lived for so long. She whispered aloud to the brilliant empty morning and the wide Roman sky.

'Why?' The word was very soft. 'Why call me a whore? Was it me, or her? Or did she just recognize something in the picture, something I was too young to see myself?'

But she received no answer to the question she had avoided for over twenty years. The memory of that happy, thoughtless remark had lost none of its ability to hurt; Kirstin's wide impersonal smile was as fresh on the crisp air of Italy as it had been in the dirty New Mexico kitchen, and had just as much power to wound.

You almost asked her once. Remember?

Kirstin had been dying, her liver riddled and gone, her skin hanging off bones that for too long had been fed grain spirits instead of calcium. She lay in a clean white bed, her hair brushed back, looking unnaturally clean. The hospital room was the antithesis of all institutional rooms, bright and sunny and incongruously cheerful with its print wallpaper and white wicker furniture, and Emily had been obliquely thankful for that. Emily had come for a visit, the young artist making an unwilling pilgrimage home. Gary was at her side, the young rising lawyer, aloof and detached from anything messy or painful even then. They would be married in less than a month.

She sat and held Kirstin's hand, feeling awkward and hypocritical, for they had never used the language of touch to communicate. The hand was cool and dry, as small as a child's. Gary, ill at ease and showing it, stayed at the far end of the room. Her mother's eyes, no longer clouded in the approaching darkness of her last extremity, swivelled to regard him.

And you're a whore.

Emily opened her mouth to speak, but the hand she held suddenly tightened, her mother's nails digging into her palm. Kirstin sighed, deep and long, wracking herself with it. Emily looked down at the head on the pillow, seeing with acuity the lank blonde hair, the parchment skin, the sudden wide smile that came with such an effort.

'I just don't know, Emily,' Kirstin said quietly, and the smile died to emptiness. 'I don't have the faintest idea. Don't ask me.'

She turned her face into the pillow, relaxing into sleep.

As Emily released her mother's hand and rose to her feet, she thought she heard something from that small broken shape, a single questioning word; she opened her mouth to speak, not knowing what she would say, knowing that something must be said. But the nurse came in then, and Gary took her by the arm and led her quickly out. Emily was never to ask her mother anything else, for she died in her sleep three hours later.

And what had she meant, with that final statement? It could have been an apology for Emily's life, for her own life; it could have been general or specific, referring to everything or to one thing. Had she meant Gary? Or had she been talking about a past now gone? There were no answers, only questions, and it was too late for questions.

On the Palatine Hill, Emily realized that both her legs had gone to sleep. The physical discomfort was Heaven sent, a blessed spur to the real world; she stretched them out in front of her, shaking them gingerly, trying to restore the circulation and drive the tingling away. As she hobbled around in small circles, wincing and gathering up the debris of her untasted morning picnic, she wondered vaguely what had happened to the hilltop watcher.

CHAPTER THREE

No earthly enterprise
Will cloud this vision.

(from 'No Earthly Enterprise')

Emily stayed in Italy for nearly a month. It was not that she discovered any particular sympathy for the land itself; the country, beautiful as it was, struck no inner chords. She was, quite simply, fascinated. The Italians were so different from town to town, the culture such a peculiar mixture of majesty and raucousness, that she found herself exploring them as a child might who was trying to catch soap bubbles in the air.

The weather turned colder, winter coming in decisively. The Mediterranean autumn had been unusually mild that year, a fact repeated with tiresome regularity in every local paper from Sicily to Gibraltar. Emily, possessing a decent command of French but little else in the way of languages, wrestled with the papers and began to make sense of Italian by way of the weather reports. The Roman shop windows boasted sweaters in gorgeous colours, boots in butter-soft leather; Emily, seeing the chic smartness of the women who roared through the traffic on their motor bikes, gave in to a whim and bought herself boots, gloves, a cashmere sweater with red birds flying on the sleeves.

On Christmas Eve, following what seemed a normal

impulse, she joined the huge throng of people at St Peter's for mass, listening to soaring voices that rang out in song, of which she understood perhaps one word in ten. And, on New Year's morning, she looked out across the city from her pensione window and saw the seven hills dusted with snow.

A week after her arrival in Rome, Emily bought a sketchbook. She had owned such things before, principally because anyone claiming acquaintance with an artist assumes that sketchbooks make useful gifts; the studio, now probably a games room for the teenagers of the people who had bought the house, had contained a nineteenth-century sea chest full of such things, all virginally clean and unused. But she had never before deliberately bought one herself, preferring instead the spontaneity of loose bits of paper.

She had made a conscious decision, before leaving America, that she would do no work on this journey, which the voice in her head insisted on calling a flight. Her agent, a calm, stately woman named Gina Wade, had gotten rather shrill about the decision. But Italy defeated her, Italy with its contrasts and contradictions and endless beautiful colours. After she found herself sitting on the bathroom floor of the Pensione Marco, desperately carving a bar of soap into the features of an old man she had seen that day before she forgot what he looked like, Emily gave in. She could neither control the need to put visceral reality into cerebral flesh nor assume that paper would be handy when that need arose, for there was simply too much of Italy to risk missing.

So the sketchbook took on life. She drew everything from odd architectural angles near the Spanish Steps to the hands of an old woman selling flowers. And there were birds, flapping and soaring, crowding the stiff vellum, jostling for pride of place under Emily's fingers.

She decided to leave Rome for the south after ten days, tiring of it abruptly. Her excuse to herself was that she wanted to see Tuscany, and Pompeii, and Herculaneum. There were also Florence and Naples, mountains and museums. After all, she had come to see, hadn't she? That was the whole point of this trek, wasn't it?

She put this question to herself as she sat sipping morning coffee on the roof-top terrace of the Pensione Marco. The snow had cleared, although the morning was chilly; she had chosen the terrace for privacy, trading the necessity for breakfasting in a coat for the desire to avoid the tourists in the local cafés. Seeing her up there, the waiter had clucked, and chattered, and shaken his head. Emily, with unwonted firmness, had demanded and obtained food and drink.

Unfortunately, she was not alone on the terrace; a few minutes after her first sip of coffee, a woman in a mink jacket had strolled to a table not five feet away. Equally unfortunately, the little voice in Emily's head answered her unspoken question with a sharpness that approached virulence.

Who are you kidding? The purpose of this trek, as you so picturesquely call it, is to run away from yourself. You could have come here before, if you'd wanted to. You've had the time, and the sale of one large commissioned piece would have paid for it. So you can call it whatever you want, sweetie, but we know better.

'Bullshit.' She spoke softly, under her breath, and hastily took a sip of coffee. Her hands were cold. The woman at the next table, slender and fortyish and almost too fashionably dressed, glanced at her curiously. Silently, Emily cursed the little voice. There she went again, answering herself out loud. This was a new habit, a very unwelcome habit too, one which was going to have to stop unless she wanted to end up in a rubber room somewhere, drawing birds on the walls with crayons.

The voice went on, small and clear and inexorable.

You aren't here to look at mountains or Michelangelo or anything else, and you know it. You're here because your ego took a good swift kick in the slats, because your husband decided he preferred a cuddly little moron who'd gotten tired of playing in the big nasty corporate world and wanted to play with her dolls and her toy dishes, because you didn't want to deal with everyone you knew making sympathetic noises while discussing you at aerobics class. You don't even have the excuse of a broken heart for being here. You ran away from home the way you ran off to California when your father disappeared, because you're a coward, a moral wimp, a . . .

'Shut up! Damn you, shut up!'

'Excuse me.'

For a moment, Emily, tortured by the internal barrage of accusations, was too disorientated to understand that the words, in English and politely articulated in a faintly musical accent. had been spoken aloud. She unclenched her fists and looked up into the face of the woman in mink.

Oh, Christ. I told her to shut up, a perfect stranger, she probably asked me how to get to Vatican City or something and I was too busy arguing with my own head to hear her and now she probably thinks . . .

'Do you mind if I join you?'

The woman was smiling faintly, looking neither anxious nor confused. Her white wool trousers had clearly come from a designer's salon, her hair was arranged with a simplicity that could only have been the work of a master; her boots and bag, understated and elegant to swooning point, would have cost the average American a month's salary. She was completely elegant, so elegant in fact that Emily wondered briefly why it looked so natural this early in the day. And the smile was so obviously genuine that to refuse would have been impossible. Emily gestured at the empty chair beside her with a shaking hand, and took the bull by the horns.

'Of course,' she said. 'Please do. I'm afraid I was arguing with myself, I do that a lot, but I don't usually do it aloud. My name is Emily Moon-Bourne. Would you care for some coffee, juice, a pastry?'

'Certainly, if you will allow me to buy.' The woman raised a scarlet-tipped hand. As if in response to a conjuring command, a waiter appeared to take her order. When he had gone, the woman lit a cigarette and cocked her head at Emily.

'A pleasure to meet you, Ms Moon-Bourne. I am Dolores Aguilar. I'm sorry for this intrusion, but I felt I must come over and reassure you. You see, I knew exactly what you were doing; I found myself doing the same thing at the Trevi Fountain last night, and I wondered if we were not, perhaps, similar. I have been wandering for weeks, and have found nothing and no one I thought was like me in the least, not even my own conscience. It would relieve me greatly to know that I am not the only woman in Europe with a conscience.'

The sophisticated smile unexpectedly and briefly became an enchanting grin. 'My conscience – I call it that from habit, although my therapist insists it is a young and hungry Dolores who has been too long ignored and clamours for attention – says inconvenient things. Sometimes the words are the truth of real horror, or so I think; sometimes I hear what is even worse, words that may be truth or may be distorted paranoia. I must add that little Dolo, as my therapist calls it, habitually speaks out at inconvenient times. There were tourists by the fountain last night, Germans and Americans I think. They moved away from me as if I carried the plague.' She extracted a cigarette from a slim gold case and offered the case to Emily. Her voice was reflective. 'I find that few people have any imagination at all.'

'That's the truest thing I've heard in weeks.' Emily, fascinated and relieved, accepted a proffered cigarette and moved the ashtray to the centre of the table. 'In years, actually. And please call me Emily. Have you always heard your little voice? I have, but it seems to have gotten louder recently. In fact, the older I get, the louder it gets. And I find that . . . worrying.'

'Ah. Something triggered it, I presume. A divorce, a death, an unhappy love affair?' Dolores languidly moved her napkin aside to make room for the tray that the waiter was trying to deposit. '*Grazie*. Good, the juice is freshly made. You understand that I do not mean to pry. But I have spoken to no one of anything important for too long, and it would be a great comfort to me. So that you will know that I am not morbidly curious, allow me to confide. I am here to break the news to my son that I have left his father. My son is here, at this pensione, and I am afraid he will not be pleased.' She shrugged gracefully. 'His reactions, however, are his own affair. I am not answerable to my child, or to anyone else, for my happiness. On that, at least, my therapist and I are agreed.'

'You're damned right you're not.' Emily had never been given to confiding her feelings, but the urge was strong in her now, and there was something elementally attractive about this strange woman. She took a deep breath. 'Mine is a divorce. My husband, who was rich and boring and conceited, decided that he wanted babies. Since I declined to produce any, he impregnated someone else, in this case a congenital twit with the moral awareness of a toilet-seat cover. A common little story, isn't it?'

Her voice was bitter. Dolores touched her hand, briefly and lightly.

'No, it is not common. For each of us, unhappiness is unique. So too are outrage, and anger, and hurt feelings. Remember that, and do not denigrate your own life by diminishing the shocks it provides; if you do that, you will learn nothing from them. I, too, found that my husband had become enamoured of someone else; in my case, it was my sister's husband.'

Emily stared at her. 'Wow!'

'Do you know, that is one reason I made myself familiar with the English tongue? One can say so many perfect things in English, all of them economically expressed. "Wow" sums it up quite well. I found them in bed together.' There was nothing but calm in the musical voice. 'A pity that we could not introduce your husband to mine; if the sticky question of babies is omitted, they sound made for each other.'

'Did you love him?' Emily, a lifelong devotee of avoiding personal entanglements, was distantly amazed at herself. Could it really be her, Emily, speaking like this to a perfect stranger? 'Should I say I'm sorry, how terrible for you, all that?'

Dolores sipped orange juice and took a dainty bite of pastry. 'Ah, the sun is finally beginning to give warmth. Sorry, terrible? No, not at all. I stopped loving Francisco within weeks of my son's birth, when I came to know that he saw me not as Dolores, my own woman, but as a beautiful and well-born receptacle for his seed and his precious family lineage. I am afraid that Diego has inherited more than his father's lineage and looks. He is inclined to be pompous, and stuffy, and to consider foolish things important.'

'I don't like children.' This confession, never before made even to herself, came out with force. Emily blinked. 'Do you know, Dolores, I've never admitted that. I don't know where you come from, but in America, women are supposed to like children. And I *don't*. I never have. I'm a bit afraid of them, and I don't really trust them, but I've never actually said so before. It feels damned good to say so, too. I guess your therapist would tell me that my voice knows how I feel, maybe even resents the way I feel.' She shook her head slowly. 'You know something? I'm really glad I met you.'

'I think perhaps that we should both be glad at this meeting. For myself, I am quite fond of children; I like the way they look, their perfect smallness and their curiosity. But really they are only children for a few months. After that they are people, strange people who must be selfish to survive, and I cease to enjoy them. They are like everyone else, only more so.'

'That's very well put.'

Dolores lifted the cover of the coffeepot. 'We have drunk up all the coffee, and I must go down and annoy my son with reality. May I buy you dinner tonight? I am leaving Rome tomorrow for Barcelona, there will be a grand fight for Francisco's money to deal with and publicity that will make him quite wild. I shall enjoy that, but I should not enjoy dining with Diego, who would lecture and preach until I am forced to remember that I am his mother and slap him until his ears ring. That would be tiresome, and put me at a disadvantage. Considering these things, I would much prefer to dine with you.'

Emily grinned at her, a wide happy grin as much for the sheer pleasure of Dolores' company as for the unaccustomed silence in her head. 'I'd love it. Pick me up here at about eight, and not too fancy, because I don't have the wardrobe for it.'

That dinner had gone a long way to restoring Emily's sense of being present in the real world. Before her head-on encounter with Dolores' charming realism, Emily had not realized how dislocated she had become. Having been forced to confide clinically in her own scarcely known attorney, she had spoken of the shocks of the past year with no one else. That dinner, in a small trattoria with excellent seafood and the smell of strong harsh wine on the smoky air, took on the talismanic significance of a Rosetta stone, a touchstone, a precursor of answers.

So they ate, and talked, and moved on to profiteroles and espresso. For days afterward, Emily was to wonder what had been responsible for the incredible loosening of her usually inarticulate tongue. Something stronger than simple loneliness relieved, something more human and less comprehensible, had been at work that evening.

And the small voice, eternally hovering with its sharp and brutal perceptions, had remained silent. Emily was never to remember all of what she herself had said, although most of Dolores' contributions were clear in her mind. In the weeks that passed, things would trigger that conversation, recalling with a sudden, starkly lit clarity a phrase or a feeling, but the whole was lost to her beyond reclamation. Whatever the words had been, the inner critic had apparently agreed.

And her companion held strong opinions about the voice. Give it a name, Dolores had advised her. To argue, or to listen to insults, from a disembodied voice you cannot identify is very much like receiving a threatening phone call from a complete stranger and being unable to hang up. Once it is named, it is personified, and easier to deal with.

And the voice, the carping demanding voice, had stayed silent throughout Emily's absorption of those words. By its silence, it had given Emily her chance, and the voice was now Emmy Deer. The name had come complete, without thought, and she still hadn't begun to consider why.

It was not until Emily herself had left Rome that she was able to make what, to her, was a startling self-admission indeed. There had been a kind of love in her feelings for this woman who had so briefly, so strangely, touched the edge of Emily's life. There had been several kinds of love there, muddied and mixed, undeniable, impossible to name. She didn't know, was never to know, what percentage of that love was sexual, what percentage maternal; after a time, she ceased to care. The feeling had been strong, and nourishing, and that was all that mattered.

But, if she could not recall her own words or identify her own feelings, Dolores had been less of a puzzle. Emily remembered every word the elegant Spanish woman had spoken, for she had used words as only one who speaks in a language not naturally their own can do. The result was weight, meaning, nothing wasted or empty.

And it was at Herculaneum, studying the wedding-cake layering of archeology and bones smothered beneath the ashes of Vesuvius, that shc thought back to that evening and with total astonishment realized that she had spoken of her father, and of the brother she was not sure she'd had.

She stood at the fringe of a tour group on a sandy beach, a chilly wind lifting her hair. She was idly examining the arches beneath which the population of the town had sought shelter on the day the volcano had gone mad. The guide was Italian, probably British-educated; his accent was pure and clean, with a musical lilt.

'. . . a little girl,' he was saying, his voice pitched to reach every listener. 'Very undernourished, with three copper bracelets around her wrist bones. She was likely a slave child, serving a wealthy family. The poorly developed bones and bracelets tell us that, also her poor teeth, of which many are missing. But the baby she was cradling in her arms when the ashes buried her was very likely a child of the noble house she served.'

Emily knew the story of Herculaneum, at least in broad outline; how for centuries the historians had assumed that the ashes of erupting Vesuvius had blown toward Pompeii, allowing those of Herculaneum, on the other side of the mountain, to flee for safety. For nearly a millennium that theory had held, until someone had gotten the bright idea to excavate what appeared to be solid sandstone on the beaches of the town. The sandstone was dried ash, hard and weathered by time, and huddled behind and beneath its suffocating weight was the population of Herculaneum. They had escaped as far as the beaches, and no farther. Emily touched her lips with her tongue, and wondered if she imagined the faint tang of hot ash on the wind.

'. . . no, certainly not the girl's brother,' the guide said. 'He was a well-fed baby, perhaps two years old, with gold ornaments and the remnants of expensive clothing.'

'Oh, that's so sad.' An elderly woman with a strong Scots burr and a Nikon dangling around her neck turned to her husband. 'That poor little girl, trying to protect that dear little baby. And it wasn't even her brother, poor little mite. Oh, Henry, I can just see it!'

The man at her side patted her hand, made soothing

noises. And suddenly Emily, whose own imagination had been busy with the relentless ash and terrified crowds, was back in a Roman trattoria, and Dolores Aguilar was opposite her, and Emily heard her own voice saying, 'His name was Bear. If he existed, if my father was telling the truth and my mother wasn't, then he died a year before I was born, of something called Foetal Alcohol Syndrome, and his name was Bear Dancer Moon . . .'

A few feet from Emily, a man turned to watch her. She had not noticed him, she didn't notice him now; the past was suddenly present in odd, disorienting colours that gave no place to the present moment. It was not as if he was an easy man to miss; he was fantastically tall, strongboned and dark-haired, and he wore, of all things, a frock coat. But he looked at Emily freely, so freely that he might have been invisible to the rest of the group; a man with theatrical clothing and deep mobile eyes, a man who might have been any age. His face bore a faint smile, the merest imprint of something that spoke of knowledge and wild freedom. Then, as he had done on the Palatine Hill, he gave a tiny shake of the head and turned away, walking quickly. He had disassociated himself from the group and disappeared into the bright cool Italian sunlight without her ever seeing him.

And Emily, standing at the rear of the noisily respectful tour group, thought for the first time in fifteen years about that trip to Alamogordo to see the petroglyphs, about the discovery of a brother who had lived and died without her even knowing of his existence, about herself and, most of all, about her father.

Running Deer Moon, of Cherokee extraction and forcibly baptized by a Christian priest as John, had been the hardest person to place in all of Emily's life. If Kirstin had been a hazy alcoholic mystery, John had been as much of an enigma as the ancient Indian petroglyphs clustered throughout the American south-west.

He was not mysterious, not in himself. Emily, mixing his Indian bone structure and capacity for secrets with her mother's real-world Scandinavian possibilities, had understood the mask, if not the man behind it. He was undemonstrative, and taciturn, but neither of those traits are uncommon among the male sex, and neither those nor his seeming lack of interest in the modern world around him had made him so difficult for Emily to understand.

Part of it was the disappearances. John Moon would take a job – throughout the first sixteen years of his daughter's life, he had worked as everything from a dishwasher to an accountant, and never for more than a year at a time – and then he would follow a routine so predictable as to be ritual. He would deposit the bulk of the money he had earned during the job's tenure in a bank account in his wife's name, nod at Kirstin, touch his daughter briefly on one arm, and leave. Sometimes he would be gone for a few weeks, sometimes for six months. During those times he might have been anywhere, for they never heard from him. He would always return before the money ran out, take another job, and repeat the process all over again. He had never, to Emily's knowledge, been fired from any of the varied jobs he had done; he had done everything methodically, and well, and apparently without interest or commitment. On one occasion when he seemed to have been gone for ever and a twelve-year-old Emily had hysterically questioned her mother, Kirstin had shrugged with an alcoholic's irritation and given her vague, watery smile.

But he had always returned, at least until Emily left home for college. She had wondered, when she grew old enough to speculate on such things, whether he had returned all those years out of some inscrutable sense of duty to his child. Certainly she was later to believe that, with the coming of her majority and its attendant freedom, a like freedom had been granted to him. And there was nothing to contradict that theory, that lack of any deep personal feeling in him, except that trip to Alamogordo.

And it was on that trip, standing in a lunar landscape and surrounded by hundreds of carvings done by twelfth-century Mogollon Indians who had worshipped their earth and had long since been received into its forgiving bosom, that he had stood beside her, his hand cupped to his brow, staring out over wonder and saying, in a dead, flat voice, 'Your brother Bear would have loved this.'

'. . . had not escaped, after all,' the guide said. Emily, startled back to the present, shook her head to clear the echoes of the past and pushed them away from her. How long had she stood there, trapped in her own incomprehensible history? The sun had shifted perceptibly in the sky, and the light was no longer the clear Italianate of an earlier hour, but something more alien.

. . . not escaped not escaped not . . .

The tour group was suddenly too dense, too close, and the wind seemed to carry a threat of tears on it. She turned swiftly and walked, having to restrain herself from running, back toward the town itself. She did not want to think about John, not yet; it wasn't the time, she simply wasn't ready.

It was the baby boy that triggered this, the boy back there. At least the slave girl was sure he existed. Did she see him as her baby brother, that hungry abused child?

Emmy Deer, this time, held no overtones of accusation or anger. Emily lifted a hand to her face and was physically shocked to find that her hand came away wet with tears.

She wiped the tears away hastily and made her way back to the centre of town, suddenly dizzy and desperately wanting the comfort of her pensione bed.

There was something going on in the piazza; a small crowd had gathered, and were watching with obvious interest. Emily, threading her way through groups of people and murmuring '*scusi, scusi,*' under her breath, stopped to look. It seemed to be a small troop of street actors, wearing costumes in the bright colours and fine lines of an earlier time. Twelfth century, thirteenth? Emily, wishing vaguely that her sense of history was stronger, scanned the scene. The acting troupe was small, six people only, four men and two women.

Emily, some ten feet away from the action behind a group of tiny Japanese tourists, let her eyes range over the scene. An impromptu stage set had been erected, something red and gilt that was right out of a *commedia dell'arte* revival, and the actors were speaking Italian. There was something familiar about it. Emily wracked her memory, and came up with fragments; Webster's *The White Devil*, a Punch and Judy pantomime, something from *The Ingoldsby Legends*, a book that she had loved as a child? All were similar, but none rang quite true.

It was obviously a morality play of some variety, perhaps a medieval replaying of the temptation of Eden. Here were the lovers, discussing with portentous curiosity what treasures might wait behind the vividly painted cardboard door; there was the Serpent, in unrelieved black, urging them to violate their instinct toward caution and explore. The lovers consulted, gesticulated, nodded. The man reached out with a tentative hand and wonderingly touched the door.

And here, true to myth and spirit, was the unleashed Devil, the price of temptation, the dark side of knowledge.

He came out from behind the door with movements of grace and threat. And Emily, her eyes caught like a fish on a hook, stared until her vision blurred.

He was tall, easily six foot five. He was black haired, and dark eyed, and the bones of his face were mobile stone. His devil was obviously a creation of sophistication, elegantly clad in a black frock coat and tight trousers that accentuated his astonishing height. He began to conjure with speed and skill, sleight of hand that produced an apple, a ring, a bright gold chain; he juggled, he smiled, he offered these things to the entranced lovers who had forgotten their fears. The Japanese tourists laughed and took pictures; the locals shouted and applauded. The man in black, the Serpent, circulated his gaily tasselled cap through the crowd, smiling and encouraging at every contribution.

Emily saw none of this. She watched the Devil.

The Devil turned, looking over the heads of the lovers and the Serpent and the watching crowd in the piazza. He smiled directly into Emily's face.

Never moving her eyes, she reached into her bag. Fingers that were chilled and trembling found her sketchbook, closed over it, drew it out. She began to work with frantic speed, taking her eyes from the Devil's face only long enough to glance at her page, feeling herself on the verge of some tremendous discovery.

Because she knew that face, those impenetrable eyes, that smile of wild happy freedom. She knew those bones, those hands that made mystery, knew them with a deep personal familiarity that was beyond naming. Somehow, somewhere, she had seen this devil before.

CHAPTER FOUR

And all the magic unfamiliar land
Was ours by distant heritage and ours
By deep love close at hand.

(from 'Memory of England, 1940')

Where do you go when you're trying to run from the ghosts of your own life?

Emily asked herself this question, and received the answer to it from Emmy Deer, as she sat on her pensione bed, staring at a face in her sketchbook and shuddering convulsively. She had finished the drawing in a matter of minutes, creating a mystery from a mystery, only to find herself faced with a conundrum.

For sometime between the time she opened her purse to drop the sketchbook in and the time she glanced back at the piazza her model had disappeared. At one moment he, and the rest of the troupe of actors, were finishing their play and bowing to the applause; the next, only two of the half-dozen remained, the Serpent to dismantle the set and the female lover to count the proceeds gathered in the passed hat.

And Emily, amazed then and for ever after at her own temerity, had marched directly up to the man in black and addressed him.

'Pardon me? *Scusi*?'

The Serpent looked up at her. At close quarters, he was

not nearly so elegant as he had appeared during the play; the mixture of greasepaint and distance had performed its usual magic and fostered that illusion. Seen face to face, he was two inches shorter than she was, and his sun-roughened skin beneath its glistening layer of sweaty make-up was pocked with old acne scars. But he smiled at her, showing a brief flash of perfect teeth, and spoke broken English.

'Hiya. I help you, please?'

Emily, wondered briefly if she was losing her mind, clutched her purse. 'Your play. The man who played the Devil?' What was the Italian for that? '*Diablo*? *Diavolo*?'

'Oh.' The man tilted his head, anxious to help. '*La Inglese*, you mean? The English man?'

'No, I don't think so. At least . . .' English. Something about that build, that smile, that slender length of bone . . . was it possible? 'Is he English? Do you know his name? I think I, I may have met him before and I was wondering . . .'

Her voice died away in shocked embarrassment at his disbelief. For the Serpent's doubtful smile had deepened into something darker and stronger. He grinned at her, a purely masculine arrangement of facial muscles in an unholy alliance with predictable attitude. '*Si*, yeah, he English. He just here today, don't know him before. He *molto elegante*. You like him, huh? You think he sexy?'

'Please . . .'

'Sure, *si*. You ask about him. His name? He said Martin to me, call me Martin. That's what he said.' He winked at her. 'He go somewhere, don't know, maybe food someplace.' He waved a hand around the piazza. 'You go fast, you find him maybe.'

Well, there you go. First try at assertiveness, one hell of a result. How do you like being a dirty joke? How does it feel to be leered at by an Italian longshoreman?

'Thank you.' Suddenly horrified at her own daring, she reached for wallet and pulled out a banknote. She thrust it into his hand, her body itching as if corrupted by some invisible pollution. '*Grazie*, *gracias*, *merci bien*, whatever. Thank you. Goodbye.'

And she fled for the safety of her pensione, feeling her legs tremble, knowing that the Serpent's impudent black eyes followed her progress.

She sat on the bed, her shaking legs crossed firmly at the ankles. She stared at her sketch, which stared back with the same dark eyes that had crinkled up at her in the town square. The unpleasant taste that the Serpent had left at the back of her throat faded, overlaid by a larger sense of urgency. There was no doubt about it, she had seen this man before. In the flesh, as an actor? Where and when had this exquisite work of bone and magic crossed her path?

And, as she held the drawing, something like a physical memory took shape under her fingers. The small comfortable room dissolved for a moment around her, transmuting by some alchemy into an untidy kitchen in New Mexico. She sat, she drew, and Kirstin drank and smiled across the room. The distant Italian traffic, the soughing of the breeze through the open window, even the annoying and distant murmur of the tourists in the next room, vanished like mist under the spur of remembrance repossessed. She heard her mother's voice, so clearly that Kirstin might have stood once more at her shoulder, even as she had done in that kitchen half a lifetime ago.

It's very good. He's very beautiful. And you're a whore.

The past receded, the present returned, and she discovered she had wrinkled the edges of the drawing in the clutch of convulsive fingers. She smoothed the paper, forcing herself to take deep breaths.

She looked at him, at the picture of the man who was

possibly called Martin. Martin, wild and happy and free in charcoal pencil strokes, looked back at her. There could be no mistake, any more than there could be another face like this in all the world. Was he even flesh, something that could be reached for, touched, spoken to? Or had the oddities of her own life these many months past, the sudden undeniable need to muse about where she had come from, conjured him up out of the antique Italian landscape?

And is he going to pop up again, and do you want him to, and a whole bunch of corollaries. Don't forget those.

'Where can I go?' She spoke aloud, softly, as if there was someone to hear her answer. 'I thought I was exploring. Now I know I'm running. But I don't know what I'm running from . . .'

Maybe you're not running from anything. Maybe you're running toward something.

Emily gave a little jump, and spoke to the empty room. 'You're the one who's been accusing me of running away from the divorce since I got here. Make up your mind.'

There was no answer to this. Emmy Deer had been silent all the afternoon; throughout the play and its aftermath, she had said nothing. Perhaps she had simply been smothered by the power of Emily's reaction. Now she had spoken, offering Emily an explanation of sorts, and she refused to bargain or to argue. Had she spoken calmly? Sympathetically? There was no way of telling.

But the words made blinding sense, and Emily considered them. What sorts of things did one run toward? Fate, destiny, adventure? One thing was sure: coming or going, she was being pursued. In Greece, in Rome, and now among the paint and ashes of Herculaneum, all along the line. The past was dogging her, step for step, and would not leave her be.

So . . . 'Where do you go when you're trying to run from the ghosts of your own life?'

Emmy Deer responded immediately, producing the answer with the ease and elegance Martin had displayed in producing the apple, the ring, the gold chain.

England, of course. The land of civilized ghosts, the land where your mother's ancestors pillaged and looted when they got bored on Saturday nights. And the Serpent said he was English. Where else?

'England.' Emily, suddenly aware that both legs had fallen asleep under her weight, hurriedly stretched them out and began to hobble, shaking the pins and needles out of them. The picture lay beside her, enigmatic and watchful. She looked down at it, considering, balanced precariously on one foot. 'England.'

Rarely had she found a decision so painless to make. She pulled her two suitcases from beneath the bed and began to pack. Her hand hesitated over the picture, whose disposition had from nowhere assumed a vast importance. Flat in the suitcase to keep it from creasing? In her bag, folded but closer to hand in case she wanted it?

Why don't you just stuff it down you bra, wear it next to your skin like a witch's charm? Maybe you can conjure him up at Heathrow when you hit London.

'Maybe I can,' Emily said cheerfully, and folded the picture small. On an impulse, she opened the folds once more, spreading it out, rubbing a faint charcoal smear away with one hand, giving it another stare. Give it a name, Dolores had said to her that night in Rome. Personify it, and it becomes easier to deal with . . .

Martin. It suited him.

Emily's first encounter on British soil was not with Martin.

She emerged from the Rome flight, tired beyond reason and empty inside, wanting a bed and a bath and, above all, food. There was a nagging pain in her stomach and her eyes were strained. So hollow did she feel that even the thought of airport food was not enough to deter her.

Food there was, and in quantity; Heathrow appeared to consist primarily of luggage carts and restaurants. Emily staggered through immigration, exchanged odd-looking Italian currency for British, and looked around. A vagrant scent of cooking caught her; she followed it and found herself looking into a café. It looked as if it might serve hot food above and beyond sausage rolls. Emily entered, dropped wearily into a booth and considered the menu.

Her mind was as sluggish as her body. Although the flight from Italy had been reasonably short, it had been bumpy, and because she had left Italy on the spur of the moment, a seat had not been easy to obtain. She was halfway over Switzerland, flying through a howling storm and trying not to be sick, when she realized that she was arriving in a country where hotels are either terrible or hard to find. She had no reservations, no plans, no knowledge of the endless teeming city into which she would be waltzing, nauseated and exhausted.

The waiter arrived, and Emily ordered fried eggs, toast, tea. The tea came first, hot and sweet, and it revived her to such an extent that her exhaustion altered perceptibly to dreaminess and she was able to think clearly, albeit remotely, about her immediate situation. Check into an airport hotel for as long as it took to find a short-term rental; surely that was the wisest move . . .

Dreaming, lazy, she lifted a slice of toast and felt something warm and alive crawling on her hand.

Her reaction was immediate and unreasoned. She slapped at her right hand and jumped, hitting the floor and rolling; there was an angry hum in her ears, unnaturally loud and much too close for safety. She got to her feet, ready to crush whatever it was, completely unnerved but set for battle. She looked up wildly, ignoring the sharp concerned exclamations of the other diners, and saw a black and yellow tube of a body, hovering in the air not three feet from her face.

And then the waiter had interposed his body, swatting ineffectually at the buzzing darting thing, killing it finally with the dish towel he carried over one arm. He hurried back to Emily, who was swaying on her feet. Her left shoulder throbbed dully where it had met the floor.

'Are you all right? Did it sting you, ma'am?'

My God, she thought weakly, it was real, he saw it too. A wasp? In an airport restaurant? In *January*? 'Fine,' she said, breathing hard, rubbing her shoulder. 'No, it didn't sting me, I'm fine. You know, this is my first trip to England. Do you often have wasps in the middle of winter?'

'Never seen one this time of year in all my life. I thought wasps died off around October. My word, we had snow three days ago. I don't know where it could have come from.' The waiter, a solid-looking man in his forties, was obviously very shaken. 'Bloody hell, pardon, sorry. It gave me a bit of a fright, that thing. Have you come from the tropics? Could you have brought it with you, in your luggage or clothes, maybe?'

'I came from Italy, it was just as cold there as it is here, and I didn't see a wasp the whole time I was there. We had snow there a week ago so, no, I don't think I brought it with me.' She looked at the body of the wasp, lying on the floor; it was the largest of its kind she had ever seen. Memory, fright, so much to feel; for a moment the antennaed head took on Gary's features as they had looked during that damned Independence Day barbecue, tight and malevolent.

And was it her imagination, or did the bloated furry horror actually twitch, as if sensing his potential victim's eyes on him? Emily lifted a hand to her brow.

'Excuse me,' she said, and heard her own voice thin and wavering, 'but I have to sit down. I have to sit down *now*.'

As if from miles off, she heard the waiter exclaim and felt his hand cup her elbow, supporting her weight. The brightly coloured plastic of the restaurant was revolving, moving in dizzying intolerable circles, and the booth shook under her weight as he lowered her into it. He said something about more tea, fresh toast, on the house of course; he hurried off for a whispered consultation with his co-workers in the kitchen.

Emily took a taxi into London, after all. The wasp had decided her against anything to do with Heathrow Airport; reservation or no reservation, she refused to stay here. Anything at all, whether it be the sleaziest fleabag in town or the Ritz, with its astronomical prices, would be better than this dreadful sense of personal threat. Absurd as it was, she could not shake the certainty that the wasp had been there, waiting for her and her alone, waiting to sting and sting and sting . . . She would get as far away as this huge comfortable cab would take her, and spend all of next day finding decent accommodation, if necessary.

It wasn't. The taxi driver, a slender Pakistani with beautiful manners and an even more beautiful voice, asked where he was taking her. When she told him her situation, he asked her how much she wanted to spend and how long she wanted to go on spending it. He then took her to a block of restored Edwardian flats a few blocks south of Sloane Square.

The proprietress, short and plump and almost comically comfortable, came out to greet them. She showed Emily into a small but beautifully furnished flat with a view of the river, quoted a list of prices that was high but not exorbitant, and waved goodbye to the cabbie. She then recommended restaurants in the area, explained how the electricity and telephone were billed and, figuratively speaking, vanished into the woodwork.

Welcome to the land of civilized ghosts, sweetie. Not bad, especially if you don't mind wasps out of season.

Emily sat down on the sofa, a scroll-backed piece of stiff satin pseudo-Empire, and looked around her. The walls were apple-green with pale yellow stripes, the carpet a thick green pile; experimentally she took off her boots and socks and pushed her bare toes into the shag. The warmth of the room met her bare skin with a physical shock and travelled up her body in a short, intense tremor. The traffic noise was thin and distant; in the tiny kitchenette, the small fridge emitted a steady, comforting hum. Slowly, lazily, she unpacked her clothes and took a long, hot bath. Outside, it had begun to snow lightly.

When she emerged into the quiet street, full darkness had fallen and London was coming to life around her. She stepped off the kerb, was nearly crushed to a pulp by a car whizzing past her, and remembered the English drive on the opposite side of the road. After that, it was easier than she had expected to remember to check traffic from the opposite direction.

She ate dinner in, of all things, a pizza parlour; the food was hot and surprisingly good. She wolfed down a large pan pizza and a side order of sautéed mushrooms, deriving a good deal of amusement from the dainty way in which her fellow diners cut their pizza into tiny bits with knives and forks. She finished her meal with custard and espresso, letting her mind wander dreamily, setting some of these staid people with their perfect table manners in a Tennessee rib joint, where the food came wrapped in newspaper and a request for a fork would be greeted with a blank stare from the pork-bellied redneck behind the greasy counter. Replete, at peace with the world, she tipped lavishly and went back out into the London night.

It was still snowing, a soft light drift of white that hit the damp pavement and dissolved into nothingness. Emily, who had studied a book of London streets in her flat and who prided herself on her sense of direction, stood and took her bearings. That department store on the corner was Harvey Nichols; surely, if she turned right, her feet would take her south, toward the Thames and Chelsea and her flat?

She walked into the light cold wind, her scarf drawn around her chin, relishing the crisp bite of night air. As she drew closer to the river, the air grew appreciably colder, and she saw fewer and fewer people. She looked at her watch under the wavering fog of a street lamp, and found it was nearly ten.

She walked on. She passed a bobby on his nightly rounds, and smiled at him; cold but stolid, inured to his duty, he smiled back. She turned down her street and paused before her block of flats, mentally greeting her windows and walking on. At the southerly end of the street, she hesitated. The streets here snaked and wound like concrete rivers, following no logical pattern. She looked at the plaque on the corner house. Sloane Gardens. Well, she might as well walk toward the river, and take her chances. If she got lost, she could always stop someone and ask directions.

She came to the river abruptly, turning on to the Embankment just as the snow stopped. For a long while she simply stood and stared; at the dark, moving expanse of water, at the bridges that spanned its living length at fairly regular intervals, at the four spires on the other side that she recognized as being the stacks of Battersea Power Station. She was warm and happy, wrapped against the austerity of the weather in sheepskin and lambswool, and her cheekbones, the only portion of her left uncovered, burned and tingled with a kind of joy.

To the east, on a bridge whose name she had no way of knowing, a train racketed from south to north; it left a shower of blue sparks whose reflection danced on the river's surface, and Emily imagined that the ground beneath her feet rumbled. She knew a sudden urge to run toward the lights on the bridges, singing and laughing at the winter, and wondered why she felt so completely at peace.

They call it freedom, sweetie. You feel happy because you feel free, and the two go hand in hand. There's no one to hurry home to, no one to ask you questions, no one to explain anything to. And then, strangely, *I'll bet Martin's like that all the time. What do you think?*

Emily jumped. She had forgotten about Martin, actually forgotten his existence for a few short hours. Now he came back into her conscious mind, flooding it, inhabiting it totally. She was in England, where the Serpent had said Martin came from. Was he here now, somewhere in this vast cold place? Was he, too, standing somewhere where his eyes could take their ease from bridges and stacks and vivid blue sparks? And why should he be, after all? There was no reason in the world for her to assume that he was not, at this moment, stepping out from behind a brightly painted screen under the merciless light of an Italian sky. Why should he come here?

Why shouldn't he?

'How the hell should I know?'

And that was true, he could be anywhere. Logic,

reason, these things said that he was most likely in Italy, where she had seen him not forty-eight hours earlier. She had no reason to assume that he had been anything more than a fluke of history, a ghost she would never see again.

But nerve and blood told her differently. He had come to her, materializing from a paper napkin in New Mexico to a street show in Italy. He would come again, perhaps he had been there all along, watching her in the California garden, the Greek hillside, the courtroom where her eyes had fallen on Dodie's long-suffering expression and swollen belly and then moved away at once, as if blushing at something improper.

Yes, he would come. She didn't know why she was so certain, but certainty was there, as solid and undeniable as the river that seemed to be calling a welcome.

She walked home quickly, smoking a cigarette clumsily with her gloved fingers. She slept deeply, without dreaming. In the new morning, cold but very clear, she made herself a cup of bad coffee and lifted the edge of her curtain.

Martin, with a gaily coloured muffler around his throat, stood some fifty yards off, watching her window.

The visceral shock of her reaction was like a sharp blow over one ear. Emily's hand slipped from the curtain with an uncoordinated violent gesture. She pressed her back against the elegant wallpaper, eyes closed, chest heaving. She stood in a mist of mental numbness and physical intensity, feeling with remote wonder the sudden slamming of her heart against her ribs, the intolerable weakness in her usually reliable legs, the sound of her own voice whispering from a universe away, it can't be, no, there's simply no way in hell, that isn't him it can't be him can't can't can't . . .

Oh, yes, it can. But there's no one there now; if there was anyone there, I'll bet you he's gone now. Go on, look. Look down and see for yourself.

'Oh, Jesus.' Emily, a hand covering her mouth as if to physically force back some part of her that wanted out, pushed her cheek between the poplin folds and leaned against the window pane. The glass was cold, too cold; it left a streak of condensation against her skin.

But Emmy Deer was right. He was gone, the slippery pavement where he had stood had been emptied of him. At the end of the street, a milk float made its morning rounds; directly below her, on the front stairs of her own block of flats, a ginger cat sat washing its face with meticulous care. There was no one there, and nothing else to see.

Maybe he was never there at all. Maybe you've caught some wacko type of spiritual midlife plague, maybe you're losing your marbles, maybe you're obsessed or demented or hallucinating or . . .

'Shut up.' The words were sharp and fierce. She stood for a moment, hugging herself, willing her shuddering body to normalcy. There was exhilaration, not unmixed with terror, in her every move. Emmy Deer could say what she liked; mad or sane, obsessed or not, he had been out there, and she had seen him, and she was damned well going to splash some hot water on her face and put on her warmest and most comfortable winter clothes and go see for herself.

Hold it right there. You're not thinking.

Emily, struggling with a boot, paused. Dolores, she thought suddenly, had been right. You don't feel nearly so stupid answering a disembodied voice if you can call it something. 'Of course I'm thinking.'

Nope. Reason it out. If that was actually Martin, if he's actually following you around and somehow found out that you left Italy and came to this particular room on this London street, then he's got a reason.

Emily pulled a sweater over her head, listening to her own voice in an undertone muffled by the heavy folds. 'You think you're so smart, what reason?'

Don't know. But if it is him, and he keeps showing himself and then running away or disappearing into the ozone layer or whatever the hell he's doing, he's obviously not doing it for the fun of it. Have you stopped to consider that, wherever he comes from and whatever he's up to, he's not ready for a mano-a-mano, *encounter yet? That when he wants to make real contact he'll stick around long enough to do it?*

'I don't have a clue, and I don't give a flying damn.' She hunted around in a drawer, found some leather gloves lined in soft rabbit fur. 'Right now, strange as it may seem, I'm not interested in his wants or his reasons. I'm interested in mine. And watch whom you're calling names. I'm a woman, not a mano.'

Thank God for small favours. Are you going to search London, from Chiswick to Walthamstow, until you find him? And aren't you talking about a full schedule, sweetie?

'It would be, if I was dumb enough to try it. Only I'm not nearly that dumb. After all this time, you really ought to try and know me better.'

She tucked her London A–Z book in her bag, checked for money and keys. Emmy Deer's voice in her mind had an odd note; uncertainty, sarcasm? Just for once, had she actually confused that hectoring, demanding piece of herself?

Then what are you going to do?

'Follow my nose,' Emily said cheerfully, and went quickly out into the morning, turning off the lights and locking the door behind her.

CHAPTER FIVE

I think I will learn some beautiful language,
useless for commercial
Purposes, work hard at that.

(from 'Intention to Escape from Him')

'Platform four, ten fifty. Next!'

'One day return to Salisbury, please. With a connection for the bus to Stonehenge.'

'Eighteen pounds forty, please, and we don't sell tickets for the bus here, that's the special excursion bus. Here you go, platform twelve, ten fifteen. Ask the British Rail people at Salisbury where to catch the bus for Stonehenge, they'll fix you up. Next!'

Emily pushed money through the small window, accepted the cardboard ticket from the cashier, and hastily moved away from the seemingly endless line of commuters waiting behind her for transport. Around her, Waterloo Station rumbled and whistled and echoed in a constant dance of hurrying feet and luggage carts.

She had never seen anything like a London train station before, and was disconcerted and amused to find the sight intimidating. While the place was obviously in pursuit of a simple purpose, the noise and hurry and apparently aimless beetling about of its patrons superimposed a mocking air over the busyness.

Additionally, the station's physical reality struck Emily

as very nearly a memorial to excess. The roof, like the buttressed and corbelled cover of some futuristic, begrimed cathedral, soared off into the heavens; the floor was streaked and dirty from the feet of the millions who gave themselves to the amenities of British Rail's South-western Region. There were kiosks and suitcases and people glancing wildly at the huge clock, voices that shouted incomprehensibly and uniformed porters looking importantly bored.

Between the many doors that opened and closed and the tracks that stretched off into the outside world, it was very chilly in the station. Emily felt it only on her cheekbones and nose; the rest of her was wrapped tight and warm against the weather. On her second full day in England, she had wandered up to Knightsbridge, thinking vaguely of the department store she had seen after her pizza. She had found it, and much more too; shops, and boutiques, and the long green mausoleum that was Harrods. There were gorgeous glittery evening dresses, and well-cut coats, and fantastic jewellery fit for the throat of an empress.

And Emily, for the first time since early in her marriage, had succumbed to the insistent urge of a shopping frenzy as might a shark in blood-streaked waters. For a woman who for years had considered her appearance so little as to be abnormal by societal standards, the flash of sensual pleasure she found in these new possessions was astonishing.

So, in the windy vastness of Waterloo, Emily waited for a train in brand-new clothes. She had justified the enormous amount she had spent by thinking of her upbringing in a warmer clime; after all, she reasoned, she had not been born to this weather, she was thin-blooded, she certainly didn't want to catch another cold. Emmy

Deer, pointedly silent during the ecstatic trying-on of leather jeans and cashmere sweaters, had finally lost patience when Emily tried to talk herself out of spending a small fortune on the softest, most expensive pair of lambskin boots imaginable. Emmy Deer's advice, which was excellent, was to shut up and just for once buy whatever was wanted without attaching a moral issue to the purchase. Emily had startled a haughty saleswoman by muttering, 'Oh, shut up yourself, of course I'll buy the damned boots,' and then immediately bursting into laughter.

'Platform seven,' a loudspeaker articulated, slow and careful behind its electronically induced distortion. 'The Inter-City express for Southampton, no stops, is presently boarding at platform seven. Thank you.'

No, no, Emily thought ironically, thank *you*. She had already noticed the premium the British attach to surface good manners, and was wryly amused by it; it seemed such a silly thing to hold up as an icon of cultural superiority. She looked at the faces hurrying by, and wondered: Suppose this superficial politeness was taken to its logical extreme? What would happen if the people in the station, the entire faceless horde of them, turned simultaneously toward the source of that polite, pedantic voice and screamed, 'You're welcome'? Would the event warrant so much as a footnote on the pages of *The Times*, or would a veil of silence be drawn over the incident, as if some shocking thing, some breach of cultural prerogative, had occurred?

The truth was that Emily was having some difficulty with England. London was a great city, that was true, but she had never cared much for cities, at least not for their own sake; after all, one could only admire period architecture and municipal monuments for so long before the brain grew glutted and resentful. It was the culture and history of a place that made it interesting. The people were the root and foundation of a culture, and so far she had been completely confounded by the people of London. She had tried sinking what little she knew of the English, from books and movies, into an impersonal non-judgemental limbo; suspecting her own knowledge as unfairly stereotypical, she had tried to form a fresh view by observing them and reading their newspapers.

So far, she had come up empty. The newspapers were contradictory, either garish and vulgar or else laced with a wit so dry as to elude humour altogether; her own eyes, to this point, had told her nothing. In Athens, in Rome, the people were also bewildering, but there they were supposed to be bewildering; they spoke different languages, and that fact alone defined them as foreigners. But these English were different, they spoke the same mother tongue as Emily and yet she could find no common meeting ground, no sense of communion. Here it was the city's physical reality, rather than its inhabitants, that struck a chord, and that chord was a cold one.

So she was off to the countryside, to the ancient town of Salisbury and the windswept reaches of Salisbury Plain, to see if England's green and pleasant land, now iced in under winter weather, would speak to her.

'Platform eighteen,' said the loudspeaker. 'The train from Woking will be arriving in six minutes on platform eighteen. Mind the ice on the platform. Thank you.'

Emily cast an irritated glance at the speakers, wondering why that precise voice so perfectly encapsulated her annoyance. Perhaps, she thought, I'm over-reacting. These English were likeable people, on the face of it, reasonable and quirky and good-humoured, but there were things about them that, to Emily's mind, made for confusion. For all their staidness, their seeming straightforwardness, they simply did not cohere.

She had already picked up a tight-lipped primness on the subject of sex. Well, she thought, that was all right, that was common enough for the thin-blooded children of the north. After all, she was not exactly a passion flower herself, and her own genetics were on the calm side. But the British attitude bothered her; it was directly contradicted by an unhealthy fascination with the subject, a kind of unpleasant pseudo-naughtiness personified by the sloppy and big-breasted nudes in their newspapers, by the veiled references in the doorways of Soho. They seemed to prefer to regard sex as something to be hinted at and somehow defiling, titillating and tawdry, rather than a function of the universe. And that attitude seemed somehow typical of other attitudes.

It was frustrating. The keystone, she thought, the Rosetta Stone. That's what I need, if I'm ever going to understand these people.

Come off it. Since when do you care about understanding these people or any people? You don't know sweet jack about reality, and you care less; you've spent your whole life carving bugs and birds. What's really bugging you is that you're having trouble placing Martin in that way of thinking. You're just not comfortable imagining him pursing up his mouth to look prim while his eyes hunger and slobber . . .

And that was true, Emmy Deer had as usual fingered the immediate source of Emily's discontent. She was looking at England through a Martin-coloured glass, and the image was distorted. That smile, that air of freedom, had not been repeated on a single face she had seen in London, or in any attitude of mind she had found here. That she might also find some clue to Kirstin, whose forebears had rampaged from Orkney to Plymouth and sown the seeds of their own lineage as they made this land their own, had faded from her mind when she had drawn back the curtains and seen Martin standing below her window. She had forgotten why she had come; possibly, she hadn't really known why in the first place.

Tiredness suddenly swept over her, weakening her, and she leaned her head back against a cold tiled wall. Alien, alien, all of this was strange and wrong and pointless. What in God's name was she doing here? Why was she standing in this glittering automated barnyard, running off to someplace she had never seen and wasn't particularly interested in? Why wasn't she back in California, house-hunting, sculpting, coming to grips with the wreckage of her life? And why this sudden urge to go to Salisbury?

Because you're changing. Because you're looking for Martin. Because you're looking for yourself. Because for the first time in your life you've opened yourself up to instincts beyond chisels and wood. Because you're looking for all kinds of things, things without faces or labels or names, because because because . . .

'Platform twelve,' said the polite, mindless voice on the loudspeaker. 'The local to Salisbury, with stops, is presently boarding at platform twelve. Mind the ice on the platform. Thank you.'

'Oh, get stuffed,' Emily said in exasperation and wearily made her way to platform twelve.

Emily turned the corner that led to the bus station in time to see the Stonehenge bus disappearing in the distance.

Typical, she thought bitterly, this was typical. If the trip down was anything to go by, this sort of thing probably happened four times a day. First there had been ice on the tracks, then a two-minute stop at a small country town had mysteriously become twelve minutes. And now there was no bus for another two hours. Considering the distance between the train and bus depots, you'd think they'd hold the damned bus. Considering that the train was the only London connection, you'd think . . .

'Miss your bus?'

Emily's stomach contracted in shock, but only for a moment; even before she turned around, her mind had registered that this voice, female and strangely accented, was not the one she'd been waiting for.

The girl, small and round-faced, smiled up at her. She looked to be no more than twenty. Wisps of corn-gold hair slid from beneath the hood of a down Parka and waved in the cold air; light blue eyes watered a bit in the wind. Her face held humour, and a good deal of intelligence. Emily found herself smiling back.

'By about one minute. The train from London was late. I hate to sound critical, but wouldn't you think they'd have let the bus people know?'

'Well, that's the Poms all over, talk big and screw up on the smaller things. Whoops, there I go again, being parochial about the Motherland.' The girl stamped her feet and hugged herself. 'Cold, isn't it? We don't see this kind of cold in Sydney. Damn, I must have left my gloves on the bloody train.'

'I know, I'm freezing my ass off too. We don't get much of this in New Mexico or California, either.' The depot was filling up with people now, probably all passengers on the London train, and all looking disgusted or dismayed. 'So you're from Australia. I couldn't quite place the accent. Did you come down from London, too?'

'Oxford, by way of London. I'm doing history there, and today was a lecture on British colonialism, so I thought I'd give it a miss.' The girl grinned suddenly. 'Bad for my blood pressure, revisionist history is. I'm Judy Waite, by the way.'

'Emily Moon-Bourne.' Emily glanced around her, noting the black clouds, the iron-grey sky, the tourists wandering aimlessly in disconsolate little groups. Overhead, casting a stark shadow, a solitary bird wheeled and made off toward the west. It was going to snow again; Emily could taste it in the air. 'You know, the next bus isn't for two hours. Let's go find a hot cup of tea.'

The town itself was extremely pretty, lovely in fact. Emily, who had seen nothing of Salisbury but the starkly dirty section by the railroad tracks, was surprised and pleased. The streets wound and curved, the older buildings were interesting and inviting, and near the centre of town a kind of gazebo caught the eye and held it. Women with woven shopping bags stamped and blew and made their way in and out of greengrocers' and haberdashers'. The entire town, in fact, managed to pull off an effect of old-world charm while avoiding the usual pitfalls that would have led to it being labelled picturesque or, worse, quaint.

They found a tea shop near the centre of town. Judy, peeling off the muffling layers of down and wool, was revealed as an exquisitely made little creature, full-breasted and slender-waisted. For all the liveliness of bone and smile, her body possessed a certain stillness, an inner calm. She slid into the booth opposite Emily, caught her companion's fascinated look and raised her eyebrows.

'Something wrong?'

'I was just wondering if you've ever sat.'

Judy blinked. 'Beg pardon?'

'Sat. For a portrait. You've got the bones for it, and the contained expression, You'd be wonderful to paint or, even better, sculpt.'

'Oh, I see. You're a painter?'

'A sculptor. I don't usually do people, though; mostly things that fly, birds, insects, the occasional dragon if someone commissions it.' The people at the next table were spooning clotted cream on hot scones, and steam rose in fragrant gusts from their white mugs. Emily's mouth watered. 'God, look at what they've got! Whatever that stuff is, I want some.'

'Isn't it gorgeous? It's called a cream tea and it tastes as good as it looks.' The waitress set a pot of tea down on the table, took their order and rustled away. Judy brushed the hair back out of her eyes. 'You know, that's interesting, I mean about what you do. The last statue I saw that made an impression on me was an insect. And do I mean an impression? No worry!'

Emily gulped down the scalding tea; it sent warmth and life through her system immediately. 'Sounds interesting. Was it that good? Whose work was it?'

'Haven't got a clue, mate. As for good, that might not be the right word. I mean, it was well done, but it was the ugliest thing I've ever seen, too right it was. I actually had a nightmare about it.'

Emily laughed. 'You may not know this, but you're paying the artist a huge compliment. Was it that scary?'

'Too right it was.' Judy shuddered and wrapped her hands around her teacup as the front door opened and shut, sending a blast of cold air moving around her head. 'I kept dreaming it was trying to sting me.'

Emily looked up suddenly, her teacup suspended. 'Sting you? What do you mean?'

'Well, that's what wasps do, isn't it? Sting people? What's the matter, see a ghost or something?'

'Maybe you did.' Emily shook her head slowly. 'A wasp. Koa wood, on an ebony stand? Head and tail forward, back arched? A stinger like something out of a blue movie?'

'That's the one. Must be, there could hardly be two of those, could there?' Judy was watching her closely. 'You see it too?'

'I carved it. I'll be damned. That's the most . . . look, Judy, where did you see it?'

'In France.' Judy was staring at her. 'South of France, Nice. A little gallery in the old town there, near the tower.

Damn, what's the place called? Oh, right, the Tour Bellanda. Huge place on the hill by the port, beautiful mosaics, Phoenician I think. There's a maritime museum there, too. But I honestly don't remember the name of the gallery. Sorry.' Judy moved the teapot aside, making room for the waitress; she set scones, jams, cream on the table and moved on. 'You carved that thing? Sorry, I didn't mean to criticize your work or anything. It was just . . .'

'Ugly as hell? It was meant to be. I sort of based it on my ex-husband, at that time my not quite ex-husband.' Not thinking, she spread marmalade on a scone and put it down again. 'Goddamn. In France? I never knew who bought it, it was an anonymous buyer. That's crazy, the most absurd thing in the world. That's *nuts*.'

'I don't see why. Must be nice, knowing your stuff's getting a wide look-in.' Judy snapped her fingers suddenly. 'Solferino. That was it, the Galerie Solferino. Rue des Something or other.'

'By the tower, you said, The Tour – what was it?'

'Bellanda. The street leads right up to the door.' Judy hunted in her backpack for a pencil. 'Here, where's my napkin, I'll write it down for you, draw you a map . . . Emily? Are you all right? You've gone all white.'

'Another ghost, that's all.' Emily swallowed hard. Here it was again, images superimposed over images; a young girl with a pencil, sitting at a food-strewn table, scratching away. All that was needed was Kirstin across the room, right about where the front window of the tea shop was. I'm being followed, followed, followed . . .

She glanced up at the window, frightened, unable to help herself. She knew that her mother's small white shade would be watching her, waiting to meet her eyes. The glass was frosted, interior warmth meeting exterior cold, clouding and obscuring. Her breathing was harsh in her throat.

There was someone out there, peering in. Hands pressed against the glass, and a face. A man's face. A tall man's face, lips familiar even through the white mist that clouded the panes, the red mist that clouded Emily's eyes.

She got up so quickly that Judy spilled her tea. 'I have to go. I've just seen someone I know outside, and I must catch him.' She fumbled in her purse, threw a five-pound note on the table. Why was she moving so slowly, her legs felt like rubber, the air itself seemed to have turned to an ether-like substance designed to hold her in place. 'I'll be back or else I'll see you at the bus depot before the next bus goes, this shouldn't take long. Here. Bye.'

'Take the napkin.' Judy, oddly, seemed unsurprised by Emily's urgency. 'You may need it later. Happy hunting.'

Emily fought her way to the door, wrenched it open and pushed past an incoming couple and out into the street. She stood there, her own breathing too loud in her ears, straining her eyes through the softly falling snow.

He was gone. Of course he was gone. Whatever his reasons, whatever game he was playing, Emmy Deer had called it right; she would see him when he chose to be seen, confront him when he chose to be confronted. Nothing would happen before that moment. She could do nothing but wait, passive and frustrated. Tears stung her eyes, chilling her.

Had he even really been there? What, after all, had she seen? A pair of palms pressed against a window, lips that had looked familiar because she wanted them to, needed it that way. Maybe she *was* losing her mind, cracking up, having some kind of early midlife breakdown. Maybe her need and her loneliness and her shattered ego had come together in a touch of madness . . .

A passer-by looked at her curiously, and she dashed the tears away, ducking her head. As she did so, her eyes fell on the pavement and her breathing shortened, stopped and started again in painful jerks.

Footprints. They were disappearing under the fall of new snow, but there they were, unmistakable, the imprints of a man. Her eyes moved upwards, finding the outer glass of the tea shop, seeing the smears there, where a pair of hands had tried to clear the frost away.

What are you waiting for, you coward, an invitation? Follow the damned footprints. Win the grand prize. X marks the spot. And you'd better hurry, chiquita, because in about six minutes there's going to be a nice fresh layer of virginal white snow to look at, and nothing else. So make like a St Bernard. Track him. Find him.

'No.' She spoke softly, hearing her own small voice carried away on the moving weather. When she spoke again, it was in her thoughts. 'No. I'm not going to chase him. I won't play that game. I can draw him when I choose and see him when he chooses, but I can't catch him and I don't want to. It isn't time yet. Aren't you the one who said that I wouldn't see him, connect with him, until he decided it was time? So I won't follow the footprints. No.'

She went slowly back into the tea shop, sliding into her seat just as the waitress returned with a fresh pot and the bill. Judy took one quick look at Emily's face and busied herself with pouring tea.

'Here, you must be frozen. God, we must be mental, chasing out to look at dirty old rocks on a day like this. Did you find your friend?'

'No. No, I missed him.' Again, she thought, again. How long had he been there, moving unseen on the periphery of her life? Judy's face held a kind of impassive shrewdness, not unmixed with sympathy, but Emily saw no curiosity there. She realized that she had taken quite a liking for this child, with her tact and good humour, and smiled suddenly.

'This may be a mistake, you may run screaming for the men in the white coats, but I'm going to tell you something. The man I mentioned, the one I keep seeing? Well, I'm not even sure he's real. I mean, I keep seeing him, I've seen him in Herculaneum and London and now here, but every time I try to approach him . . .'

Judy lifted her brows. 'Playing games with you?'

'How quick you are. Yes, in a way.' And Emily related the entire story, all the way back to that first placemat sketch, twenty years before. When she was done, she felt cleansed. She spooned clotted cream on a scone, noting with detached pride that her hands were perfectly steady. 'Now tell me I'm loopy as a loon.'

'Why?' Judy's surprise was so obviously genuine that Emily felt tears of gratitude burn her lids. 'We all have these little guideposts along the road, don't we? We may not know where they come from, or what they're for, but we've all got them. Sometimes it's animals, pets I mean, and sometimes it's just a kind of remembrance, I guess what they call *déjà vu*. With me, it's a song. When I was a little kid I kept dreaming that someone, a man, was singing to me. It wasn't a real song, I mean, not one that I've ever heard anywhere else. And I've never forgotten it, the exact sound of it; I'll know it if I ever hear it. Sometimes I dream about the singing voice again, if something bad or stressful happens. Loopy? No worry. I'd more likely think you were nuts if you didn't have a few of your own.' She handed the hovering waitress money. 'Here, keep the change. Half an hour to the next bus. I'm ready if you are.'

The moment she saw Stonehenge, Emily knew why she had had to come.

The bus was full of tourists. Most of them had recovered from their disgruntlement at having missed the earlier connection, and the air was full of noisy, polyglot chatter. Emily, in a window seat with Judy serene beside her, idly rubbed her gloves against the glass and tried to make sense of hedgerow and ominous sky.

Had it not been for the steamed windows, she would have seen it first from the bus. She caught a glimpse of something huge and dark, held in an open hollow, as the bus crested a slight rise and turned a corner. The flash was of size and potency, nothing more; the snow softened the edges of the world, and a clear impression was impossible to get.

'Stonehenge.' Judy, who had been quiet, leaned across Emily's body and pointed. 'Damn, you can't see. We'll be there in a moment.'

The bus turned sharply, pulled into a parking lot, and stopped. It was snowing steadily now, a dry heavy powder that promised to stick. Emily pulled the hood of her jacket over her head, let the bus empty out, and followed Judy down the steps into the darkening afternoon.

The shock, the physical slap of internal awareness, would stay with her; even at this distance, across the road with a two-lane strip of asphalt separating her, the sense of recognition was immediate and powerful. If Emmy Deer spoke, prompting her, Emily heard nothing of it, for such prompting was unnecessary.

Alamogordo. Stones, ancient stones, a windswept vista that was rocky and wild. A place of breathing ghosts, of dead hands that cut and carved, of minds that were busy in ways no modern mind would ever understand.

She was unaware of Judy's presence beside her, unaware of the milling, exclaiming crowd of visitors. She had no memory of having moved through the tunnel beneath the road, of emerging from the dark underground into the swirling snow. She stood before the wire fence, her gloved hands clutching, gazing into memory.

There were stones in Albuquerque, plenty of them; if one wished to see petroglyphs, there was no need to leave town. But her father had announced, shortly before her high school graduation, that when that rite of passage had been accomplished he and Emily would drive down to Alamogordo to see the stones there.

Kirstin had not been a part of that invitation, and she had not asked to come; Emily remembered her foolish, enigmatic smile, remembered, too, that she had as usual been annoyed by it. And 'invitation' was the wrong word; it had been an announcement, a statement of fact. Chiefly, her reaction had been one of astonishment. John had never suggested such a thing before.

So, on a brilliantly sunny morning late in June, father and daughter had climbed into the car and driven to the south-east. The trip had taken several hours. John had stopped twice along the way, once at a roadside gas station that served food, and once at a scenic overlook on Highway 25. Here he got out of the car without a word and stood staring toward the Rio Grande for some moments. When he came back to the car, he gave Emily the twitch of the lips that passed for a smile with him. She asked him nothing; he was taciturn to the point of surliness. Experience had taught her that John Moon spoke when he chose, and only then.

After a few hours of driving, he broke the silence.

'When I said Alamogordo, I was being misleading. We'll sleep there tonight, but that's not what I want you to see. The stones are really at Three Rivers.'

'OK.' Emily, at a loss, did not really mind. This trip was a new experience and, like all new experiences, it required a period of internal absorption. She cast a quick glance at her father's profile and ventured a question. 'The stones at Three Rivers. Did your ancestors carve them?'

'No.' The highway before them was nearly empty, but he kept his eyes on the road. John Moon, who did everything well, was an excellent driver. 'The Mogollon carved them. Twelfth century. You'll see.'

'Um.' Emily asked no more questions; her father had retreated into taciturnity. For the next half-hour neither of them spoke. Then John pulled the car into a parking lot, turned off the ignition and sat staring ahead at the bush and rocky scree in the distance.

'We're here?'

He answered by climbing out of the car. Emily followed hurriedly, shutting the car door carefully, adjusting her stride to match his.

The next little while was devoted to scrambling. They moved through a picnic area, where a few families sat eating and talking, until they emerged on to a trail. John moved along the trail, over a thousand yards long and rocky, with the sure feet of one who had walked this route before. He stopped in front of her, so suddenly that she bumped into him, on a stark ridge that was strewn with boulders.

And here, at last, was the pride of the long-vanished Mogollon. The boulders were carved, thousands of them, tumbled across the landscape. Emily had seen petroglyphs before, but never in such a wild setting. Moved by impatience, by inexplicable need, she edged round her father and began to explore.

The stones were warm under her hand, speaking of sunlight and dust. Emily saw lizards, and deer, and human figures in bizarre ceremonial dress. Some of the stones had been tampered with, chipped away by obvious souvenir hunters or with graffiti carved on them, and this produced in Emily something akin to rage. She let her fingers trail over carvings, savouring them. On the ridge above her, John stood watching, making no move to join her. There was something tactful, delicate, about this avoidance; he seemed to be distancing himself from her to allow her time and space to react to this ancient place.

She made her way back up, finally, coming to stand breathless and oddly disturbed at his side. She was aware of him, as she had never been before; aware of his regular, even breathing, his dark weathered skin, his hollowed-out black diamond eyes. She said nothing, for she had no words.

And suddenly John Moon, who rationed words as the white man had rationed whiskey among his own fore-bears, turned to his daughter and said, 'Your brother would have loved this.'

Twenty years later, in the hard-driving snow of an English winter, Emily could feel that long-vanished sun beat brutally down against her uncovered head. The day was blazing, merciless, without shelter, she heard the angry drone of insects, a distant chattering of birds. Some-where behind her, near the picnic area, a dog was barking. She turned to stare at him.

'I don't have a brother.'

'You did.' Without taking his eyes from the dust-hazed horizon, he reached into his work shirt and pulled out a cigarette. 'He was two years older than you. He died the day your mother found out she was pregnant again. His name was Bear.'

A cloud of mosquitoes whined around Emily's head. She ignored them, knowing they would not touch her; insects never did. In seventeen years spent in a land infested with these creatures, she had never received so much as a flea bite. She stared at her father, taking in his profile, his stillness, wondering if he had gone mad or if she had. She spoke slowly, clearly.

'I had a brother? Named Bear?'

'Bear Dancer Moon. He died of FAS, Foetal Alcohol Syndrome.' And now he did turn to look at her, his dark face a mask of a fire left banked too long. He smouldered in the sun like a breathing icon of this place in which he stood. 'I should have married an Indian woman. Are you all done? We have to drive to Alamogordo and find a motel.'

And that was all.

'Emily?'

She came out of it slowly, hearing her own name repeated twice. Judy stood beside her, shivering but entranced.

'The bus back to Salisbury is due in ten minutes, and we still have to go back under the road. Ready?'

'Yes.' Was this what taking drugs was like? A long dream of connection, followed by sharp dislocation? All those opium eaters, those morphine users, those drinkers of absinthe in *fin de siècle* Paris, was this what they sought so urgently? Her feet sank into the snowy path as she left the open field for the warmth of the bus. She climbed aboard, taking an aisle seat. She did not look back at Stonehenge as the bus swept toward the world of lights and movement.

CHAPTER SIX

Stricken with noise, confused with light.

(from 'Exiled')

There was a connection. Somehow, in some arcane way, there had to be a connection.

All through the slow ride back to London and a scratch meal with Judy, Emily pushed the thought away from her. Yet it remained real and solid, a snake coiled in readiness for the strike. It crouched somewhere between her waking mind and the dark recess where Emmy Deer lived, waiting patiently for her full attention.

There was a logic to all this, as quirky as anything found in Lewis Carroll's little syllogisms. The fracturing of the life she had known, which had sent her careening across Europe, was connected to all those unresolved memories of her mother and father. Those memories, in turn, were connected to the flesh or spirit that was Martin, who was probably connected to all those empty years of marriage to an empty man. That sense of need, the desperate desire to screw all those loose ends into their appropriate sockets, was becoming an obsession.

She gave Judy her number, telling her that she'd probably be there another two or three weeks before leaving for France. Signposts, Judy had said, guides along the way. Well, that was logical too. The knowledge of her own work's presence in a resort town on the French

Riviera – and that particular piece of work above all others – had pointed out in which direction she must travel. That she was not yet done in England, she knew; she had no sense of completion here, there was something yet to be found, or gained. But France was calling to her, and to France she would go. She promised Judy, when they parted at the restaurant door, that she would send her an address in France, care of Judy's college, when Emily was settled there.

The dinner itself was not without interest. Judy, like Dolores before her, had things to say. It was amazing, Emily thought, that after twenty years of not exchanging a single word of importance with anyone, these strangers should show her the treasure of spoken communication in all its power.

Judy had done so. Without a single questioning word, she had drawn Emily out of herself, making her talk about things long buried. She had accomplished this by making remarks about herself, a verbal equivalent of forcing a key in a lock; to have kept silence in the face of such cheerfully fearless frankness would have been poor manners. Like women in a magazine, but with certain differences, they had talked about sex.

'I love sex.' Judy, her yellow hair amber in the dim light of a Fulham restaurant, held a goblet of Calvados in one hand, swirling the drink in a gentle lapping tide. 'I don't much care for men, having to listen to them and cope with them and gratify their egos. I'm not really interested in reassuring people. But I simply love sex, the whole thing, fire and ice and the whole nine yards. I mean, isn't it great?'

'No.' Emily, thinking painlessly about Gary, was surprised at the spontaneity of her answer. 'I don't think it's great, it hasn't been great in my experience. Of course, I don't exactly have a huge bank of comparisons to draw on. I met a boy in my first year of college and stuck to him. We got married when I was in my twenties. But I sure as hell didn't marry him for the sex. To tell you the truth, I always found it boring and embarrassing.'

'Boring?' Maybe it was the dimness that now made even Judy's light eyes seem amber. 'Embarrassing? Lovey, I hate to say this, but you have a real problem here. I mean, either this bloke wasn't worth the sheets he slept on, or else you didn't like yourself too much.'

Bright child, isn't she?

'Clever, clever girl. Do you know, I never stopped to ask myself which one it was. And there's no way to know now, unless . . .' The words tailed off.

'Unless you take another lover? Not a bad idea, take it from someone who did just that. Of course, it might not prove anything, because no one's the same person at forty that they were at twenty.' Judy grinned suddenly, a gleam of teeth and shifting of muscle in the shadows. 'But who cares whether it proves something, as long as it's fun? How about this mysterious vanishing playmate of yours? You think you could maybe get a yen for him?'

'I don't know!' There it was, the spur, the dark winding road. In all the years with Gary, she had never felt more than a fleeting few moments of desire, and the bare truth was that the desire had not been directed specifically at him; it had been a universal flash of feeling, impersonal and weak. Finely grained wood had been a greater spur to lust than any man had. Was that normal?

In the face of Judy's perception, the thing was sitting on her shoulders like a bird of ill omen. It was huge and demanding and undeniable. She wanted Martin, wanted him as she had wanted nothing else in her life. The Martin-coloured glasses had a burning smoky tinge to them, and when she thought of him, it was with her whole body.

And you're ashamed of it.

Judy was watching her, quizzical, impossible to snub. Emily pushed her dessert around on her plate, looking down, thinking. She was on the edge of a revelation here, there was something of vast importance to her life, an answer that lay buried, just visible beyond self-examination. Don't think, she told herself. Don't. Just open your mouth and say whatever comes out, no matter what it is. Maybe it will be the truth, or maybe the Four Horsemen of the Apocalypse. Who knows, who cares? Just do it.

She spoke slowly, carefully, listening to herself.

'That last day in court,' she said. 'That last day, when the divorce decree was handed down. Dodie was in court, you know, Gary's little fertility factory. Playing the poor patient woman, *hugely* pregnant. God knows what she was doing there, maybe trying to sway the court in saving Gary a few bucks. If that was the idea behind her little game, the plan backfired in a big way.' She smiled suddenly, a small tight smile, but genuine in its sour amusement. 'Oh, boy, did it backfire. The judge was a woman, one of those upright sensible ladies in her fifties who was raised with a much simpler morality. So Dodie's little scam didn't work. Her Honor was not impressed, nor was she moved.'

'Yes.' The word was neutral. It held no judgements; it could have meant anything.

'When we were all leaving, I was watching Gary, like a hawk with its eyes on a mouse. He was his usual tight-lipped, tight-assed self; Mister Big-Shot Lawyer, who didn't like the court's decision, seething. Half a million bucks! God, it was glorious, he was such a rage . . . I hadn't felt that good in months, years maybe. Now, you tell me; is that reasonable, or just vindictive?'

'Oh, definitely reasonable,' Judy responded immediately. 'I would have been howling with mirth, myself. Did something happen, some kind of confrontation?'

'I glanced over at Dodie. I hadn't done that, not once, I'd been concentrating on sending Gary the blackest possible death vibes. I swear I felt like Darth Vader and I loved it. But I felt, I really felt that if I let myself look at that little moron, I'd just let go and deck her one.' Emily struggled to explain. 'It wasn't that she'd broken up my home, or any of that crap. I don't think anyone can do that to you, not if you're solid. You do it to yourself. But I hated her for what she was, for what she represented. You know, the so-called liberated woman with the feminist rap. It was *such bullshit*. She was a middle-class girl who'd taken a shot at playing with the big boys. Now she was tired of that, so she wanted to call it quits and go home and play with her toy dishes and her little dolls.'

Judy was grinning, a huge delighted smile. 'Good on you, girl friend! I'd have smacked her one.'

Emily smiled back, but with an effort. 'I've never hit anyone in my life, but I was afraid I was going to that day. I hate women like that, I just hate them. Anyway, we all brushed past each other in the hallway, my lawyer had his arm around my shoulder and was cheerleading like a mad thing, and I was smiling at Gary. I could feel that smile, it was so savage it hurt. He shot me a look like a laser beam, and I looked away from him and my eyes landed on Dodie.'

Judy was still grinning. 'I wish I could have been a fly on the wall! It sounds like a real party.'

So clear, so very clear . . . Emily spoke slowly, clarifying her thoughts with every word. 'All my life, I'd been hearing the Great American Myth about pregnant women. Maybe you've heard it too, all the way Down Under.

Childbirth is God's great blessing, a wonderful thing. A pregnant woman is glowing, and radiant, and blah blah blah. Well, that myth went west for ever when I looked at Dodie.'

'How did she look?' Judy caught the waiter's eye, and tapped her glass for a refill.

'Drained. Pinched. There were huge blue shadows under her eyes, and her ankles were swollen. She looked as if a vampire had been at her for weeks. And for a minute I actually felt guilty, do you believe that? Like her tired feet and morning sickness were my fault?'

'Don't you believe it.' Judy, between gulps of Calvados, was comfortingly robust. She had an assurance, a clarity of view, that was incredible for a girl of twenty. 'And don't go blaming Gary for it, either. She did it to herself, bought into it herself, chose it herself. She probably *was* sick, and drained, and all that. Babies *are* vampires, Emily. I ought to know, I'm the eldest of seven, and I can't remember my mum looking healthy a day in her life. But it's what she created for herself. If I were you, I'd be more worried about finding out why sex seems embarrassing and boring. I mean, you might not like the answer, but it's one you need to find out. How old are you?'

This last question came abruptly, and startled Emily into an honest answer. 'Thirty-eight. Thirty-nine this Hallowe'en. Why?'

'Just wondering. From what I've heard of the forties collision course, you're on the young side for it. Still, you never know; everything you've told me sounds suspiciously like the midlife fork in the road to me.'

'Midlife crisis?' Emily thought this over, aware of a sour taste at the back of her throat. 'Me? Now?'

'You, now. What's so surprising about it? You've had

a shock. Everything's upside-down, your memory's gone all neon and a signpost has taken on flesh and is following you all over Europe. So you're open, you see, you're vulnerable to things right now. I'm told it hurts like hell, that state of mind. But why not turn it to your advantage? Why not be an explorer? I know that all the books say it has to be hell, but those books were mostly written by men. If you ask yourself some hard questions now, you may get the answers. And, if you get the answers now, it may make your thirty-ninth birthday a whole lot easier.' She checked her watch. 'Jesus, look at the time! If I don't get going, I'll miss my train. Write to me, will you? For both our sakes, write to me. You need an outlet.'

Emily reached out and hugged her. 'Maybe I do need an outlet. But why for your sake? What do you need?'

'Me? Nothing at all.' Judy kissed her lightly. 'I'm just nosy.'

A raised hand, a fleeting smile and she was gone into the cold London night.

And Emmy Deer spoke clearly and lucidly.

Maybe she was wrong about one thing. Maybe Martin's not following you. Maybe he's leading the dance.

Why not be an explorer?

The more Emily pondered the question, the greater sense it made. She had started this journey in a state of numb loneliness, of self-denial. With Martin's first appearance in Italy, loneliness had transmuted into something resembling the feeling of a fox fleeing the hounds. The difference in state of mind was not so great, not nearly great enough; both, after all, were negatives.

Here was a suggestion to change things, a recommendation toward the positive pole. Explore, explore. Take the reins, damn the torpedoes, seize the day . . . Emily turned this over and over in her mind with increasing pleasure. Like Dolores, Judy had hit the nail on her head. Name it, personify it, ask yourself. For once in your life, be in control of it. It doesn't have to be bad, and you don't have to be a victim.

So, the day after Stonehenge, she bought herself a car. The only car she had ever purchased was shortly after her wedding, and she remembered it as a hideously complicated procedure. But this was easy enough. She borrowed a paper from her landlady and scanned the classified columns, marking off four possibilities. The first two numbers she called had messages on answering machines, stating that the automobiles in question had already been sold. The third number, a ten-year-old Citroën, was still available. It had recently been completely serviced, the mileage was low and the price reasonable.

Emily took the Tube to North London. She fell in love with the car at once; its resemblance to some kind of alien insect seemed like an omen. She asked the owner some tough, pertinent questions and drove the French import with its elderly leather seats experimentally around Muswell Hill and Highgate. By the time she had adjusted to the sensation of driving sideways on the wrong side of the road, she had fallen in love with this coffee-coloured, bug-eyed monster that was so comfortable and responsive.

Fortunately, the owner was perfectly willing to take traveller's cheques. Emily drove the car back toward Chelsea, sweating nervously, but exhilarated at her own daring. Seize the day, she thought, be an explorer. Emily de Leon, that's me. Stout Cortez in the modern age. Fountain of youth, here I come. I've taken my first step toward El Dorado.

After that, England opened up. Armed with road

guides and Ordnance Survey maps, Emily drove to Cornwall, to Yorkshire, to Wales. She strolled the Lake District in Wordsworth's footsteps, bought cashmere in Edinburgh and took pictures of Hadrian's Wall. She spent a delirious Saturday in Oxford, wandering in and out of bookshops with Judy, rediscovering old favourites that, over the years, had taken on new meaning.

It was Judy who found the book, in a stall of battered hardcover editions of poetry. Emily, who loved books, was conscious of her nomadic status and mindful of the consequences attendant on burdening herself with too many volumes. An hour of browsing contentedly among the dusty shelves of Godbody's Used Editions, Ltd., had produced nearly twenty books she coveted; sternly mindful of reality, she had limited herself to only two.

'Oh, lovely!'

Emily, on the verge of paying for her purchases, turned towards Judy's voice. She was standing by the stall of fifty-pence hardcovers, a book open in her hands. She was smiling, an odd distant smile. Emily moved to her side, curious.

'Find something?'

'An old favourite of mine. I used to adore this one, but it never meant anything really; I guess I was too young.' Judy brushed hair out of her eyes and handed the book to Emily. 'Funny how things take on different meanings, isn't it? Sir Thomas Gray.'

'The *Elegy*? Lord, it's been years!' Emily scanned the poem, last read some eighteen years ago in a college course on literature. Immediately she understood what Judy meant; what had been a pleasing exercise in meter at her last encounter had indeed become something else. The words held power, and regret; the stillness and sentimentality were merely the mask for depth and knowledge.

She scanned the verses, searching for that often-quoted couplet, and found it at once.

'Full many a flower is born to blush unseen . . .' Judy, reading her thoughts or perhaps her face, prompted her softly. Emily raised her eyes from the page, staring at Judy. Her feelings were mixed and potent.

'. . . and waste its sweetness on the summer air,' she finished.

'*Desert* air,' Judy corrected. 'Waste its sweetness on the desert air. You know something, love? I think this bloke's been reading your mail.'

The perspicacity of that remark, appalling as it was, was so typically Judy that Emily could take no offence. Desert air, indeed! That was turning your back on the mirror with a real vengeance. No wonder Judy had corrected her quote. How long had she been sitting in the hot dry sun, her memories distorted and withering, empty, without self-knowledge? She turned away toward the sales counter, feeling a spot of colour high on each cheekbone.

Judy, at her side, touched her sleeve lightly. 'Sorry,' she said softly. 'I talk too much sometimes.'

'You're usually right.' She added the anthology to her other books, and paid for them. Together, they walked out into the frosted sunshine of the street.

'Judy,' Emily said abruptly. 'I know I was going to stay for dinner, but I've changed my mind. I think I need to be alone somewhere for a while. Can I take a rain check on tonight and buy you a meal next week?'

'As long as I haven't mortally offended you.' The girl looked really anxious, and Emily took her hand.

'I'm not offended at all. I've just been struck by some gentle lightning, that's all. Call me Monday or Tuesday?'

'Too right I will.' Judy, relieved but still perceptive, immediately turned away. Emily stood on the pavement, staring into space, until with a sharp jerk of the mind she realized that Judy was no more than a dot in the distance and that matrons whose progress she was impeding were giving her dirty looks.

The book was an anthology, dog-eared and discarded by some unknown schoolgirl when her requirement for reading Poetry for the Masses had been legally fulfilled. The *Elegy* was marked with notes in the margins, banal observations designed to please a schoolteacher, carefully written down in a round schoolgirl's hand. Other pieces had been commented on, as well; the book contained a remarkable assortment, from Villon to Spenser to Blake and all the way through Dorothy Parker.

Back in London, Emily stopped at a takeaway kebab place, wedged the Citroën between two cars, and shut herself in for the evening. Emmy Deer was silent, the streets outside were grey and streaked with cold rain and the windows of the houses across the street showed misty lights.

Emily ate her kebab, savouring the peculiar spices at the back of her throat. When she had washed the faint greasy residue from her fingers, she made herself a pot of strong coffee and curled up on the sofa with the book.

Emily had read poetry before; there was, it seemed, no escaping the American educational system without it. But that had been of necessity, and not of choice. She was a sculptor, a visual person, and the magic of words had always eluded her. She had dutifully ploughed her way through the classics, memorizing their structure while confounded by their substance. Shakespeare was a struggle, Virginia Woolf a depressing muddle; at eighteen, at twenty, she had wanted no part of what these purveyors of thought and feeling had to say, for they had succeeded only in making her uneasy.

Times certainly do change, she thought. Thomas

Nashe, for instance; what in her youth had been no more than a sonorous exercise in rhythm had become vivid and real and pertinent to Emily, the woman. *Dust hath closed Helen's eye, the plague full swift goes by.* Another piece, too, sent some interior bell pealing faintly, something about going into the world of light.

She read on, greedy, frankly guzzling the sweet liquor of words that had come bearing hidden gifts and wearing magical new strengths. A quote from Marlowe, speaking with a veteran's voice to a new woman. *But that was in another country, and besides, the wench is dead . . .*

That's me, Emily thought. Her ashtray was overflowing, scattering grey dust across the polished table; her coffee was cold and her limbs ached with stiffness. Another country, and that wench that married Gary and went to Alamogordo is dead, dead, dead. Maybe not buried . . .

She stood, stretching, and rinsed her cup. Far from her own thoughts, she was yet caught deeply and completely by new awareness. The anthology was chronological, running from *Beowulf* and Grendel to T. S. Eliot's cruellest month and a lovely saucy villanelle by Sylvia Plath. Emily dried the cup.

You're ducking again, sweetie.

Except for that single observation about following and leading, Emmy Deer had been silent all day. Now the cold little voice sounded in Emily's head, startling her, making her jump. For the first time she was aware of resentment, as if a friend had presumed too closely on friendship itself and gone into a place into which she had not been invited.

'I'm absorbing, that's all. And I certainly don't think I'm ducking.'

Oh, yes, you are. What was giving Emmy Deer's words that iron tinge of patience stretched too far? *Remember why you bought the book in the first place? Desert air, instead of summer air. Your own personal desert, the place where you lived so long. What Judy said, what you said. About exploring, about why you found sex boring at best and distasteful at worst. You were going to think about it, remember? How do you plan to be an explorer if you're afraid to cast your boat from the safety of the shore?*

'No.' Emily spoke strongly, loudly, to the empty room, the inner voice. The book was solid in her grip. 'I'm not afraid of that. But I need time to absorb things. What in hell's the use of leaping into things without understanding?'

For a moment, there was no answer. Then, *So what do you do next?*

The coffee she had drunk was doing odd things to Emily's stomach, sending off little gurgling sounds. The kebab had been delicious, but it was useless in absorbing the quantity of acid produced by six cups of coffee at ten o'clock at night. She rummaged around in her tiny cupboard, found herself an opened box containing a Swiss roll, and cut herself a large hunk of the gooey chocolate confection.

Well?

'What a stupid question.' Emily shook her head, pleased to find that the omniscient and constantly critical Emmy Deer was capable of fuddling her own interior logic. 'A really stupid question.'

You haven't answered.

'This afternoon you offered up the idea that Martin wasn't following me. You said that maybe he was leading. And maybe you're right.'

So?

'So I let him do the leading. I don't do anything until he does, that's all.'

Ah. Passive aggressive.

'Bullshit!' Emily was shocked at her own flash of anger, and even more shocked at the irrationality of it. What in hell am I doing, she wondered? This voice, it's me, part of me, a separate self maybe but the key word is still self, isn't it? Just who or what am I getting mad at?

Good question, sweetie. You tell me and we'll both know.

'Oh, shut up.' She ate the last crumbs of Swiss roll, rinsed off the plate. The room was warm, too warm. The smoke of too many cigarettes clouded the air, turning it blue-grey. Emily wandered over to the window, pushing the curtains aside to lean her heated cheek against the chilly glass.

Look out!

Emily leaped backwards with a stifled cry, the curtain slipping back into place. There was something outside the window. It hung at eye-level, hovering; the sound of its wings beating a thousand times a minute was muffled by the separating glass, but still audible. The whine was deadly, hungry, speaking of terror and need. Emily, her hands at her mouth to push back the nausea rising fast in her throat, watched the shadow of a tiny body darting angrily closer to the window and away again.

A wasp, a hummingbird? Had it really even been there?

A wasp or a hummingbird. In February, in London? Oh, good suggestion, kiddo. Really brilliant. Maybe it was a flagship for a race of invading elves.

'It's no dumber than the wasp at Heathrow.' Not a hummingbird. Nothing so benign as that could have produced that instant reactive fear in her. 'It was a wasp. I don't know how, or where it came from. It was a wasp.'

A wasp. Yes, all right. So what?

Emily stared around the flat, her eyes wide and vacant. 'I'll tell you so what. I'm going to France.'

CHAPTER SEVEN

And when the lights begin to show
Up from the town,
I will mark which must be mine
And then start down!

(from 'Afternoon on a Hill')

There were no wasps on the ferry ride from Dover to Calais. The first hint of spring came to Emily as she stood at the rail and watched gulls chasing white-caps, her muscles tautening and responding to the small gusts of a wind that grew insensibly warmer with every lunge of the unwieldy craft Emily rode on. She saw no wasps. The only thing present with the capability to sting was the salt sea air.

The ferry was crowded, overweighed with bodies that wandered from deck to deck and a cargo-hold full of parked cars that would carry their owners and families on leisurely jaunts across the Continent. It had cast off under a Turner sky, speckled with clouds that were hugely obese and distantly tinted with the purple-red that spoke to Emily of storms in the distance. She had been at the loading dock shortly before nine, her eyes gritty with a short night's sleep and the expectation of culture shock. She had expected a bumpy ride; she had expected to be sick.

The journey was exhilarating, from the slap of white-capped breakers against the side of the ferry to the sensation of riding atop a bottomless well. Emily, growing up inland and too shuttered in her studio as an adult, had little experience with sailing. Gary – this was the first time she had really thought about him since the divorce, and she was astonished and pleased at how painless it was – had been a poor sailor.

True, true. But is this really what Judy was talking about, this kind of confrontation with yourself? Well, maybe. Maybe.

It's a start, Emily thought, and continued playing with the memory. He had discovered this weakness the hard way, with a gratifying smack to his self-esteem, when a senior partner in his law firm invited both Gary and his secretary out for an afternoon cruising San Francisco Bay. How fearfully pleased he'd been, puffed and strutting with self-importance; he'd been virile that night, amorous in reaction to the attention he'd been paid by a man Emily privately regarded as a status symbol with feet. He'd actually gone out and bought a pair of deck shoes for the event . . .

Ten minutes on a glassily calm surface had proved, beyond doubt, that he was not Captain Blood or Jacques Cousteau. According to a titbit dropped by his gossipy secretary, he'd spent the remainder of that sail retching over the side, the colour of pea soup. His own inability had galled Gary enormously; not, however, enough for him to try to conquer it by perseverance. So they had never sailed, he and Emily, and the very question of seaworthiness, by tacit agreement, had been left alone.

She smiled reminiscently. Gary, with his lop-sided view of justice, would certainly have considered Emily's reaction unjust. She turned this picture over in her mind, the smile growing into a legitimate grin. It was a pity she couldn't simply force a picture into his mind long distance; watching how happily Emily weathered what, to him, would have been physical torture would have sent him into a frenzy.

She sucked in a huge gout of the foam-flecked air, revelling in the salt caking on her lips and the bucking of the deck beneath her feet as she had once revelled in the feel of a horse beneath her. Another memory surfaced, pleasantly spiteful. That was something else Gary had avoided doing, had tried once and only once, another physical activity that had ended ignominiously for ego and physique alike. If he wasn't Captain Blood, he certainly wasn't Roy Rogers, either. Emily remembered the incident with pleasure, cupping her hands around her lighter as the smoke from her cigarette drifted and mingled with the tendrils of north-riding fog.

They'd gone riding together once, at Emily's suggestion. It was just after they'd gotten married, at a public stable near San Francisco. Emily's mare had been beautifully mannered and very responsive for a hired ride. Gary, on the other hand . . . the staid elderly gelding Gary had picked with a spurious air of confidence had rid himself of his burden in something under five minutes. Gary's cursing and swearing, distressing at the time, made for a nice memory.

Emily puffed and smiled, unconscious of the people that strolled the deck around her, chatting and pointing and trying to decide whether to button their coats. Gary, dear old Gary, approaching the unknown art of horsemanship like a Rough Rider. He'd been sore for days, his backside so swollen and discoloured that even the famous birthmark had been indistinguishable from the surrounding welter of bruises . . .

A cormorant called out harshly, hidden behind the aft tower of the ferry, startling Emily back to the present. She took a deep breath, closing her eyes to feel the spray settle damply on her lids. She realized, with some surprise, that she had fallen into a mood of relaxation and calm. God, it had been a long time since she'd felt anything other than numbness or pain.

Spring's coming. Isn't that amazing? It was still winter, back there in England; you couldn't go outside without covering every extremity. Here in France, there's spring waiting just over the horizon.

Not France yet, Emily corrected Emmy Deer lazily. This isn't France, it's sort of nowhere. This boat's afloat in the Sea of Erewhon. We're about half-way between the two countries, a kind of international limbo. A fragment of verse came into her head, from Lewis Carroll this time; from *Alice*, wasn't it? 'The further off from England the nearer is to France . . .'

. . . 'will you, won't you, will you, won't you, will you join the dance?' That's the rest of it.

Well, France waited somewhere, perhaps just beyond the next breaking wave, and Emily was as ready to make a grand entrance into Paris as Napoleon had been after his escape from Elba. She had changed her English pounds for French francs; she, who ran from Italy to England with no plan in mind and no place to go once she got there, had planned this leg of her journey like a general plotting strategy for a military campaign. She had gone to a famed travel agency near Leicester Square, she had arranged for her car's passage and her own, she had perused a list of holiday rentals in three different *arrondissements*. On the advice of the travel agent, who was familiar with Paris, she had chosen a two-room *pied à terre* a stone's throw from the Eiffel Tower and the École Militaire, whatever that was. Everything had been pre-arranged, down to the smallest detail, for the first time since her travels had begun.

Unusual for you, Ulysses. Did you maybe smell something different, something important, about this leg of things?

'Who asked you, anyway? Look, there's something on the horizon. I think it's France!' There was land up ahead, a thin black line now separating what, a few minutes ago, had been the sketchy grey haze between earth and sky.

As if in response to this thought, the stacks of the ferry blew a single piercing blast. Emily wrapped her sheepskin jacket firmly around her – milder though the weather definitely was, it was still barely March and no amount of jaunty bravery was going to make the English Channel any warmer than it really was – and headed indoors to the ship's bar for a careful perusal of her road maps and a cup of tea.

As Emily nosed her car into a space on the Avenue Bosquet, the thin drizzle that had begun not five minutes after setting foot on French soil, and which had accompanied her drive down from France's north coast, faded and died.

It was nearly six in the evening, and the weak light of early March was transmuting into something darker, more mysterious. The drive had been simple and straightforward enough, but she was nervous; all of her automotive adventures in the Citroën had been from the other side of the road, the pavement of the highway was slick, and traffic, as she grew closer both to the City of Light and the impatient crunch of the legendary Parisian rush hour, was increasingly thick and hard to navigate.

On the edge of her peripheral vision, she was aware that a place of balance and exquisite beauty was unfolding on every side of her. While her complete attention was required for locating the correct exit (the Porte d'Orléans, marked with yellow Magic Marker on the small spiral-bound road atlas given to her as a courtesy by the London travel agent), she paid no heed to the ugly industrial outskirts of the city. Once she was in Paris proper, however, the street names she had memorized from her map simply pulled her towards her destination, freeing corners of mind and eye to take in fleeting, tantalizing glimpses of gorgeous monuments bisecting the skyline, fabulously carved bridges across the Seine, the uppermost tip of the Eiffel Tower sliding in and out of view.

She climbed out of the Citroën, pulling two of her smaller suitcases from the trunk. Across the two-way rush of traffic, she saw the shops and amenities that would become an integral part of her life for the next little while: East Indian and Italian restaurants, a bistro whose small glass-topped tables huddled beneath a gaily striped awning that flapped in the breeze, a *pâtisserie* with amorphous, tasty-looking things arranged in the window. A woman in a leather coat walked by on low-heeled boots, leading an Afghan hound with its nose in the air; two small children chattered to a harassed-looking man carrying a basket with a huge loaf of bread protruding from either end.

Welcome, sweetie, welcome. You're here, your car is safely parked, and it's time to get your ass in gear. So do it. Now, which one of these imposing-looking buildings has your bed in it?

It was a good question. Emily set her bags on the pavement, scanning the blue-tiled number plate above the entrance of the nearest building. 137, 135, good. Here it was, nearly at the corner of an interesting looking little street called Rue de Grenelle.

She hesitated a moment, scanning the name-plates on the bells. The names were representative of many nationalities, many cultures: Hakim, di Vincenzo, Wilmington-Gates. Ah, here it was. Concierge; that looked right.

The woman who came to the door was small and plump and birdlike. Emily, not immune to the rumours of legendary French rudeness to strangers, felt her misgivings lighten; anyone who so resembled a robin must have at least the potential for basic cordiality. She smiled, opened her mouth to speak, but was forestalled.

'Madame Moon-Bourne? *Ça va*? I was expecting you.' The woman's English, though heavily accented, was perfectly correct in idiom. Emily found herself caught between the conflicting emotions of relief at not having to communicate in a language she suspected had become rusty with disuse and disappointment at not being allowed to try. And what was the French for Ms? Was there one?

The woman smiled up at her, the bright dark eyes lost briefly in the pleasant crinkling of deeply etched laugh lines. She reached out a hand and shook Emily's. 'I am Juliet Maubert. Please call me Juliet. I hope you had no troubles coming down from Calais, and that you found a place to put your auto.'

Emily shook hands. 'I'm pleased to meet you, Juliet. *Heureuse de faire votre connaissance.* Please call me Emily. No, no problems; I've got a French car, a Citroën, and it seems to like the roads. By the way, I do speak French, if you'd prefer, only you must be patient because I haven't used it in years and I suspect I'll sound terrible until I've practised for a while. And how did you know I'd driven?'

'English will be good, better than French in fact, at least for me. I must practise, you see, because my daughter is studying at the university in Edinburgh and she writes her letters to me in English. As to the auto, the agent who made the booking for you asked about a garage, so I assumed . . .'

The explanation died away. Juliet took one of Emily's bags, and gestured around the entrance hall with her free hand. Emily, following with her eyes, saw a high painted ceiling, a wide marble staircase that curved upward into a well-lit stairwell, a small lift with an ornate bronze grille. She glanced down at Juliet.

'Am I on the ground floor?'

Juliet, shaking her head vigorously, led her toward the lift. '*Non*. Quite opposite. Opposite? Is that right?'

'Quite *the* opposite. You left out the article. You mean I'm all the way at the top?'

'At the very top, all the way up next to the sky, with the birds and the sun for company.' Was the startlingly poetic cast of the sentence the result of a poetic soul, or did it merely reflect an imperfect grasp of the language? As Emily briefly considered this question, Juliet elbowed the bronze grille open, revealing a diminutive oak-panelled box with a shaded lamp fixture. It looked capable of holding no more than three adults and a grocery bag. 'There are seven levels and then there is the garden apartment, which is where you will be.'

'I have a garden? On the *roof*? That's amazing!'

'*Oui*. But it is mostly plants growing in pots. And you will not need to water them, so early in the year; the weather will attend to that for you.'

The lift whirred past pebbled glass doors, each with a number painted on it. It bumped to a stop, shuddering as it did so. Juliet pushed the grille apart, opened the glass door, and led Emily into a densely carpeted hallway. At the end of the hallway was a thick wooden door.

'I think, I hope, that you will be comfortable here.' Juliet pulled a key off the large ring that dangled at her side, slipped it into the lock and clicked the door open. 'You will tell me if you need anything, yes?'

'Wow!'

The apartment was gorgeous. Every door in the place had been flung wide, a gesture that Emily found oddly welcoming. There were two rooms, a living room/kitchen combination and a bedroom; each room had a skylight, and the apartment, with its overheads not yet turned on, was bathed in the Parisian dusk. A pair of glass doors at one end of the bedroom opened out on to a roof-top garden some forty feet in length, railed in wrought iron and edged with potted greenery. There was a café table and two candy-striped chairs; there was a bird feeder.

Juliet looked up at her. '*Comment*? You like it, I think. But tell me, please, what is "wow"?'

'*C'est incroyable.*' Emily, suddenly reminded of Dolores and her reaction to that same word, set her bag down. The bathroom, she thought, the bathroom alone was worth the cost of admission; directly off the kitchen, it had a yellow dormer ceiling and a sink that was topped with marble and a claw-leg tub big enough to sit in without bending one's knees.

There was even a lavabo, painted with scenes of a hunt in the forest. Glossy chestnut horses reared and bucked, pursuing an unworried-looking stag under a cloud-flecked sky. Where, she wondered ecstatically, where did these riders and their dogs cavort? Normandy, Champagne, the well-tended forests she vaguely associated with the château country?

Juliet rambled on, explaining how the electricity and telephone were billed ('very expensive, I am sorry to tell you'), praising certain local restaurants ('avoid the *tabac* on the Rue Saint Dominique, it is full of Arabs who sell drugs'), and explaining how the parking meters on Avenue Bosquet worked ('you pay for all day'). Emily, listening with half an ear and making vaguely encouraging noises, noted the small but perfectly functional kitchen, the pots and pans, the lack of built-in closet space that was compensated for by a vast Victorian free-standing wardrobe that was almost certainly a refugee from a country estate somewhere.

Juliet finished her peroration by pointing out that there

was complimentary coffee and tea in the cupboard, reminding Emily that she had booked the apartment for a month but that an extension was possible if desired and offering to help Emily with the rest of her luggage. This accomplished, Juliet gave Emily building and apartment keys and told her to call if she needed anything, by pressing the button on the phone labelled 'concierge'. She then vanished downstairs in the tiny lift, leaving her new tenant alone in a state that bordered on ecstasy.

The first thing Emily did was to set a kettle on to boil and fling open the roof-garden doors. Somewhere on the roof of the apartment, hidden from her view, pigeons were cooing; she heard a flutter of wings, a scrabbling overhead as some winged thing – could there actually be a nest up there, this early in the year? Off to her right, fabulous against the darkening sky, was the eccentric and beautiful skeleton of Monsieur Eiffel's famous folly. On the café table was a glass vase with fresh roses in it; she must remember to thank Juliet for that. Traffic sounds, dim at this height, floated up from the street as soothing bits of indistinguishable sound.

The kettle, with a piercing shriek, brought her feet somewhat closer to earth. Happy, more awake than she had felt since she had last laid hands to wood and tools, she went indoors to make herself a cup of coffee, leaving the pigeons and the skyline to await her return.

Emily fell into Paris as the Duke of Clarence had reportedly fallen into his butt of malmsey: head first.

The City of Light, unanimously portrayed by Hollywood and the American media as populated by bad-tempered, xenophobic people whose favourite pastime was being as rude as possible to Americans, opened itself to Emily and welcomed her inside. She went out that first evening, with the vague intention of exploring the quarter-mile boundary of her neighbourhood and stocking up on a few essential groceries. Beyond that, there was no thought but that of her bed. She had been awake since another time zone, she had driven for hours in a strange land. Her mind was hazy, functioning distantly and outside any plane of physical reality; her body wanted sleep.

It was not to be, of course; Paris is a place designed for the undoing of virtuous intentions. From the moment she turned left instead of right at her front door, the city made nonsense of her sensible planning and her fatigue. She wandered down Avenue Bosquet, stopping idly to peer into windows; she stopped at a small shop and bought milk, eggs, butter. She turned left on Rue Saint Dominique, and emerged into an ambassadorial-looking avenue imposingly called Avenue de la Bourdonnais.

She turned toward the river, hearing a distant music; was Paris singing around her, she wondered? There was moisture in the air, and a light mist that grew more tangible as she approached the Seine. She passed a side street, a dark little alley lined with large and indistinct residential buildings. There were no shops here, not even a café to draw the eye; there was nothing to look at, nothing to see.

Except that, at the end of the street, was a sparkling, hulking pillar of light and a distant sound that might have been someone singing. Emily hesitated, seeing the mist-dampened lights of traffic whizzing by on the Quai Branly, by the river and only a block to her north. There was life there, and energy, and constant enchanting motion. These things beckoned, laughing, urging her to further exploration. But the pillar had called first and more loudly, and Emily turned her steps that way.

The Eiffel Tower met her with the impact of a colossus. The pillar of light was a leg, one of four, seemingly rooted into the earth of this astonishing place. Tourists wandered around in little groups, taking photos and exclaiming in polyglot tongues, scanning the menu and astronomical prices on the menu of the Restaurant Jules Verne. Enormous, contemptuous but indulgent of these tiny life forms scurrying beneath its vast elegant bulk, the tower stretched itself to the heavens and welcomed all comers. The singing resolved itself into just that; a small girl, carefully watched by a young couple, chased a dog round in circles, carolling with energy and happiness.

For a little while Emily merely stood where she was, trying to absorb what she saw and felt. Emmy Deer, perhaps giving her alter ego time and space, was blessedly silent. So much to see, so much, and all of it beautiful. There was a carousel, and a hot-dog stand; there was the glorious stretch of lights from the fountain-stuffed sweep of the Trocadero just across the river. A wrought-iron elevator, looking dangerously fragile through its clear plexiglass walls, clanked and hummed its way up one leg of the tower toward the summit. Off to the south, in the Parc Champ de Mars, a group of young men were playing soccer.

It occurred to her, vaguely and distantly, that standing in the chilly evening by herself, eyes blurred and mouth agape, would be earning her curious stares almost anywhere else. But Paris, famous for its eccentricities, is in this sense not hypocritical; it loves an eccentric, and Emily was right at home. Aware of this sense of belonging, remembering the comestibles in her bag, she was suddenly ravenous. She headed for the hot-dog stand, waiting her turn impatiently, her mouth watering at the smells. Her agent, who loved Paris, had once told her that good food in Paris was available anywhere there were lights. Hopefully, that dictum would extend its writ to takeaway food.

Apparently, it did. The hot dog, spicy and delicious, was slathered with a hot, pungent mustard and stuffed inside an entire baguette. She took the steaming food to the river's edge, crossing the Pont d'Iena as she munched, stopping for a few minutes to wave over the edge of the bridge at a *bateau mouche* whose water-borne tourists, delirious with adventure, waved frenetically at the watchers on shore.

After that, any intentions of heading home to bed were irretrievably lost. She walked up the Trocadero, laughing at the skate-boarding locals, smiling and shaking her head at the Africans who sat with blankets before them, selling oddities such as leather bullwhips and brass belt-buckles. The Trocadero ended in stairs that came out into a rushing circle of traffic and people. People, heedless of the damp and the chill of the evening, sat at outdoor tables sipping coffee and eating beautiful confections, watching her even as she watched them. She looked to the east and saw Paris, alive on every side.

In the end, almost without realizing it, she walked to Place de la Concorde. The city glittered around her, the reds and blues that were the wake of passing tour boats turning the night into a fantasy streaked with fairy lights.

Here's another snatch of poem for you to chew on; isn't there something, somewhere, about being miles from home?

Emily came back to herself with a start. She looked to one side of her and saw the darkness of the Tuilleries, looked to the other at a wall of bistros and restaurants, one with the famous name of Maxim discreetly set above the door.

Hit by an unexpected wave of exhaustion, she leaned against a lamppost and closed her eyes. Emmy Deer was right, she was miles from home. So was the Citroën. And she was certainly not going to start her intended exploration of the Métro when her eyes watered and her legs trembled . . .

So call a taxi. Look, there's the Hotel Ritz or something, right at the corner, and you're practically right outside Maxim's. From the look of it, this may be the easiest place in the world to get a taxi. So go on, what are you waiting for?

Emily hoisted the grocery bag against her hip and turned toward the glittering façade of the hotel. How far had she walked, entranced as securely by Paris as Merlin had been by Nimue? Two miles, three? It didn't matter; nothing mattered but a cab and her warm bed. She reached the corner, lifted a hand; a Mercedes with a blue light atop it pulled over.

She was half-way inside before she became aware of the presence of another potential passenger in need. They had both lifted their hands, summoning the cab at the same time; she was actually pulling herself into the back seat of the Mercedes when she saw a man's hand closing the door from the outside. Apparently he was conceding her rights to this particular cab.

'*Merci*,' she murmured, closing her eyes momentarily against the sting of weariness. No doubt she should thank this gallant Parisian more formally, but she could barely remember her own address at this point, much less remember enough French to be fulsome. He would just have to be satisfied. '*Conduisez-moi à la 131 Avenue Bosquet, s'il vous plait. Merci bien, monsieur.*'

His reply was distorted by the window glass and the roar of the Mercedes' engine starting up. It came in a well-bred English voice, deep without booming, cultured without caricature, utterly masculine without a hint of machismo.

'Not at all,' it said happily. 'Why thank me? Actually, I quite enjoyed being able to help you. Get home safely, and sleep well.'

Open your eyes, woman. Open them very, very fast.

The taxi pulled away from the kerb with a lurch. Emily wrenched frantically around in her seat, a movement so abrupt that she felt a quiver of pain in her neck. She ignored it; exhaustion was forgotten, set aside, for every sense she possessed was stretched and jumping. She peered through the rear glass, the grocery bag forgotten on the seat beside her, eyes searching the pavement. The glass fogged with the proximity of her breath; she smeared it with her hands, trying to clear the space for vision.

A crowd, small and insignificant, all going in different directions. One shape, different from the others, taller, stranger; it stood with hands jammed into deep pockets, seeming to stare after the cab. A man in black, long slender legs, what seemed to be a frock coat.

Unaware that the driver had begun chattering about the weather in rapid-fire French, Emily pushed her face toward the rear windshield as closely as it would go. Her shaking hands were balled into fists. It was, it wasn't, it couldn't be, oh God oh God . . .

Journeys end in lovers meeting. You did the right thing, coming here, in case you had any doubts about it. Now go home and get some sleep.

The taxi shot out into traffic, leaving the man who might be Martin but couldn't be Martin behind it, indistinct against the night.

CHAPTER EIGHT

April
Comes like an idiot, babbling and strewing flowers.

(from 'Spring')

'*Bonjour, monsieur. A combien faut-il affranchir une lettre pour l'Angleterre? Bon. Merci.*'

The letter to Judy had been written in bits and pieces. What had begun its life as a short note containing little more than a return address had evolved into something between an epic and a running diary. Emily, who rarely wrote letters at all, was stunned to discover that she had produced nearly thirty pages, which would no longer fit into a standard envelope. She had to buy a legal-sized brown one to accommodate its girth.

Wednesday, 13 March. I'm sitting at a small table at a chic little brasserie called Delphine, on the Champs-Elysées. The waiter – who is so gorgeous that even I noticed it – has just scurried off to bring me an astounding-looking confection called a Mont Blanc, which probably has about eight million calories and is almost as gorgeous as the waiter is. Everything in this damned city is beautiful, from the people down to the food, which is something I knew or should have known from all those old movies, but still . . .

The Mont Blanc, a whitish, hill-shaped pile of what

tasted like a cross between whipped cream and hazelnuts, was wonderful. She ate slowly, relishing it, her eyes moving with slow languor up and down the glittering boulevard. To her left was the Arc de Triomphe and the endless multi-lane traffic circle of Place Charles de Gaulle, to her right a busy infinity that ended in the Concorde and the Tuileries.

> My apartment is staggering. I swear to God, I was expecting some dark dingy little rat-hole; you know what holiday rentals are. Instead, I'm in this fantastic little eyrie, with the Eiffel Tower watching over me at night while I sleep and the sound of invisible birds to keep me company. In the morning I take my coffee out on my roof garden. I can hear the city waking up around me, and the air is golden and expectant, and I don't think I've ever been happier in my entire life.
>
> I'm staying in the seventh – Christ, doesn't that sound snooty, using just the number of the area? What that means, naturally, is that I spent the first three days exploring Montmartre, clear across town. Does everyone save the local stuff for last, or am I just perverse?

The waiter – really, he was almost too handsome, with sooty blue eyes under heavy lids and muscles rippling in his upper arms – brought her a *café noir* and the check. He smiled at her, a purely Gallic smile that Emily, in a single week, had already become accustomed to. It was a warm smile, an appraising smile, an acknowledgement of delightful femininity close at hand. It was sexy and suggestive; it held a faint shade of impertinence, but nothing of insult. Emily smiled back and sipped her coffee, resuming her letter to Judy.

> . . . may find it difficult to believe, but I think I saw him,

my first night in Paris; not only saw, but heard! I'm not going into details on that one, for some reason I have the feeling it might be unlucky to discuss it at this point. But I'm virtually certain it was Martin.

God, that Mont Blanc was good; I think maybe I'll wander down to the next café and order myself a *bombe glacé* or something. Oh, right, now there's an oddity for you. I can't figure this out, because I've never noticed what I ate, but for some reason I've been ravenous ever since I got here. I've been going from curry to pasta to cassoulet like a child in a candy-store fairyland, stuffing my face with whatever takes my fancy. Is it because everything looks and tastes good? I don't think so; the food in Italy was gorgeous and tasted like heaven, but I hardly ate when I was there. I just wasn't hungry, but now I'm hungry all the time. This place is so seductive, even the food gets into you and plays with your sensibilities. The odd thing is, I haven't gained an ounce! If anything, my clothes are actually looser . . .

She looked at the total owing, noted the '*service compris*' acknowledgement printed on the bottom of the bill, and left a small tip anyway. After all, he had not only been nice to look at and pleasingly flirty, he'd brought her a clean ashtray and not even laughed at her French. Stepping on to the east-bound pavement, she was immediately drawn into the constant stream of pedestrian Paris, going by on busy, expensively shod feet.

Still Wednesday, a few hours later. I decided against another café, mostly because by sitting down you miss going somewhere, so I'm picking this up on a park bench in the Tuileries. Do you know, I haven't driven once since I got here? My poor little Citroën must think I don't love it any more. On the other hand, I haven't stopped walking, except when I'm so worn out that I succumb and take the Métro, which fortunately is the single most efficient mass-transit system I've ever encountered.

I just tried to figure out how much walking I'm doing, and if my calculations are even close I'm averaging about eight miles a day. Would you believe it, last night I walked all the way from my place down the Boulevard Saint Germain, to the Latin Quarter and then to Notre Dame? It took two hours and of course by the time I got there I was starved, so I tried Greek food, something called *brochettes à la fruits de mer*; lobsters the size of Mirage jets. Maybe that's why I'm losing weight; it's all this exercise.

I'm telling you, those espadrilles I got in Greece have saved my ass *and* my feet. The first long daylight walk I took, I made the mistake of wearing heels, and after about an hour I felt like an Indian fakir. You know, the fire-walking guys? Hot coals?

Anyway, after I left Delphine, I went to the Louvre. In case you want an artist's opinion, I'd like to use a small thermonuclear device on that God-awful pyramid in the courtyard; that's not architecture, it's an abortion. I saw maybe a fifth of the museum – the *Mona Lisa* is incredible, but I think I prefer the *Madonna of the Rocks* – and I'm still in shock. I felt a stab of something totally unworthy of me: blind ambition. I mean, I looked at all those damned Greco-Roman statues, not to mention little irrelevancies like *Venus de Milo* and *Winged Victory at Samothrace*, and I just had this vicious little surge where I thought, Damn, I wish they'd put something of mine in here. A bird, a bug, anything at all to keep company with those others and wait the ages away . . .

The Louvre had been mobbed. Emily, who abominated

large crowds, never noticed the people milling around her; from the first moment of hesitating on the grand staircase in front of *Winged Victory* and trying to choose a direction to follow, she had felt herself alone in this vast palace with its silent company of ageless genius. She saw paintings by Delacroix and Bosch, sculpture by Rodin and Canova; she promised herself, as she had been doing since England, to visit the Rodin Museum, fifteen minutes' walk from her apartment. When she had glutted herself past bearing with the Museum's treasures, she had hurried out of doors, lit a cigarette, and planted her aching body on a Tuileries bench.

I've been thinking about our conversation, the one when we talked about sex. Well, *you* talked about sex; in all honesty, I just shied away from the whole idea. And I have been thinking, Judy, I really truly have. Maybe it's because this city regards sex the way you do, as something delightful and enjoyable and full of variety. Paris, maybe all of France, is permeated with it. But it's not threatening, even though it's everywhere from the looks on people's faces to the endless advertising posters on the walls of the Métro.

Anyway, whatever the reason, I have been thinking about it a little bit, asking myself a few questions. I've got glimmerings of answers, but nothing really solid. One good sign is that Emmy Deer, you remember my hungry little interior nuisance, hasn't been giving me as much grief since I got to Paris. Usually she's a complete nag, but since I've started confronting a few things she's only been nudging me with questions, and I don't feel as self-judgemental. Maybe I'm heading in the right direction. Wouldn't that be nice?

So, said the lady sculptor as she drew a deep breath and

girded her loins – can women gird their loins, or do you need a testosterone count for that? – I'm going to set down the one solid conclusion I've drawn so far. Here goes. Because my view of sex meant my view of Gary for my entire adult life, and because my opinion of Gary is that he's an embarrassing bore, I've come to equate sex with Gary, and that means the above-named adjectives. Dear me, how pompous and scattered I'm getting; I just reread that last sentence and, semantically, it reeks. Still, you know what I mean, don't you? Tell me, talk to me, grovel, plead. I need some input here.

Emily paused in her writing, letting her pen fall into her lap. The day was warm still, only an occasional breeze stirring the sheets of her letter. She was lazy, and calm; was it the weather, the long walk, the release that even the smallest of confessions brings to a troubled mind?

More likely it was that Mont Blanc you crammed into yourself.

Emily gave a small jump, and cast her eyes around in the now unconscious ceremony of making sure that no one was watching. Emmy Deer had been silent all day, minding her own business, unintrusive. Instead of justifying herself, Emily picked up her pen again; something, a vagrant notion, had come to her.

I've just had a strange idea, hard to explain, so bear with me. You know, all my life, I've invested Emmy Deer's remarks with feelings and opinions. I've taken her words, some of them unpalatable and hard to listen to – she can be pretty brutal – and said to myself, Oh, she's blaming me, she thinks I'm stupid, she's impatient. Occasionally, very rarely, I've said, Oh, she's sympathetic. What I'm trying to say is that I've responded to her words as if to an actual human voice, coloured by human perception and response. I've been personifying her.

But that's ridiculous. It only just occurred to me, but that really isn't right. It can't be. Because Emmy Deer isn't an invading spirit, or the ghost of someone else; she's just me. So it's my own perceptions and responses I'm hearing. It's my own voice. I've assigned her a persona, a life of her own, and the bottom line is that she doesn't have one. When I argue with her, tell her to shut up, it's me against me. She's just a part of me, a split somewhere in my own mind, my own self.

What does that mean, Judy? Does that make me a textbook schizophrenic? Am I crazy? I don't feel crazy, and no matter how clearly I've always realized that other people might think that Emmy Deer was some kind of aberration on my part, I've never felt abnormal. It was only after the divorce, when I started assigning a dangerous, accusing note to what she said because her truths became hurtful to listen to, that I started feeling threatened. Maybe I should just ask her, say to her, what are you? Would she answer?

Don't ask me, sugarplum. It's your mind, not mine. I'm just along for the ride.

Emily stuffed the letter into her purse. She was too close to her own question, too near some kind of revelation, to continue writing. It was time to be up and going. The thought moved through her mind, that she was running away once again; Tough shit, she thought, too bad. I'm not going to sit here and poke at barely covered wounds on a public bench in the middle of Paris. If that's cowardice, then I'm a coward and proud of it. So be it.

She salved the fear that had invaded her in the classic manner of those with money to spare: by shopping. Her feet took her eastbound down the Rue de Rivoli and into several small shops; she bought a Hermes scarf, a silver pin, a flask of perfume. That she never wore perfume was dismissed as irrelevant; the bottle was lovely, crystal with a crystal dove serving as a stopper, and the scent of the perfume itself was as light and teasing as a finger down one's back.

By the time she had acquired enough material objects to distract her attention from her own inner turmoil, she was laden down with packages, physically weary and slightly footsore. She paused to get her bearings. There was the glorious fountain and the traffic roundabout of Concorde, familiar yet different in the sunlight. There was the outrageous façade of the hotel (it was the Crillon and not, as Emmy Deer had suggested that first night, the Ritz) where she had hailed the cab and seen Martin – she was certain, now, that it had been Martin. There was also a Métro station.

There was a crowd on the hotel pavement, but then there were always crowds in Paris. And there would be cabs, lots of them, one of them undoubtedly waiting to be put to use by a tired American woman with too many packages to wrestle with a jam-packed train during the onset of the busiest time of the day. She turned her steps from the arcade shops on Rivoli towards the hotel.

The crowd outside the Crillon was very thick. And they were not lined up waiting for cabs, they were watching something. They seemed to be primarily tourists, and many of them held their cameras raised towards the outdoor gallery that ran along the front of the building. A celebrity, most likely; wasn't the Crillon where the élite meet and greet?

Then why did every muscle in your body just send off a red alert? Because Jack Nicholson or Warren Beatty or Dan Quayle is waving graciously to the hoi polloi?

It was true. Emily's breath had shortened, coming in

small painful pushes of air forced from a tight diaphragm, and her legs were trembling. Tiredness? No, this was something else. Clutching her packages, wondering distantly at herself, she manoeuvred her way out from behind a knot of men a head taller than herself to where from her distance she could better see what the others were watching.

Celebrity indeed. There were several people on the gallery, holding glasses, talking among themselves, seemingly oblivious of the human ant farm on the street below. Emily recognized a world-famous Italian director, a screen siren with three Oscar nominations and a Palm d'Or under her belt, the actor generally considered the sexiest in France.

No. No, you wouldn't be reacting like this, from basic instinct, not for them. They aren't important to you. There must be more. Keep looking, keep looking.

A small knot of people, three women, two men, gathered in conversation at the periphery of stardom. One of the men detached himself, came to the railing, looked down at the milling throng below. His eyes searched, lingered, moved on. They found Emily and rested there; he lifted a hand and, as if greeting an old acquaintance through a shop window, waved casually.

There, you see? Ghost laid, reaction explained. There he is. You do realize, don't you, that you're not surprised?

There was no point in trying to gain admittance to the hotel or the terrace. Shocked though she might be, aware that she had finally found him while he stood still and that she could therefore do something about him, Emily was perfectly aware of that. During the suspension of time that seemed to separate both Martin and herself from the rest of humanity, she considered it. She saw herself and her armful of packages trying to explain the inexplicable to a haughty doorman, saw herself contemptuously and humiliatingly herded back into the street with the rest of the great unwashed.

He was watching her, hand still upraised, acknowledging her presence. And Emily knew, as surely as she knew that she could get no nearer than she was right now, that he had stood on that terrace in the full knowledge that she had been coming that way. That this was impossible made no difference at all to the reality. She felt the warmth in her stomach, the pure satisfaction that only comes when one has hit upon an unarguable truth. There he was, having somehow known that she would come, and here she stood. She could get no closer, not now.

Those thoughts, those comprehensions and realizations, took only a fragment of time to complete. Emily lifted her hand, over the heads of the people in her way, and waved back. This done, she turned her back abruptly and went to find a cab. She had done what she could, done what she must; she had performed the only assertive option open to her, and she could do no more. She stared in front of her, forcing herself not to look back, until the cab had crossed the Pont de la Concorde and swung its way to the south-west, until the hotel was completely lost to view.

It was only when she had arrived home, had unpacked her purchases and poured herself a large glass of mineral water and taken it out on the roof, that Emmy Deer spoke up with her own version of the truth.

Maybe he wasn't waiting for you. Maybe he called you. Maybe you went there because he wanted you to.

'And maybe you're right,' Emily said to Emmy Deer and the unseen pigeons asleep in the eaves. 'Maybe he did.'

. . . so I called the Crillon, of course, to find out what that little party had been in aid of. I'm not sure why I did,

I guess I just thought it might be helpful. And it was, Judy, it was; turns out the Crillon, and probably the other *luxe* hotels, get a lot of that this time of year. It was a sort of pre-Cannes party, you know the film festival? Apparently there's a movie in production, and they're going to be hyping it at Cannes next month. And Martin was up there, he was with them. I thought, for one moment, that I was having a heart attack . . .

Remember when we missed the Stonehenge bus and talked over the teacups, down in Salisbury? You said something about guidelines, signposts along the way; I'm ashamed to admit I can't remember the exact words. Well, is this a signpost, or what? I mean, it's practically outlined in neon arrows! You saw my wasp statue at a gallery in Nice, and Nice is just down the road from Cannes – yes, I've been looking at maps – and I come to Paris and here's Martin, with a group of people who are on their way to Cannes . . .

Now, please don't tell me to hold my horses, or be logical, or consider the other possible alternatives. I've already been over all that, and I'm not going to be careful or any of that crap. Because I've realized that, whatever is happening here, the *last* thing I ought to do is be logical about it. Martin's either a signpost or a goal, I've come to believe that. He has something to do with my instincts, not my brain. And if I'm not going to follow my instincts, then what the hell am I doing here?

Emily set her pen down, shaking the cramp from her fingers. The terrace doors were open, and the evening flooded the room, belling out the curtains. She smiled, and picked up the pen once more.

Juliet – my landlady, I told you about her earlier on in this great American novel – has been incredibly helpful. I was dreading trying to find accommodations in Nice. I mean, what do I know about Nice? I want an apartment down there, not a hotel, because I have the feeling that something's going to happen down there, and I don't want to be anywhere but in a room of my own when it does. In American sports, we call it the home-field advantage.

Anyway, Juliet's sister and brother-in-law own a building in Old Nice, and they keep a few of the apartments vacant for holiday rentals during the Season. I should have guessed. After all, concierges have this international reputation for being able to handle anything – isn't there a story about some rock group demanding a live sand shark from the concierge of a Paris hotel and him procuring it without a blink? In my sheltered, provincial way, I never stopped to think that an incredible talent like that might extend to residential concierges, too. Apparently, it does. Juliet is a marvel.

The Cannes festival starts on April twentieth this year. So Juliet called her sister, and *voilà*! As of April 15, I'm the proud occupant of a three-room apartment at 302 *bis*, Rue Desboutins, Nice. Juliet tells me I'm right by the sea and close to everything of interest. The building even has an underground garage, which is vital, since parking in Nice is said to be very expensive.

I thought about trying to rent something in Cannes itself, in case you were wondering. That turns out to be impossible. One doesn't simply stroll into Cannes during the festival and expect to sleep anywhere but in one's car, because everything during the festival is booked six months in advance. And, anyway, Nice feels right. I know, I know, I've already explained my current feelings about instinct *ad nauseam*. I won't bore you with any more of it.

So, if you're going to write back – and I hope to hell you will, Judy, because you're the first person in many years that I've really wanted to know – then send your letter care of the above address in Nice. Marie-France, Juliet's sister, has promised to hold my mail for me until I get there.

In a way, leaving Paris will be a wrench. I've fallen in love with it, with every building, every street, every idiosyncrasy. I'm at home here, comfortable, the kind of comfort where you don't notice little things and everything seems familiar. But I've got three more weeks before I take off for the south, and believe me, I plan to enjoy myself. It ought to be easy, because I feel – no, I'm sure – that I won't see Martin here again. I honestly believe that the minute I made that reservation for Nice, he left Paris. It's a strange sensation; I feel deprived, but I also feel relaxed, and very, very free . . .

So, angel, I'm going to end this letter here and mail it, before it reaches unmanageable proportions. I realize that I haven't asked you the usual letter things, how you are, how's university, what you've been doing. You'll take those questions as stated, and tell me all about it when you sit down to answer this pile of inconsequence. Notice my self-assurance and arrogance; you will answer, won't you?

P.S. – the first spring flowers have arrived.

Emily laid down her pen, straightened the unwieldy pile of ruled paper, and addressed the envelope. The glass doors to the roof were propped open, the drapes billowing slightly in a warm wind. She flexed her cramped fingers, and headed for the kitchen to make herself a cup of tea. She had discovered that writing was thirsty work.

Martin, she thought, Martin. His picture, the now rumpled sketch she had done of him at Herculaneum, had been tacked up on the kitchen wall, safely away from the dangers of being splattered by cooking grease yet able to watch her as she moved about. She stopped by the picture, touching one edge with the tip of her fingers; the gesture was not a kiss, but it came close to a caress. He smiled down at her, his odd wild face as comforting as a Catholic's rosary.

Soon, she thought, it's going to be soon. Her letter to Judy had performed a miracle in Emily's life; the admission of her own feelings toward Gary had crystallized the problem, given it flesh, and the flesh was a good thing. She had ceased backing off from considering the physical reality behind the mask of the man.

She looked up at the picture, and was sorry that she had not drawn all of him, legs stretching finely veined skin over long potent bones, hands that could touch in miraculous ways. Since the moment she had lifted her hand and waved back to him, he had ceased to be a *doppelgänger* and become a man. And a man, this man, was something to be considered, and desired, and touched. That gesture, that simple lift of her hand, had given Emily back her womanhood. It was the first truly assertive connection she had ever instigated.

After all, you've been looking for him all your life. Well, haven't you?

'I don't know,' Emily said aloud. She looked up into Martin's charcoal-pencil eyes. 'Maybe I have. Anyway, for the next three weeks, I'm totally free. No ghosts, no hauntings, nothing following me or wanting me or conjuring me up like a prop in a magic act. Twenty-one days, and I can do whatever I choose.'

Well, what do you choose?

'For starters, I'm going to stay in tonight. I'm going to cook myself a lamb chop and some of those spring peas I bought. Martin's going to watch me while I cook, and then I'm going to take my dinner out on the roof and devour it, because that Mont Blanc wore off hours ago.'

What about for afters, if that's for starters?

'Maybe I'll go to the Luxembourg Gardens tomorrow, and sketch the first spring flowers. Maybe I'll stop off and get some cheese and bread and juice, and have a picnic. Maybe I'll go to the Rodin Museum, and stare at the statue of Balzac. I don't know, and it doesn't matter.'

Doesn't it?

'Nope.' Emily lifted her arms above her head, stretching out to her capacity. 'It doesn't matter because I'm free. I thought I told you that.'

CHAPTER NINE

I will touch a hundred flowers
And not pick one.

(from 'Afternoon on a Hill')

If it hadn't been for Emily's appetite and a horrendous traffic jam, she might never have discovered Avignon.

She left Paris before sunrise, suspecting that a gruelling day of driving loomed ahead. If the road between Calais and Paris was typical, she was in for ten to twelve hours of clutching the wheel in perpetual bumper-to-bumper misery.

Except for a few spots where road repairs were being performed, however, the drive south proved painless. Once away from the roaring tangle of Paris, she found herself moving leisurely through a Cézanne landscape that changed in shape from mile to mile without once losing the essence of whatever made it so extremely French.

When will you ever learn? This country isn't typical; nothing that's happened to you in the past year has been typical. If you can be sure of any one thing about your life these days, it's that whatever you expect will have kinks in it.

That was true enough, Emily thought, but she paid Emmy Deer no mind past that agreement. There was too much around her to engage her attention.

Spring had arrived in earnest, a glorious flaunting of colour that had been splashed against the world's face by a brush heavy with paint. She drove past distant hills, as dark with ancient forest as they were bright with new-growth shrubbery. The sky, an endless streak of cobalt, reflected roses, and pines, and things less familiar. There were rest stops, some mere patches of ground, others bristling with gas stations and restaurants and shops that sold the specialities and crafts of their respective regions. All boasted beautiful views.

Shortly after three, Emily stopped for petrol at a rest stop south of Lyon. She had developed a bad headache, a result of sitting in a motionless line of cars just north of the city. The road here was being repaved, and a three-mile stretch had been closed down to a single lane in either direction. Those three miles had taken nearly an hour to achieve, a nerve-wracking period of cars inching forward and drivers watching their temperature gauges with grim faces. By the time Emily emerged into freedom, her head was throbbing and her stomach grumbled. As if to add insult to injury, the gas tank was bordering on empty. Emily swore aloud, suppressing an urge to cry.

Hunger, fool. You're tired and cross but above all you're hungry. Why not stop for lunch?

'*La plein*, fill her up, the works,' Emily told the station attendant, and added an internal coda to Emmy Deer. 'I am not stopping for lunch in Lyon. I am not stopping for *anything* in Lyon. I have taken what Judy would probably call a proper scunner to this city, in fact I loathe the very sight of it. If that's unfair, I don't give a damn. I don't care if every second café in bloody Lyon serves the best food in Europe, I refuse to stop here, so don't nag me. *C'est tout*!'

She pulled the Citroën back out on to the highway. Unfortunately, if Emmy Deer's suggestion was unacceptable, her logic was irrefutable. Emily was very hungry indeed, her stomach rumbled and complained in counterpoint to every pulse of her temples. The pain was enough to make her vision seem untrustworthy. Furthermore, she had no aspirins in her purse. And, now that she came to think of it, she had been driving damned near for ever and she wanted a cup of espresso.

Come on, be sensible. OK, so you don't want to stop in Lyon, that's reasonable. But it's at least four hours from here to Nice, assuming you don't run into any more road work along the way. Do you really want to arrive starving and grumpy, in the dark? Why not find a town along the way that looks appealing, and spend the night there? That way, you're all fresh and rested and fed, and you can deal with Nice in broad daylight. Juliet's sister will guess why you don't arrive tonight.

Emily took the road for Avignon. She knew nothing about it, except for a vague memory of a charming song in which it was mentioned. It would have restaurants, and hotels, and there would be the steady gurgle of the Rhône, slipping toward the sea. Besides, whatever its iniquities, it had to be preferable to Lyon. It couldn't possibly be worse.

Due to some confusion in changing lanes, she missed the northern exit for Avignon and was obliged to take the southern. The ride into town was subtly depressing, and Emily felt her spirits sink. Why in the world would anyone write a charming song about auto dealerships, or seedy-looking shops, or industrial complexes? If the centre of town was as dull as the road leading to it, she might just as well have stayed in Lyon. And she had been foolish enough to think that all of France was going to be beautiful . . .

The outer walls of the medieval city met her with such a shock that she almost sent the car into a tree. Nothing about the drive in could prepare the traveller for this. Twenty feet tall, weathered with the centuries, the great walls ringed the centre of Avignon, enclosing the beating heart of the life sheltered within.

Emily drove slowly along the outer perimeter, one eye on the towering structures to her right. She had no map of Avignon, no clue as to where to go; at the first break in the walls, she drove between the towers and found herself in fairyland.

Avignon was beautiful, after all, and her earlier disappointment was forgotten. Bemused, enchanted, she drove slowly along a shadowy boulevard lined with oaks. At a cobbled intersection, a street musician stood and strummed on what might have been a lute, or a hurdy-gurdy. The young player had a surpassingly beautiful face and a golden ponytail down to his waist. There was something of Martin here, not so much a presence as a memory. After a moment's struggle, Emily pinned it down; it lay in the freedom of his smile, echoed on the face of musician. She cranked down her window, yearning toward the music and the lights.

She pulled the Citroën into the first space she saw. This was indeed the centre of town, and Emily needed no map to tell her so. Everything here moved, and was busy, yet there was none of the numbing desperation of big-city activity. The sense of smallness, of a place sitting in the palm of a god's hand, was unaccompanied by any feeling of claustrophobia.

Ahead of her, the oak-lined boulevard widened out into a pedestrian zone, studded with café tables under billowing fabric tent canopies. There were artists and artisans, selling their wares; there was a carousel, whirling and gaudy with fairground colours. Emily's headache had disappeared entirely, and she began to walk.

The first hotel she saw boasted three stars and a modern façade. She booked a room for the night and obtained a detailed street map. After dumping her overnight bag on the bed and splashing the dust of France's highways from her face, she hurried back out into the streets.

It's a comforting sort of place, isn't it? A nice version of the land that time forgot. Look, real live hippies! Men with beards and long hair, barefoot girls, street musicians. There's a little stall with silver tragedy- and comedy-mask jewellery! When was the last time you saw anything like this? It must have been back in the sixties.

The whole place smelled wonderful, redolent with food in various stages of preparation. Emily made a beeline for the Place de L'Horloge, the pedestrian area she had noticed earlier, stopping for an ice-cream to stave off the hunger pangs. It was just past five, an impossible hour for dinner in France; still, she thought, if she didn't put something in her stomach, there would be film at eleven.

Licking happily, she made her way to the top of the square, where she stood for a few minutes, watching the vividly painted animals of the carousel circling to music. There were stairs at the top of the square, and a twisting little lane, lined with stalls and craftsmen, offering their products for sale.

Emily climbed the stairs, dawdling over tables of woven scarves and painted miniatures. One woman, young and dark and very Gallic, sat at a table full of tiny marble statuary, and Emily paused for several minutes at this booth. Really, she thought, the stuff showed a lot of promise. There was an amazing amount of detail in these pieces, none of which were larger than Emily's hand. The artist herself, smiling placidly, relaxed in her folding chair. She put no pressure on Emily to buy; apparently, admiration and interest were as acceptable as money.

Emily picked up a tiny statue of the god Pan. He was an exercise in exuberance, his pipes at the ready, his horns perfectly ridged. It was odd, she thought, that she had never before seen a rendition of the god of the woodlands that was neither cute nor threatening. She was examining it closely when a loud, pitiful squeak nearly made her drop it. She jerked her head up and saw the artist reaching into a knitted string-bag that was propped against the leg of her chair. Murmuring softly, clicking her tongue in a sound recognizable anywhere in the world, she rummaged in the bag and pulled out a kitten.

'Oh, what a sweetie!' Emily, delighted, hurriedly set the Pan down on the table and tentatively reached out to stroke the small squirming bundle. The woman, giving Emily a radiant smile, immediately put the kitten into Emily's hands; it was black, all feet and ears and long white whiskers, and its yellow eyes blinked frantically.

Emily gathered it in, fighting back an inexplicable urge to burst into tears. The kitten was smaller than the palm of her hand, and its heart beat strongly against her fingers. She tickled the soft fur beneath its chin, whereupon it stretched its neck, mewed plaintively and began to purr with a shattering rumble of sound.

'Chou-chou,' said the woman, apparently in explanation, and Emily nodded. She hadn't much experience with pets, but Cabbage was probably as good a name as any.

Emily bought the Pan; she would rather have bought the kitten, but that seemed impractical. She handed Chou-chou back to his owner, who promptly set the kitten atop one shoulder. He scrabbled wildly for a foothold before curling up and beginning to nurse on the woman's ear.

The statue was remarkably cheap for so fine a piece of work, and Emily paid without haggling. Then, waving to the kitten, she tucked Pan into her purse and turned back toward the square. She had caught a glimpse of some massive structure at the top of the lane, but it was after six now, and the mingled aromas coming from the various restaurants were too persistent to be further ignored.

Four courses and two bottles of mineral water later, Emily resumed her exploration of the city. She was replete, sated, and her progress was slow and rambling. Her street map proved invaluable, for Avignon was no carefully planned modern plotting of intersections and geometric logic; it had grown according to need over eight centuries. Tiny alleys opened with bewildering suddenness into wider streets, which seemed always to become new tiny alleys. It was a place of idiosyncrasies, always managing consonance.

Someone, something, had a sense of what was proper in this place, for many of the buildings had been exquisitely painted with life-sized scenes and people. Emily saw troubadours, and mounted crusaders in medieval armour, and ladies in farthingales who appeared to be leaning out into the street to receive a minstrel's admiration, or to throw posies of flowers. There was liveliness in every brushstroke, and sense of unapologetic joy.

She walked in circles for two hours, wishing for a camera; the place was indecently visual. Eventually, she found herself on the doorstep of her hotel, thought about sleep, and decided against it. She had walked south and west; she had not yet gone north.

There was something called the Palais des Papes which she had not yet seen. A papal palace; hadn't she read about a distant period of history, during which the Church was centred in Avignon? And it was close by.

The Palais des Papes turned out to be the massive structure she had glimpsed at the top of the lane some hours before. It was ghostly in the moonlight, overbearingly white and still, its turrets and windows reflecting blindly out on to the cobblestones. She stared at it, shuddered, and moved on. The Rocher des Doms, now; here it was, something big marked on her map, only a few minutes' walk away. And if she went that way there was the river, too, just waiting to be communed with . . .

She was walking north, toward the Rhône, when she spotted what seemed to be an enormous lump of a building, irregular in outline and massively tall. But was it a building? It seemed both shaped and oddly formless, as if someone had set a partially carved sculpture down and then cowered before the enormity of having to finish it. It hung above her, as if poised in readiness for some kind of lunatic action. Emily, who had been momentarily frozen in place, took an involuntary step backward.

That's not a building, that's a rock. And one hell of a rock, too. Grandma, what big teeth you have. Someone tried to make a building out of it, and didn't finish. Maybe they saw how it was going to turn out, and were as spooked as you are.

Emily approached it slowly, realizing with dismay that, to reach the river, she would have to walk directly beneath a portcullis carved from the base of this terrible pile. Her throat had gone tight, and the pace of her heart had suddenly become erratic. She couldn't do it, she simply couldn't. If anything ominous, if any shade of darkness inhabited this little jewel box of a place, it was centred here. Rocher des Doms was so big, its presence so overpowering, that she felt an actual physical sensation of threat. No, she thought, no. I can't walk under that thing, I won't. It's late, I'm tired, and I want to go to bed. Some other time, when it's light.

What other time? You make it sound as if you live here. You're just a wimp, that's all. Stop making excuses and admit that it scares you.

'OK, so it scares me,' Emily muttered. She continued

to back away from it, walking in a kind of nervous sidle. The traffic, whizzing by on the other side of the portcullis, might have been separated from her by an ocean, so remote did it seem. 'So I'm a wimp. Tough. I'm not going near that thing, not in the dark. Sorry, no way. It's a lovely rock, a handsome rock, a damned fine rock. I'm sure it's charming and well behaved. I don't give a damn. I'm getting out of here, and I'm going to bed.'

Rocher des Doms glittered dully, then darkened as a cloud obscured the moon. From its heights, some winged thing fluttered skyward and wheeled toward the river. Emily edged backward, completely unnerved; absurd as it was, she refused to turn her back on it. She kept one eye on it, terrified of tripping and falling, until she had reached the end of the street. Then she turned and almost ran, back beneath the sightless staring windows of the Palais des Papes which had frightened her and now seemed so benign. Her heart was pounding, her hands sweated; she didn't get her breath back until she had reached the safety of her hotel room and locked the door.

Emily left Avignon with no regrets, knowing that she would be back. Under the spur of some compulsion she could put no name to, she had driven once around the city's outer road, parking her car just under the bulk of the stone monster that had so unnerved her the night before.

During the daylight hours, her fear seemed remote and ridiculous; huge as it was, Rocher des Doms under the bright lights of day was merely an interesting pile of stone, and nothing more. She walked beneath the portcullis, fearless and happy, wondering at her own panic during the hours of darkness. She ran her hands over its bumps and curves, pleased to find it warmed by the sun, smiling at a tour group that had climbed out of an air-conditioned bus and were circling with cameras. Then, the fear-ghost exorcized, she turned the car south toward the sea.

By noon, Emily was driving slowly along the Promenade des Anglais. She had never seen anything like Nice, which bore a far greater resemblance to travel posters of Tahiti or Miami than to downtown Albuquerque. On one side, the Mediterranean sparkled into infinity, edged with palm trees and a beach of pebbles. Down on the shore, a group of dark-skinned men were trying to raise a hot-air balloon; above the noise of the traffic, Emily heard distant shouts of laughter.

On a good-sized hill directly to her east, she spotted a vast circular tower. Something Judy had said stirred in her mind. The Tour Bellanda; that must be it. And what was it about the Tour Bellanda?

A gallery, remember? The Galerie Solferino, with your wasp from hell in it, your loving little portrait of Gary.

She had studied the directions given to her by Juliet, and found Rue Desboutins without difficulty. This was Old Nice; from the limited view available from the driver's seat, it was even prettier than what she had seen of the rest of the city.

Emily found the building she wanted, pulled into the underground garage, and once more found herself ringing a doorbell marked 'concierge'.

At first glance, Juliet's sister Marie-France was as unlike her sister as possible. Where Juliet was small, Marie-France was as tall as Emily herself; where Juliet was round faced and dark, Marie-France was gaunt and pale. Her eyes were huge and sunken, her nose verging on Roman. Could this really be a blood relative of that bird-like little woman back in Paris?

Then Marie-France smiled, a smile that was warm and wide and completely open, and the family resemblance declared itself with a vengeance.

'Mme Moon-Bourne? I am Marie-France Del Amico. Did you stop along the road last night?' Her voice was Juliet's, vibrant, high-pitched, somewhat squeaky. Although a perfect accompaniment to Juliet's tiny plumpness, it would take some getting used to coming out of this high-boned warrior's face.

Emily offered her hand. 'Call me Emily. It's a pleasure to meet you. Yes, I stayed over in Avignon. It's a longer drive down than I expected, and I ran into some road problems near Lyon . . .'

Marie-France ushered her into the lobby. 'Ah,' she said with immediate comprehension. 'One lane, I suppose, and cars for ever, and impossible to move. I know it well, which is why I always fly when I go to Paris. Our roads are a source of pride to us, but Lyon is a nightmare. At the exit for Marseille, too, the way is never clear. If you have been driving since Avignon, you will be thirsty. Let me give you an *eau minerale*. Then I will take you upstairs. You have put your car in the garage?'

'Yes, I did, because I couldn't see a parking space on the street anywhere. If I'm in someone else's parking place, just let me know and I'll move my car. And I'd love some water. Thank you. You're very kind.'

The mineral water was blessedly cold, and Marie-France's small kitchen was bright and warm. Emily sat in a patch of sunlight, washing the grit of the highway out of her throat. She leaned back in her chair, lazily listening to Marie-France talk as she sipped.

'. . . across the landing from you. Madame Delange, she is perhaps a thousand years old. She has buried three husbands, from what I hear. I believe she is a witch.'

Emily, her attention regained, blinked at Marie-France, who grinned; it was a schoolboy's look, full of mischief, and it transformed her face. 'Well, perhaps not a witch, or a thousand years old. But she is an old, old woman, and her nose turns down and her chin points up. She has three teeth, and they stick out. Also, she is a gossip, and she spends all day peering out her door to spy on her neighbours.'

Emily laughed. 'You mean a bitch, not a witch.' She stretched suddenly, feeling her body ripple; really, she thought, I feel like a cat. 'A bitch is what we Americans call an unpleasant woman who likes to give other people a hard time. It means a female dog.'

'*Comment*? Bitch? I will remember that, it is a good word. In any case, please ignore her; she is irritating, but also harmless. She had lived here a long time before Emilio and I bought this building, and under our laws we cannot force her to move away. I do not think that she will bother you, but . . .' The words trailed away; Marie-France gave the little shrug that proclaimed her nationality, and smiled apologetically.

'Don't worry, I won't let her get on my nerves. To tell you the truth, she sounds better than the imbeciles who used to live next door to me, in the States. They had a barking dog that never shut up and I never heard them talk about anything except their possessions. All in all, I prefer witches – sorry, bitches – to yuppies.'

Marie-France looked relieved. '*Bon*. Come, then, if you have done, and I will take you upstairs.'

'Upstairs?'

'You are upstairs on the fourth floor, with a little balcony.' She grinned suddenly. 'Juliet told me that when you stayed in Paris, you took the roof. That is a nice apartment, in fact Emilio and I stay in it when we visit.

So this made me think that maybe you like high places, and I put you up high. *D'accord*?'

'Oh, absolutely.' She got up, stretching once more; what was it about driving that made people so stiff? 'The higher up, the better. Will you show me the apartment? Can I go down and bring my bags up?'

It was not the spectacular apartment of the Avenue Bosquet, but it was charming nevertheless. The ceilings were high, the small balcony sunlit; by craning her neck to the left, Emily could make out a flash of blue water and clouds out to sea. Both places were very French, but there were differences, the main one being that the sense of isolation in the clouds Emily had felt in her Paris eyrie was missing here. People moved down Rue Desboutins, and she could see the tops of their heads and hear their voices. A cat slept in a shop doorway; at a café at the end of the street, people sat at small tables, and church bells somewhere close by pealed the hour. She was not remote; she was a part of the life of the street below, alive in Nice. And she was pleased, very pleased, to have it so.

As they turned back inside, a vase of flowers on the bedside table caught Emily's eye. They were orchids, tiny perfect blooms, purple striped with white; soft and exotic, they emitted a vagrant scent. There looked to be two or three dozen of them, and they glowed where the sunlight touched them. Emily sat down on the edge of the bed, smiling at Marie-France.

'Juliet was right. This is a charming place, Marie-France. I love it already. Thank you for everything, and especially for the flowers. Orchids were a lucky choice, because they're my favourites.'

'Flowers?' Marie-France followed Emily's gesture, her brows furrowing in honest bewilderment. 'You are very welcome, and I am glad that you find them to your taste.

But I cannot accept thanks for them, because I didn't put them there. The vase, yes; the flowers, no.'

Emily stared. 'Your husband, then.'

'Emilio is visiting his father in Palermo, who broke his leg. He has been there all this week, and these flowers are fresh, cut this morning. They would have come from the flower market around the corner, on the Cours Saleya.' She reached out and touched the petals of one tiny flower. Her forefinger came away wet. 'Yes, these are freshly cut; in fact, they are still damp.'

Emily stared at the orchids. There was a curious sensation in the pit of her stomach, half superstitious fear, half exhilaration. 'But . . . but if you didn't put them there, and your husband is in Italy . . .'

'I know. It is all very strange, a mystery. And me, I do not care for mysteries.' Marie-France shook her head, and shrugged once more. 'Still, if there must be mysteries, it is best that they should look nice and smell better. Are you positive you know no one here?'

'Of course I am. This is my first time in France, you know. Besides, even if I did know someone, how could they get in here to leave the flowers without you knowing about it?'

Not quite accurate, darling. There is one person you know, sort of know, or at least he knows you. And I have the distinct feeling he can get in anywhere he wants to, one way or another, wouldn't you say?

Marie-France was looking at her, so intently that for a moment Emily wondered if the internal voice had, for once, spoken aloud. 'But there are only two keys. And both are here, in my pocket.' To emphasize her point, Marie-France jingled the keys. 'This is worrying me. Who can have been in here?'

'Don't worry.' Why Emily should suddenly be so

happy, so sure as to where those mysterious orchids had come from, she could not have said. But she was elated, joyous, and it spread from her to the worried woman facing her. 'It's all right. After all, Marie-France, whoever it was obviously likes me. One of those sweet little mysteries of life; half the time, they never get solved. If anyone tries to get in without my knowing, I'll take it from there. But for now, I'll just send out some silent thanks for a lovely welcome.'

When Marie-France had left her, Emily sat on the bed. There was something in the air, that came in on the breeze through the balcony doors and mingled with the sweet scent of the orchids. It lay on her skin, a strange perfume that was sense and feeling. Her eyes were fixed on the flowers.

No, I'm not arguing. I know what you think, and I think you're right. How, why, those things aren't worth trying to figure out. But he knew you were coming, like he knew you in Italy, called you to him in Paris. He did.

'I know he did.' Emily separated a single orchid form the rest and tucked it into the buttonhole of her jacket. A street show in Herculaneum, a dimly perceived shape peering through a café window in Salisbury, footprints in the snow . . . he was as present in the touch of that flower as he had been those other times. One petal brushed against her bare collarbone. It was like a lover's touch on bare skin; something, a desire beyond her experience, took hold of her and coagulated, thickening in her blood.

She spoke aloud, very softly. 'Martin, Martin. Are you here, is this a greeting, a gift, what? Where are you? And what are you?'

The flowers offered no response. Emily took the tiny Pan from her purse, and set it on the table beside the vase of orchids. Guard them, she thought, care for each other.

Then, consumed by an inexplicable restlessness, took her purse and her keys in hand. Leaving the unpacking for a later hour, she slipped out of the apartment and into the twisting streets of Old Nice.

CHAPTER TEN

But if I weep, it will not matter, –
Ah, it is good to feel you there!

(from 'The Dream')

Emily found the Galerie Solferino without trouble. The curving bulk of Tour Bellanda, with its Phoenician mosaics and exquisite view of the city below, acted as her landmark and her guide. Emily knew that, in the days to come, it would perform the function of a lighthouse on a rocky shore, semaphoring without motion, telling the sailor how to come safely to port. In its massive friendly presence was a memory of the Eiffel Tower; since it was never out of view, it served the purpose of beacon and compass alike.

The young man in charge of the Galerie, formal and expensively dressed, was dark and curly-haired. Sicilian, Corsican, or from that same Palermo as the as yet unseen Emilio? He greeted her as she walked through the door. '*Bonjour, Madame. Puis-je vous aider?*'

'Yes, please.' Emily responded to this polite query in English, surprising herself. How had she known that this elegant, extremely French young man would speak her language? 'I've just arrived in Nice, and I was told by a friend in England that you have one of my pieces on display here. A piece that I carved. It's a wasp, done in koa wood, on a solid base.' Emily saw that he was staring at her, and her heart sank. Damn it, why couldn't she remember the French word for wasp? 'Um – *l'insecte*?'

His mouth fell open. '*La Guêpe*? Your work, you say? Then you are Emily Moon-Bourne?'

For someone to whom the thought of fame had never been anything other than faintly embarrassing, this second moment of instantaneous recognition in a six-month period sent a warm pulse of pleasure through her veins. 'Yes, I'm Emily Moon-Bourne. I see my friend was right. Do you still have the piece, or has it been sold?'

He shook her hand. 'A great honour, madame. I am Alain Verchereux. If you will come this way?'

He led her toward a glassed-in display case. 'We still have it, yes, because it is not for sale. I bought it for display, for exhibit; it is not the gallery's property, it is my own.' He shot her sidelong glance. 'It is not that no one has wished to buy it, you understand, so you must not feel pique. Several people have asked for it, in fact, since I brought it down.'

'They must be very strange people.' Emily, unaware of any incongruity in her own words, stared through the glass. God, she had almost forgotten how malevolent the thing was, how purely ugly. She had wiped the bitter angle of the stinger, the fixed red hatred of the eye, from her mind. She shivered. 'I've never done anything else quite like this, you know. To tell you the truth, I wondered who had bought it. Quite frankly I never expected it to sell at all.' She saw that he was watching her, and struggled to explain. 'I know it's very well done, one of my better pieces, but let's face it, M. Verchereux, it isn't exactly everyone's cup of tea. Well, is it?'

He obviously understood this particular idiom, for he burst out laughing. 'True, true. It is not for everyone, no? So potent, and certainly not friendly. Yet it would surprise you, madame, how many are liking this. Only this morning, a man offered to buy it.'

'A man?' Emily remembered the young waitress who had wanted her sketch of the thing, her sexual attachment to it, her fascinated repulsion. That was understandable; the piece spoke to that sour place in the female psyche. But that a human male could want to possess something so blatantly insulting to all his baser instincts was astonishing. 'How – how flattering.'

'A man, yes, and *très intéressé*. He told me to, what do you say, name my price. I confess to some temptation,' he said candidly. 'Because the English are all crazy, *étranges*, and I think I could have asked him for any amount of money, and he would have paid it. But I decided to keep the piece.'

'English?' Emily heard her own voice, casual, only slightly interested, and marvelled at the difference to her racing insides. 'A tall man, dark haired? With a smile?'

'Ah, a friend of yours.' Verchereux nodded in instant comprehension. '*Oui*, that is who it was. Very tall. He had a smile, as you say, very much a smile. Also, he had a bunch of fresh flowers. I said the English were all mad.'

'Orchids,' Emily said dreamily. 'Purple and white orchids, damp with the morning.'

'Just like the one you have put on your blouse. You have seen him, then. Well, in any case, I did not sell him my evil pet.' He looked fondly at the wasp, and then back at her; that sideways, slanting, considering look was one she had come to categorize as completely Gallic. 'Are you here for holiday, Mme Moon-Bourne?'

'Yes, in a way. Why do you ask?' He wanted something, that much was obvious. Emily, who could guess what it was, decided to retain whatever small advantage there was by going on the offensive.

'Because if you were working here, the Solferino would be honoured to show your work.' He offered her a blinding smile. 'An exclusive showing, you understand. We are fairly popular among a certain group, and it is a good time of year to do so, because of the festival.'

'I'm afraid I've done nothing but sketches since I got to Europe. And by the time I got anything done, Cannes would be over.' Martin, the group of film people on the balcony of the Crillon, Cannes . . . 'I hadn't planned on working, before I left. But I went to Greece, and Italy, and now here, and I've been considering . . .'

'We would be pleased to show your sketches,' he said, and for the first time the smooth voice was tinged with urgency. If this was butter, it was certainly the best butter. 'And perhaps a small piece or two. My friend, here,' he gestured at the wasp, 'would of course be the centrepiece of the showing.'

What are you waiting for? This is the opportunity you've been waiting for. Come on, Emily, face up to it, seize the day again. He's been here, he came, he saw the wasp. If there's a showing, your name gets advertised; that would draw him, bring him back here. He would come, you know he would. Say something, you fool. What in hell are you dithering around for?

'I'll do it.' Her fingers tingled with the thought of smooth wood under her fingers once more; it had been so long, too long. 'Actually, I'd love to do it. But I have no tools with me, and I don't know where to get wood. I've only just got here, you know. I don't know my way around yet.'

'Well,' he said, looking modestly down his nose, 'I do some work in wood myself. Mostly in the softer kinds, balsa, like that. And certainly I am not in your class. But I would be very honoured to have you use my tools, and also there is a small studio at the back of the building, very sunny and bright. That is where I do my work, because my apartment is too small. And I will procure you any wood you desire, or take you to where you may choose what you like.'

My goodness, she thought with elation, he really does want to make this easy for me. If he bends over any farther backwards, he's going to slip a disc. 'How kind,' she said aloud. 'If it wouldn't trespass on your time?'

'We are closed this afternoon. And I have a car.' Verchereux bowed, a courtly gesture that should have looked absurd and theatrical, but somehow achieved grace. 'I am completely at your service, Mme Moon-Bourne. We can go any time you wish.'

The four pieces Emily produced for the Solferino showing were done in record time.

She had chosen four exquisite blocks of wood, two of koa, one of cherry, and a stunning piece of African bubinga, grained to dark perfection. She began by attacking the cherry, producing a fat and exuberant honeybee about the size of her own hand; it was sensual, and extremely cheerful, and as a contrast to the wasp it could hardly be bettered. There was something familiar about it, some look she knew but couldn't quite place. And she had completed it in under six hours.

Emily had never worked under these conditions before. All her life, she had taken her time, deciding what she wanted to do, considering form and substance, playing with the image of the completed statue in her mind's eye before ever laying hands on a tool. A piece this size, from conception to completion, usually averaged four days to a week, and the larger pieces took much longer. Gina Wade, that unflappable agent, had learned to keep her mouth shut about Emily's slow pace.

This time, whether because of the time factor involved

or because of the spur of Martin's impending presence, she worked like a thing possessed. And Verchereux did his part; not only were his tools in excellent condition and complete in every size she needed, but his energy was unflagging. Before she had even set the thick block of cherry-wood on the table, he had drafted an ad to be placed in the local papers, and was on the telephone with someone in Cannes, haranguing the unseen listener in rapid-fire French.

It was nearly eight when she finished, and the last of the light was quickly fading. She stood back from the table and looked at the bee dispassionately. Should she smooth that faint rough edge from its back? Her hand hovered over the planer, then fell away. No, it worked. That suggestion of ruffling gave it the feeling of impending motion. She decided she was pleased with it, and ran a hand over her brow. There was sawdust on her face, and wood chips in her hair; her eyes stung and watered, whether with tiredness or with debris from her work she didn't know. She heard a slight noise, realized it was her own stomach protesting its enforced emptiness, and laughed aloud. Empty was the word, all right. When had she last eaten?

Twelve hours ago, sweetie. A brioche and two cups of coffee, back in Avignon. Hadn't you better do something about that before you fall over and die?

'Emily?' Verchereux, receiving no reply to his light tapping on the studio door, pushed it open and stuck his head through. She had insisted on first-name basis, mainly because she refused to remain formal with someone who trusted her enough to lend his precious tools. 'Are you working still? Shall I go away?'

'Oh, Alain. Come in, come in. I've finished.'

Suddenly light-headed, she sank down on a stool and

tried to catch her breath. 'I just realized I haven't eaten all day, and I must get some dinner. Here, what do you think of it?'

He came to stand before the table, scrutinizing the bee with a professional eye. Suddenly he laughed. '*Nom d'nom*, what a little miracle he is! So fat, and so friendly. I think he would not sting anyone, this fellow, for he is far too good-natured. Almost, I think, he is laughing at some joke we cannot hear.' He touched it lightly. 'A good choice, the *bois de cerise*. The grain is like stripes. Most woods would need to be polished, to bring up the grain, but not here. Shall I mount it for you? And what is he to be called?'

'She, not he.' Emily, in a bolt from the blue, had realized whey the creature looked familiar. Alain was right; a little miracle, fat and friendly. So small, and happy, with honesty in it. Ten to one, this creature would be completely unintimidated by the wasp. 'It's called *Pour Judy Waite*. And now I have to stop, and wash up, and then I have to get something to eat before I die. The last food I had was in Avignon, about twelve hours ago.'

He looked appalled. 'What, so long? Then, indeed, you must eat. There will be notices of the show in the Cannes daily paper, starting tomorrow, and printed circulars at the major hotels. I have set the date for Friday. May I buy you dinner, and a glass of wine?'

'No thanks, Alain, not tonight. And I don't drink alcohol, anyway.' She hesitated, not wanting to hurt his feelings. But the need for privacy was overwhelming, and she tried to explain. 'When I've been working this way, I always have to get away by myself for a few hours. I get tired, and drained of energy, and even in a kind of bad mood. And I always get a headache, you know, *mal de tête*. I've got one now. Until I've recuperated for a few hours, I'm not fit for human company. You do understand, don't you?'

'*C'est entendu.* I shall see you tomorrow, then? Good. Enjoy your meal, and sleep well.'

She followed Alain's directions to a small restaurant in the Port area of town. It was called Carpaccio, and that was all it served; several different variations on the original theme of raw beef, marinated and sliced paper-thin. Emily ate slowly, languorously, forcing herself to take her time despite the urgency of her hunger. The concentrated protein moved through her system, and her palate seemed super-sensitive, acutely aware of the sting of the marinade. Her wrists ached, her legs trembled, but when she had finished her dinner her head had ceased its throbbing and she was ready for the walk back to Rue Desboutins. And now, her senses rarified with exhaustion and repletion, she could look around her at this new place she had come to, could see it in all its glittering fullness.

Nice was beautiful, impressive and friendly at the same time. What had been vivid and lively in the sunlight was transformed by the spring night. There was mystery here, and peace; there was also energy and vigour. The Mediterranean was an endless sweep of indigo velvet, the sky that next touched land in Israel shot through with stars. To the east, out towards Villefranche-sur-Mer, a streak of lightning backlit the clouds like special effects in a big-budget film. Below her, in the waters of the port, small crafts bobbed at their anchorage in a tide that was quiet without being calm.

She passed the War Memorial, a strong shell set back in its own grassy park, and saw three cats; they were sitting on the base of the memorial, washing themselves, momentarily relaxed in the time of day given over to the hunt. They reminded her of Chou-chou, how his heart had fluttered against her fingertips, how his tiny pink tongue had lashed furiously against his own fur, how his body had shaken with the intensity of his purrs. She turned the corner and leaned against a building wall. What was it about that kitten that had made her feel so soft inside? That it had trusted her with its life?

You keep saying you don't like children. Maybe you do, after all.

Emmy Deer had been silent for hours. And that was one good thing about that intrusive little voice, Emily thought dreamily; she kept herself to herself when the body she inhabited was working. 'No,' she murmured under breath, 'I don't like children. But Dolores said something about babies, about being new and small and completely selfish. I think maybe she was right. There's something appealing about that, something that only lasts the first few months and then disappears for ever. It's so elemental.'

She peeled herself off the wall, just as an elderly couple leading a poodle on a leash turned the corner. They all smiled at each other, said a soft *bonsoir*, moved on. Another difference between a big city and this place of enchantment; encountering another living being on an after-dark walk in America meant a sharp sideways glance in search of weapons, a hand to make certain one's wallet was safely tucked away. Emily smiled to herself, pleased by the sight of an old pair still obviously in love, indulgent even of the overstuffed and ornately groomed poodle.

She walked down the Rue des Ponchettes, passed under a stone arch, and turned down the Cours Saleya, where Martin, it must have been Martin, had bought those orchids this morning in preparation for her arrival. It was just after ten, toward the tail end of the dinner hour, and the Cours Saleya was dotted with tables and diners and waiters and white jackets hurrying back and forth with trays of food.

A juggler moved from table to table, tossing apples in the air; the diners smiled, applauded, tossed coins in his soft cap. Emily, suddenly remembering the street show in Herculaneum, felt a wrench under her diaphragm. Somewhere, abroad in this placid spring night, those long legs moved across the land, and those far-seeing dark eyes fixed on something she couldn't see. Perhaps he was smiling, too, the tiny laugh lines creasing invisibly under the sheltering hand of darkness. What was he doing? Was he playing the devil once more, tossing apples and golden baubles into the air, for the delectation of a watching crowd?

Or for the delectation of a bonne femme*?*

'Shut up!' She bit down on the words, aware that she had spoken them aloud. A woman at a nearby table glanced curiously at her, and then away. 'Shut up, shut up.'

Well, well. A real live human emotion, jealousy no less. And from you, of all people.

Was he with someone? No, she thought strongly, no. The surge of jealousy – Emmy Deer was right, she realized with surprise, it had been jealousy – faded and died. If there was a woman, or a man, or anyone else at all, then even the weird esoteric logic attributable to this entire situation was pointless. If he loved or needed or wanted elsewhere, then what in Heaven's name was all this about, and why would he be doing this to her? There was no one else. There couldn't be.

That's right. Emmy Deer, for once, sounded quite friendly. *Just messing with your mind. Pay no attention.*

'Bitch,' Emily muttered under her breath, and walked on.

The Cours Saleya became Rue St François du Paul. Emily turned down her street, let herself into her building, took the lift – a rickety affair that she had intended to avoid – up to her flat.

As she stepped up to the door, a sound from the apartment across the landing made her jump. She turned her head sharply, and found herself staring at one half of the ugliest woman she had ever seen. The other half crouched, watchful and hating, feral as a wild animal, behind the relative safety of a half-opened door.

For a moment they stared at each other, Emily and this woman who looked like an archetype of a withered, bad-tempered Frenchwoman in a Hollywood film from the forties. So this was the infamous Mme Delange, Emily thought, aware that beneath her amusement lay a genuine jolt of unease. Marie-France was right. The old hen looked exactly like a movie witch, from the opposing points of nose and chin to the narrow brow that remained unlined only because of the harsh unyielding pressure of scraggly hair scraped tightly away from her face.

The old woman muttered something under her breath, and slammed the door. The noise was deafening; it sent echoes from ceiling to floor. Emily stood for a moment, wrestling with disbelief and the urge to giggle with incredulous panic. Only some expression of her sentiments would do; if she didn't say something, she would walk over to that blank-looking door and give it a resounding kick. Feelings must be vented if she was not to behave like a lunatic, and she proceeded to vent them.

'Good evening,' Emily said politely to the empty hall, 'you must be from Central Casting.' Spleen vented, receiving no reply, she turned back to her door.

There was a white rectangle of paper on the doormat; she almost stepped on it in her exhaustion and astonishment over the encounter with Mme Delange. She bent down with an effort, and took it up, holding it close to her face.

The envelope was stuffed full, and bore an English stamp. Judy had written at last.

Emily took her time. She brushed her teeth, took a fast shower to wash the wood chips from her skin and hair. Her nightgown felt soft and light, and the bed was deeply comfortable, welcoming the traveller to its depths. She touched the vase of flowers, let her fingers trail over the body of the small fat god from Avignon. Then, snuggling down against the pillows, she slit the envelope open and prepared to enjoy herself.

It was a wonderful letter, a heartening letter, a fine way to end what had been an endless day. Judy wrote well, amusing yet perceptive; she talked about the weather in England these past weeks ('would you believe snow, twice, what a blasphemy when the Tuileries flowers are blooming'), about a young engineering student she had spent some time with ('he's useless for anything but sex, and I told him that; he was insulted, but personally I think it must be nice to know you're good for something'), about an exhibition of African primitive art she had been to see in London ('fat leering gods with huge breasts, ugh'). Life was proceeding normally, as Judy defined normal. Her brother visited; her physics professor had gotten drunk, climbed a tree on a bet from a group of exchange students, and broken her ankle.

Judy had written on a computer, sparing Emily the trouble of having to decipher what Judy herself admitted was an appalling handwriting. Emily savoured every word. Judy breezed through her own affairs, and moved on to Emily's. What she said was straightforward, expected; one paragraph in particular caught Emily's eye, and she read it carefully, extracting Judy's wise young essence from it.

So you waved to him and walked away? Good on you, girl friend! Such a clever, clever female it is, not trying to push her way into that god-awful gilt palace and risk getting royally snubbed by some hyperthyroid bellboy with fake gold buttons on his uniform and his nose ten feet in the air. You did good, you did right. I'm proud of you.

Of course I'm talking about more than just the phone call. Walking away was right. A single wave was even more right. God, I wish I could have seen that, a casual lift of the hand and strolling away; superb, superb! Maybe you're getting answers to some of those internal questions. After all, whoever he is, whatever place in your life he came from, you can't deny that he's been calling every tune of the fiddler to this point. I guess there's something about the ability to vanish at will that makes it easy to do that.

When you were a child, did you ever have fantasies about being able to become invisible at will? Because I sure did. I used to imagine how I could control things, make things happen or prevent them, scare the hell out of people. I guess it's a power thing. I thought about moving things just out of people's reach, about singing in their ears when they couldn't see me. There was a little girl at my school, very fond of herself, and I used to wish I could become invisible so that I could pull her hair, throw ink on her, pinch her. Right, so I was a little bitch. Maybe anyone with any imagination at all has fantasies like that . . .

Speaking of fantasies, now that you've grabbed the old bull firmly by the bollocks, what are you planning to do with it? If you're reading this, you're obviously in Nice – please send my fond if shuddering greetings to that hell-born bug you carved, by the way – but what now? Do you haunt Cannes, searching for him in the cafés or on the beaches, seeing his smile on every third male face? Or do you sit back in the calm happy limbo of Nice, awaiting events? I know what I would do, but I'm not going to tell you, because you aren't me. And I have the feeling that you don't need advice. You seem to be doing just fine on your own . . .

Emily set the letter down on her bedside table, between the statue of Pan and the vase of orchids. She slept long, and deeply; the tiny stone god watched her as she dreamed, a faint smile on her face, and the flowers sent their elusive smell through the night.

She was back at the Galerie Solferino at ten the next morning, awake and alert and eager to work.

Alain had obviously been watching for her. He kissed her on one cheek, showed her into the studio and closed the door behind him. There was a wonderful tact to this behaviour, and she found herself warming to him. She warmed to him even more when she saw that not only had he cleaned and laid out the wood blocks and tools in preparation for use, he had procured an assortment of pastries and a hot cup of coffee for her. She ate a *brioche au sucre*, washed it down with a mouthful of scalding espresso, and got to work.

By late afternoon, one of her koa blocks had become a sparrow, small and bright, its wings tucked tight against its body. If the cherry bee had spoken of motion, the sparrow spoke of stillness; its head tilted cautiously up, its bright eye fixing on the world as it guarded its eggs. She had set it in a small nest, deliberately left very rough, merely sketching the outlines, and the contrast between the barely formed nest and the highly detailed occupant drew the eye and held it.

She washed her hands at the small sink before reaching for another pastry. She set it down after two bites; sugar was not what she wanted. She wanted cheese, and bread, and a big cold glass of something that tasted of the sun. She stretched once, feeling her joints crack and settle, and wandered out into the shop.

Alain was delighted with the sparrow. He ran his hands over it like a lover, making noises of pleasure and astonishment. Then, almost paternally, he shooed Emily out into the afternoon.

'Go, go, feed yourself. Look at the sun and the sea, and all the pretty people. I am a selfish pig, I have behaved very badly. You have been here since yesterday and I have kept you slaving in a small room like an eastern pasha. Why did you not scream at me? I deserve to be flogged. Go and see the sights. *À bientôt!* Come back and work more later.'

She laughed, waved, and went. A couple came in as she exited, stopping to glance curiously at the notice of the show that Alain had placed prominently in the window.

And now, dearie, hadn't you better get down to business?

Emily, who had turned toward Tour Bellanda, stopped in its shadow. Business? She'd been doing nothing but taking care of business since she got here. What business?

Something to wear. You know, to the showing? You may have forgotten that French women look like runway models even when they're wearing flour sacks. You're the star of this show. Hadn't you better look like it?

Dismayed, irritated, Emily realized that Emmy Deer

was absolutely right. She had nothing with her in that class, and she hated shopping for fancy clothes. She hated having to wear fancy clothes, in fact; her body, overly tall and too strongly built, always seemed ludicrously out of proportion to wear those exquisite creations that sat so nicely on other women. Dressing up made her feel gangly, and clumsy, and awkward. Damn, damn, damn!

Remember what Judy said, about asking yourself questions even if they're painful? Ask yourself this one: Are you planning on doing this self-hating act with Martin?

A cloud passed over the street, darkening it, chilling her. No, she thought. No, I won't do that. Even if I feel that way, I'm damned if I'll show it.

She turned back into the Galerie Solferino. Alain was busy with the couple; he saw her frantic signal, excused himself and came to her at once.

'A problem?'

'Yes. No.' She lowered her voice. 'Look, Alain, I just realized. I need to get something to wear to this showing, and I don't have a clue as to where to go. Where are the shops? Which way, where? Help!'

'Ah.' He stepped back, studying her, letting her eyes range from head to toe. The look, which would have tempted her to slapping rage from any other man, was completely inoffensive; for all its masculine appraisal, it held no glimmer of sexual awareness. He was merely considering her problem, and studying her in a way that would best provide him with an answer.

'You have a beautiful body, you know,' he said, and astounded her. 'You could wear almost anything. But I suspect you are most comfortable in loose clothing, things that are basic and have no frills or ruffles or bits.'

'You've got that right.'

'*Bon.* There is a boutique, Chez Madeleine. It is on

Avenue Jean Medicin, right near the Place Massena. Left side of the street. Madeleine looks very much like you, she is happiest in big sweaters and soft skirts, and she designs evening wear that is some of the simplest and most effective I have ever seen. Go there, mention my name to her; she is expensive, but I think you don't care about that.'

'You're an angel,' she told him, and went.

The dress was perfect. Madeleine was statuesque, very prominently curved without being blatant. No sooner had Emily explained what she needed than she was taken firmly in hand, led to a small rack in the corner of the shop and handed a hanger. Emily got a look at the price tag, bit back a whistle, and allowed herself to be indulgently but firmly shepherded into a thickly carpeted dressing room.

The dress was grey, a dense silk that seemed to be made of many layers, deeply compressed. It was the colour of the sea on an angry day, a sort of agitated moonstone; it was fitted without being tight, and the collar and sleeves stood away from the shoulders, almost like a rollneck sweater cut very deep.

She stared at herself in the mirror, at the way her skin glowed against the grey stuff of the fabric, at the way her black hair, which she had always considered coarse and boring, now seemed so sleek. Her eyes looked enormous, her cheekbones were carved and prominent, the bones of an Indian warrior; for a disorienting moment, John Moon looked at her appraisingly out of his daughter's eyes. She took a deep breath, changed back into her working clothes, and went back out to talk to Madeleine.

She bought the dress, and three others. The total for these four items came to well over a thousand dollars, but Emily paid without a blink. They were worth it; clothing that could turn a gangling duckling into a sexy swan were worth anything the maker cared to charge.

She spent the rest of the afternoon, not sightseeing as she had vaguely planned, but buying shoes to match her new dresses. She stopped off at home, just long enough to drop off her new things; there was no sign of old Delange this time, and Emily breathed a sigh of relief. Then, after a stop at a local *charcuterie* for an assortment of pâté and cheese, she went back to the Galerie Solferino, exchanged a few words with Alain, and locked herself into the studio to work through the night. The show was in less than two days, she still had two pieces to produce, and she had seen nothing of Nice. Emily, happier than she had been in years, sang as she worked, a vibrant off-key warbling that was the voice of joy, doing what it wished.

The difficulties didn't matter in the least. None of them mattered. When the show came, when Martin came, she would be dressed and ready, a centrepiece in her own right. Cinderella had gotten a dress for the ball. Let the bells chime midnight, let the fairy-dust sprinkle where it would; let the dance begin.

CHAPTER ELEVEN

My candle burns at both ends;
It will not last the night;
But ah, my foes, and oh, my friends –
It gives a lovely light!

('First Fig')

From Alain Verchereux's point of view, the showing was a wild success.

True, it went off without a hitch; people came, casually dressed during the daylight hours and more formal after dark. They chattered to Emily in a polyglot of languages, and Emily, lovely in her grey silk, talked back at them. All four pieces were sold in the first three hours, with the proviso that they remain in the Solferino's custody for the duration of the show. An elderly couple, very elegant and almost too obviously wealthy and cultured, even bought three of Emily's sketches of the Spanish Steps.

As a social event, it went beautifully. From Emily's perspective, it was torture of a variety she hadn't known existed.

Martin did not come.

She had never been in love, not even during those teenage years when love is so absurdly painful and the heart is sent racing by a familiar profile or the timbre of a voice in a crowd. She had no frame of reference for this agony, therefore, no past experience to shield her from the hideous disappointment that grew with every passing minute. It was torture, misery, the very stuff of wretchedness, and she had no weapons against it.

Alain knew something was wrong. Through the steadily growing haze of dull aching unhappiness, Emily caught his eye on her, puzzled and worried. She was unable to care, or to think beyond her crushing disappointment, although she went through the motions. She spoke when speech was required of her, shook hands, gave answers to the foolish questions ('Where do you get your ideas?'). She kept a social smile pinned securely to her face; behind that sheltering mask, her skin felt stretched to bursting point with the immensity of her effort not to crane her neck, to jump at every newcomer, to weep like a child who has waited up all night for Santa Claus, only to find the tree bare of any gift at all. None of these faceless people knew, but Alain Verchereux knew a good deal about women, and he had already come to guess at certain things about Emily. That was something eating her alive, he had no doubt.

When the doors to the Galerie finally closed, it was nearly one on Saturday morning. Emily was trembling, a tiny seismic hell that had taken over her entire body and would not let her go. She was nauseous, the bile in her throat an acrid, bitter measure of her disappointment. He didn't come, she thought, he didn't come. I can't believe it, I won't. She wanted to scream the words aloud. God damn it, it isn't fair!

'Emily?' Alain touched her, very gently, on the shoulder. 'You are tired, and unwell. Something is wrong?'

'I can't explain.' The words came out in a stranger's voice, a choked rasp that surely could not belong to her. 'I have to go home, Alain. I have to go home now.'

He was seriously worried about her now. 'Shall I walk you there, or take you in my car?'

'No.' The word was rapped out, forced from her, and she was dismayed at herself. Sick as she was, she could hardly let it stand; he had done nothing to deserve such rudeness, not from her. But what could she say? How could any woman possibly explain a situation like this to a human male? It was impossible, inconceivable, to share this pain. She took in air, and tried her best to find words that would reassure him while imparting nothing of her own humiliation. 'No, thank you. I'll be all right. I – it's just . . .'

The words died off, as she realized with horror that she was going to be sick. She made a noise in her throat, and turned wildly toward the door of the studio. Alain, understanding the problem, took her firmly by her elbow and guided her to the sink there.

The retching seemed to last for ever. When at last she regained some control over her heaving muscles, she was clammy and limp, and her entire body hurt. She made no further protest when he led her out into the street, locked the door behind him, and pushed her into his white Jaguar.

The drive took only three minutes, but Emily was very grateful for it. She allowed him to accompany her to the door of her flat, and was glad he had come; as she fumbled for her keys with fingers that felt like sausages, Madame Delange pushed open her door and peered out. Eyes narrowed, mouth tight and vicious; it was the same concentrated malevolence of the first encounter, and Emily whimpered.

Perhaps the old woman was a classic French type, after all, for Alain understood immediately, both what she was and that Emily could not, in her present condition, cope with it. He rounded on Mme Delange like a fury, spitting out the kind of French that is rarely heard outside of France.

'*Gâteuse!*' The words were hissed, intended to hurt and

scare; the elegant proprietor of the fashionable art gallery had suddenly transmogrified into a Sicilian wharf rat, tensed for a knife fight. '*Salope! Putain! Arrette ou je te fous une baffe!*'

To Emily, exhausted in body and sick at heart, the quick progression of French was too fast to follow. The effect on Mme Delange was immediate; she gave an eldritch screech and slammed her door. Alain at once turned back to Emily, leading her inside and settling her in a chair with a glass of cold water.

'I apologize,' he told her. 'I should not have used such language in front of you. But I could see that she upset you, and I wanted to get rid of her as quickly as possible. I am forgiven, OK?'

It isn't real, she told herself wearily. None of this is real. Just answer him, and maybe he'll go away . . .

'You don't need to apologize, because I don't know what you said. Too fast for me to make out.' She was aware of a faint glimmer of curiosity, and that surprised her. 'What *did* you say?'

'Well,' he replied cheerfully, 'since I have already said I am sorry for being offensive, I might as well tell you what the offence was. I called her a senile old bitch, and a whore, and told her to knock it off or I would slap her one.'

Involuntarily Emily laughed, and the dull pain around her heart eased a bit. 'Impressive, very impressive. Could you write all that down for me? It seems to work, or is that only because you're a man? Would she respond that way to a woman's anger?'

'God knows,' he shrugged. 'With a woman like that, who knows anything? *Une vrai mégère*, that one, what you would call a harpy or a shrew, and they are not predictable. But I will write it down for you, tomorrow or the next day. For now, you must sleep. Thank you for tonight;

although you are not happy, I was pleased with the showing. I shall see you again when you are well, I hope.'

He was gone on the words, closing the door with a solid snap behind him. Letting the old witch know he wasn't spending the night, Emily thought. Trying to make my life a little easier. He's really very kind.

Poor Emily. Wasting your sweetness on the desert air, or is it burning your candle at both ends? Now what?

There was no unkindness in this killing phrase; Emmy Deer, if anything, sounded dispassionate. And there was no answer to her question, not yet. Emily dragged herself to the door, and locked it. A distant clatter told her that Alain had let himself out of the building. She was alone, all by herself, on a Saturday night on the French Riviera.

On an impulse, she went to the long mirror on the bathroom door and scrutinized herself carefully. There was intensity in her gaze, an attempt to unlock the secret behind this sudden sense of loss. The grey silk still flattered, but not as it had done when she was happy with herself; her eyes were glazed, her hair dishevelled, her skin the colour of a fish's belly. She blinked, shivered, and turned away.

The next morning, after a deep dreamless sleep that left her feeling heavy and drugged, she packed an overnight bag, tossed her leather jacket over her arm, climbed into the Citroën and drove to Avignon.

It was as pretty, as welcoming, as it had been the first time. The skies of Provence were endless and wide, no clouds even on the distant peaks. She ignored the hotels; whatever need had sent her here, whatever the night ahead would offer her, she knew in her bones that sleep was not on the agenda.

She spent the day wandering, not thinking, simply

feeling. She passed by the carousel, by the painted figures on the walls, and gave them no thought at all. Something was brewing in her spirit, percolating, and it took all of her. She stopped at one café for coffee, at a second for mineral water; she waved vaguely at the sculptress with the kitten and the stone gods, acknowledging the woman's look of welcome and recognition. Her mind tried to work, but she suppressed it firmly. This was not the time for thought; somehow, she knew that much. And, inexorably, the day wore on toward nightfall.

Still, there is no way to shut down a functioning mind, short of inducing coma. Things slipped through Emily's hardly held wall of self-protection, mostly the same words, moving in snail tracks through her awareness. He didn't come. He didn't come.

Why not go to the river? Commune with that bloody huge rock that scared you so badly? Look, there won't be light left much longer. It's dusk, and soon it will be dark. You know how soothing you find the sound of moving water.

With a start, Emily came back to herself and looked around. Nearly eight, and the day was almost gone. Did it matter where she went? She had thought that this panic flight to Avignon, this putting of as much distance as was reasonable between herself and the humiliation of last night in Nice, would blunt the edge of that humiliation. Had she been wrong? Was the pain in fact less, or was this merely the nepenthe of sheer physical exhaustion?

She turned towards Rocher des Doms, passing under the portcullis just as the last of the light faded and died, and the stars came out.

It happened in a matter of seconds; one moment there was a dusky rose eternity, and the next there were dancing ghost lights. She had never seen so many stars; the sky was indigo, preternaturally clear, and lights moved above her in a crowd of luminescence past counting. She pulled her jacket close around her, momentarily cold.

I can hear the river, she thought, and indeed the soft hush of its passing edged the noise of the traffic. She glanced up at the great rock, admiring it distantly. Stars, and rivers, and huge old walls. Why in hell do I feel so totally bereft?

Maybe because you're alone?

Emmy Deer, this time, seemed almost sympathetic. And, out of nowhere, Emily was hit with a burst of terror, the same irrational fear that had seized her once before at the sight of Rocher des Doms in the dark. She was alone, completely naked and unprotected; the enormous rock was hideous, terrible. It loomed over her like a fate, and she was too close to it, under its very bulk. Its beauty and majesty had become an icon of threat. She could no longer stand here.

She turned on her heel, trying not to break into a run, and walked away from Rocher des Doms, feeling it behind her like a watching monster out of myth. Too big, she thought wildly, much too big. It wants to eat me. Walled rock, what big teeth you have. She stifled a sudden burst of hysterical laughter, and swallowed hard. The taste of fear, sour and hateful, was strong at the back of her throat.

The luck was with her, and so were the traffic lights; as she reached the kerb, they changed in her favour. Emily scuttled across the road, feeling ridiculous but hurrying nevertheless, almost running to reach what had so oddly become the fairy-tale safety of the other side. The traffic started up again, forming a barrier between her and the white pile behind her.

Safe, she thought, I'm safe now. Olly, olly, oxen free, now the monster can't get me. She stopped, breathing hard, and with a surge of impatience at her own cowardice turned to look. Rocher des Doms stood as it had always done, solid and pale, gleaming under the night sky. Why did it affect her this way? Benign in the daytime, terrible at night? There was no answer; she could only accept, and react accordingly. At any rate, her fear had done her one small favour. For a few brief minutes, the enormity of her phobia had pushed aside the consuming sense of failure, of loss, of frustration.

Now, with the childish terror evaporating as if it had never been, Emily walked to the river's edge. It's a lovely stretch of water, she thought. The Rhône danced along at its own eternal pace, dark and peaceful, paying her no mind. She listened to its voice, to the slap of water against the banks and the old bridge downstream, the cry of the night birds, the creak of wood as the motion of the river jostled the boats docked all along the line. Glancing up through the lighted window of a large houseboat, Emily saw two people.

The man was seated, obviously finishing his evening meal. As Emily watched, feeling faintly guilty, he laid his fork down and said something to the woman seated across the table from him. She was dark and lovely, and she smiled back, a beautiful transforming smile. She reached out a hand, touching his face lightly, and he snatched a kiss at her fingertips. The gesture was tender beyond definition, and almost unbearable in its extreme sensuality.

It was too much. Emily sat down on the soft grass of the verge, put her head in her hands and burst into tears.

The crying fit was brief, but shattering in its intensity. All the world had unfairly become uncaring and separate, leaving her marooned on a barren island in a distant sea. For a cold and lucid moment, she understood how completely alone she was. But I never used to mind being alone, she thought through her grief. I never used to mind.

That's what you say, dummy. And if you're stupid enough to believe that, I've got some prime waterfront property just west of Ireland that you might be interested in purchasing.

Damn it, she thought angrily, it's the truth. But Emmy Deer had regained her old irony, and Emily hated it. I never used to mind. I always thought . . .

'Are you feeling better now?'

The voice was light, musical, with a certain depth; it spoke in a British accent that was cultured, but not to parody point. She had heard it before, she knew it, just as she had known that this night in Avignon would be a Rubicon, bringing something to a point. She should have been surprised; she felt no surprise at all.

She jumped galvanically, turned, and looked up into the lively, passionless face of the medieval devil at Herculaneum, the kind gentleman who had given up his cab in Paris, the smiling face on the balcony of the Hotel Crillon.

He stood there, smiling faintly down at her, dressed in the same black frock coat, the same trousers so tight that they might have been a thin layer of flesh on his slender body. I got his hairline wrong, Emily thought crazily, I made it too far down his forehead. But the smile is just what I drew . . .

He gave her that smile, letting his question hang on the night air.

Emily stood staring, voiceless from the shock that had paralysed her vocal cords. But the shock was of recognition, not of fear. She did not even question how he had gotten there, or why. He was so inevitable, so utterly a part of this vital French night, that to question his presence would have been pointless and insensitive.

She lifted a hand and wiped the tears from her face; she was voiceless, unable to respond to anything. At this moment in time, she thought, I can do nothing but be . . .

'Here.' She had said nothing, had not had the time to formulate the words to take away the disadvantage of being found on the banks of the Rhône, crying her heart out. And there were questions, surely, logical questions that she could ask him, but she could not speak. Yet he seemed to expect no words from her, only her attention, and she kept silent. 'Here. Watch. This is for you.'

He reached into the breast pocket of his frock coat, and pulled out an enormous white handkerchief. His clothes would look absolutely ridiculous on any other man alive, Emily thought irrelevantly. But he's all length, all curving lovely bone. They suit him.

'*Violà.*' He slipped a hand under the handkerchief, performed a brief flourish, and whisked the handkerchief away. Nestled in the palm of his hand, calm and unafraid, was a small white pigeon.

Martin smiled into Emily's face, saying nothing.

She felt the blush stain her skin, a dark spread of crimson temperature; her entire body heated, wavered, stabilized. I never blush, she thought in amazement, but certainly she was blushing now. My God, my God, what, no, I know what. It was the smile. Maybe it's been the smile all along. But can a smile, such a faint smile too, really do that? To *me*? And why can't I talk, ask him, find out?

She turned her head swiftly away, dropping her eyes, confused. From the corner of her vision, she watched his hands.

He loosed his hold, the long fingers spreading in a gesture of release. The bird took wing, arching the strong muscles of its back, letting the breeze fill its primaries and carry it into flight. As Emily turned her head further to watch its passing, the pigeon gained momentum. It circled over the river, high and triumphant, arcing over the houseboat with the lovers. Then it wheeled to the south-east and was gone, a tiny shadow against the gleaming bulk of Rocher des Doms.

She stared into the clear perfection of the sky, yearning after it. To be able to do that, she thought, to fly, to simply stop and start and land whenever the fancy took you. Maybe you could even fly away from history, from time, from . . .

Say something, you fool. Speak to him, hurry up, before he vanishes again.

Yes, Emily thought, yes. You've been anticipating this, waiting for this; you came here tonight because you knew this was where he would be. Do something, say something. She drew a deep breath, and turned back to her unexpected companion. 'That was great. Sometimes I wish . . .'

The words trailed off into silence. She was alone on the bank, talking to nothing and no one. He had gone.

Blew it, blew it, screwed it up . . .

He had been there, taking flesh from the hour and her loneliness. He was like the devil he had played, a demon in a Punch and Judy pantomime, appearing and vanishing at will. It was ridiculous, absurd. I didn't imagine it, she thought, and she stood for precious minutes, trying to clear her head. I am not losing my mind, and I was not imagining things. He had a bird, and he said it was for me, and it flew away.

And he had smiled, smiled straight into her eyes, and that smile had burrowed its way into places of the soul where nothing else had ever been. It was sunlight on water, that smile, and shadow against skin. And now she could admit it, without shame or regret or intervention from Emmy Deer. She wanted that smile as she had wanted nothing else in her lifetime.

And she hadn't even told him her damned name.

Come back come back please please come back . . .

She turned on her heel, racing across the road. The lights were against her; cars screeched to a halt, horns sounded, people rolled down their windows and shouted pungent Gallic insults after her. She heard none of it.

He was here, he was here, he was, he was. I saw the bird. I saw him smile.

The plague full swift goes by. Doesn't take much to fall down and skin your knees, does it, sweetie?

'You're damned right it doesn't,' Emily said aloud, and turned toward the lights of Avignon.

The hunt through the city was frenzied at first, then methodical; towards morning, when Emily was so exhausted that her sleep-deprived body seemed detached from her conscious mind, it became peevish and aimless. She was aware of nothing but need, obsession, the fact that he had been beside her, had given her a gift, had faded out, gone away and left her standing here, taking his smile with him. That the gift had been freedom, and her acceptance a kind of enslavement, was something that would come clear to her at another time. For now, the needing was all there was.

She was glad that she had not bothered with a hotel, for she had forgotten there was such a thing as sleep and would have fought the need away in any case. She went too quickly through the Place de L'Horloge, peering like a wild woman at people seated for late drinks at the open-air tables; she only took some control of herself after realizing that a gendarme was watching her with obvious suspicion.

She went past the carousel with its lights and music,

up the hill toward the Palais des Papes. She passed the spot where the woman sculptor sat with her table and her small squeaking bundle of life, and paused there for a moment. She offered up a promise, inchoate and unreasonable. Pan, god of the wooded place and of all things wild. If I find him, Emily thought madly, I'll come back and pet the kitten and buy all her statues. I swear I will.

Step on a crack, break your mother's back. Are you offering the gods a bribe, or just being childish?

I don't know and I don't give a flying damn, Emmy Deer. Maybe I am being childish. What if I am? I've got a right to be a child sometimes, everyone does. Aren't you supposed to be the child Emily? What's the matter, are you scared of some legitimate competition? And where is it written that childish is bad?

Emmy Deer made no reply. Emily glanced up at the Palais, enormous and regal and completely empty. Martin would not be found here, neither within nor hard by its vast pale symmetry. She wasn't sure how she knew this, but know it she did. She turned down a winding side street, passing under closed windows and alcoves, watched by the painted kings and troubadours.

Once, feeling a sense of eyes on her back, she jerked her head up and for a heart-shaking moment found herself staring at his smile. But it was only a painted smile, laid down by an artist on the face of a green-mantled minstrel with a lute in a wall mural, and Emily moved on. Around her, the air grew moist and chilly, the streets emptied of people and the night thinned toward morning.

Alleys, side streets, the shadow of the city's inner walls. She peered into parked cars, into dark doorways; she passed like a slightly demented ghost under the walls of ancient churches and small hotels, and the closed windows of shops and cafés regarded her blandly. Gone, gone, nowhere to be found. If he was in Avignon still, he was hidden away, safe beyond the reach of her five senses.

Shortly before dawn, yawning and shivering, Emily conceded defeat.

For the rest of her life, that early morning drive would have the remembered precision and clarity of an out-of-body experience. Her body, drugged with exhaustion and dangerously unresponsive behind the wheel of the car, seemed a universe away from her own sharp awareness of her thighs pressed against the seat, the shadow of birds flying overhead, the distant hum of a tractor hidden behind a vast field of lavender.

Admitting to herself how tired she was, she stayed in the slower right lane. Just short of the main turn-off for Marseille, the car drifted slightly into the left lane and a furious horn blast alerted her to the extent of her own exhaustion. The warning was enough; she pulled off at the first rest stop that offered a café. Here, sitting outside, she ate an omelette and drank four cups of espresso. Thus fortified, she took to her wheels once more.

The Citroën, which had behaved so beautifully up to now, felt peculiar. Emily heard an odd little rattle under the hood, felt the engine lose compression as she climbed a steep grade near Aix-au-Provence; the problem was only momentary, however, and she put it from her mind. It was nearly noon before she turned on to the Promenade. She rolled down the window, tasting the salt tang in the air. It was welcoming cnough to give her the last burst of energy she needed to get home. The day was bright, too bright; the edge of the sun seemed particularly harsh against her eyes and her skin was misted with a light, clammy sweat. Sleep, she thought. I'll be fine after I sleep.

A hundred francs says you dream of him . . .

She ignored that, except for a single fleeting thought: I never bet against certainties. Threading her way through the winding side streets took time and concentration, but at last it was done, and she was forced to walk on legs that felt rooted to the ground. She put the car away, bought some mineral water and walked wearily up the four flights to her apartment; even in this state of near immobility, she could not cope with the lift. The landing was dim, dust motes dancing on the still air.

Sleep, sleep, Macbeth hath murdered sleep. Sleep no more, I thought I heard a voice say, sleep no more. Fat lot of good sleep is going to do you. Brightness falls from the air. I bet you dream about the Smile . . .

'Shut up.' She had actually spoken aloud this time, and she cast a guilty glance around her. If the ubiquitous Mme Delange was engaging in her usual snoop, she would think Emily was cracked, too. Well, the hell with the old bitch and what she thought. Her command of English was probably streaky at best.

She had pulled out her key, had actually laid a hand on the latch, before she saw the package on her doormat. It was small, wrapped in the soft green tissue used by all the local *pâtisseries* and tied with string.

She bent and took it up. The paper was pliant in her hand, which for some reason had begun to tremble. She breathed heavily, impatient of the green paper and the dimness and her tiredness. After a short, clumsy struggle, she ripped the tissue away.

The little bird, orange and white, nestled in her hand. It was carved, not of wood, but of sugar and rock candy. Its wings were decorously folded against its body; the profiled beak and the one visible eye were bright beads of red sugar. Here was her own sparrow, gone from hard koa wood into sugar, watching its maker with love.

Now do this properly, Emily dear. Be logical, and sensible. Be the little detective.

After a long moment of struggling with her shock, she

picked up the green tissue and turned it over. The words were there in small, neat letters; they were in green ink, nearly the same colour as the tissue itself, and she had almost missed them.

'For Emily, who can fly if she wants to. Will she fly to Bistro Marcel, Rue Mascoinat, at nine tonight?'

And the signature, his name, the beautiful happy conjuring devil-sprite completely personified, identified at last: Martin Ferrier.

CHAPTER TWELVE

Some love, and some simplicity,
Might well have been the death of me.

(from 'Theme and Variations I')

He was waiting for her.

Emily belonged to that class of people who invariably arrive at their destination much earlier than necessary. There had been times, parties and receptions and dinner engagements, when she had been forced to sit in her car for half an hour or more, simply because her conviction that lateness equalled inexcusable rudeness had led her to arrive too soon for decency. This magical, momentous night was no exception; despite the agonizing over her clothes, the arranging and rearranging of her hair, she found herself standing beneath the façade of La Cathédrale de Sainte Reparate, thirty feet from the Bistro Marcel, at eight forty.

She saw him from the corner. He was facing her, sipping a glass of something pale and bubbly, watching her approach. She hesitated for a moment, feeling awkward and suddenly shy, wondering if, after all, the leather pants and jersey tunic had been a mistake. She had changed clothes six times. An hour ago, this final choice had seemed a perfect compromise between sexy and controlled. Now, with a whole new world scant moments and a half a block away, she wasn't so sure.

This is the River Styx. Here is Charon, waiting to ferry you across. Or is it the River Jordon?

No, Emily thought. It's neither. This is what I thought, back in Avignon. This is the Rubicon. And it's high time I crossed it, ferryman or no.

She hoisted her purse, straightened her back, and walked the last remaining distance to where this shadow of her life sat waiting for her.

His first words, when she sat, were somehow just right. 'Under the shadow of the child saint Reparata,' he said cheerfully. 'Well met. Of course, there's nothing at all saintly about those trousers. You look a bit like a witch tonight, a benevolent witch.'

'Do I?' She studied him frankly, feeling obscurely that, after all, she had the right. Her drawing, that folded and creased map of his features, had been very close to reality. There *were* tiny lines around his eyes when he smiled; the eyes themselves, now that she saw them under indirect light, *did* seem to reflect unseen things. 'Saint Reparata. Do you know, I don't think I've ever heard of her? I mean, I'm not a Catholic, but she's not one of the well-known ones, is she?'

'Saint Reparata, child martyr.' He was turning the glass around in his hand, letting the reflections from the street lamps play in the yellow substance. Beer, lemonade, champagne? 'Martyred, I seem to recall, during a massacre performed under decree of the Emperor Somebody-or-other, possibly Theodosius. It usually was Theodosius, for some reason. I've always had trouble telling the various pompous Roman types apart. Martyred, in any case, at approximately aged ten. I suspect she was a sanctimonious, stubborn, irritating child, the kind you want to slap. There's no proof she ever did anything miraculous, by the way. Her acts are listed as spurious.'

She stared at him, astonished. 'What an amazing piece of pointless trivia,' she said. Where in the world was this peculiar conversation coming from, and why? It might have been scripted in advance, so painless was it. 'Are you a Catholic, or just an expert on obscure saints?'

'I am neither Catholic nor hagiologist.' He took a sip of his drink, waved a hand toward a waiter, and smiled directly into her face. Something that was part heat and part pure liquid need moved into Emily's nervous system, and settled there. 'I just like to study the competition. Now, what will you drink? No coffee, would be my guess; you've been running on over-extension and energy for far too long. A *citron pressé*? Hot tea? It's rather chilly, after all.'

'Tea, please.' A small fact, but interesting, and Emily automatically registered his knowledge; he had not offered her alcohol, and that omission had come because he knew she wouldn't drink it. Who was he, what was he? What had he meant by that odd remark about studying the competition? And how in hell did he know so much about her?

'Don't ask me questions, Emily, not right now. It simply isn't the proper time. A pot of tea, please.' She had said nothing, not a word. Did he read minds? She flushed, feeling her face engorged with blood, and he reached out and touched her hand. It was the merest brush, a butterfly of contact, but the effect on Emily was immediate and electric. She dropped her eyes, willing her mind and Emmy Deer to keep silent. If he could read minds, she would be mortified. God, oh God, why couldn't she manufacture just a tiny bit of Judy's sublime self-assurance?

The waiter arrived with a china pot and matching cup, on a tray. These he set down before Emily, pouring for her. Fragrant steam rose around her in a cloud. It was no use, she simply couldn't keep her unruly thoughts quiet. Why had she asked for tea, anyway? She didn't want tea. What she wanted, wanted desperately in fact, was a handle, a key, some kind of Rosetta stone that would give her even the smallest of ways to handle this bizarre situation.

You also want to touch him. You want to touch him like a blind woman would touch him, running your hands over his features, mapping them, absorbing them, verifying them . . .

'I'm drinking champagne, myself.' He emptied his glass, and set it down. 'When you've had your tea, I want to take you for a walk. You've been here for days and you still haven't seen anything of Nice. It's high time you did.'

'I've been busy. I've been working. And I'd like to take a walk.'

'I know you've been working. Lovely little creatures, bees and birds.'

He hadn't been to the showing, the only time those pieces had been on display. Here was one more mystery, one more unanswered question, one more thing he knew about her that, by all the rules of logic and reality, he should have had no way of knowing. She sipped her tea, watching him.

'I didn't come to the showing because I don't like crowds.' The smile this time was personal, produced for her and because of her; it was sensual in the extreme, and very tender. Emily, through a sudden flush of exhilaration, knew that she wanted to kiss him, really kiss him, not stop kissing him. She got control of herself, breathing through her nose, wondering if the body she could feel reacting so forcefully was the same numb carrier of her talents that she had grown accustomed to over nearly forty years. Martin added, casually and devastatingly, 'I'd rather have you to myself, assuming you don't object.'

'Oh, God,' she whispered, and set the tea down. Words came from her, unconsidered and reckless, the truth. 'Let's walk. Let's go away from here. I want to walk with you, with the face in my drawing, with the juggling demon king who seems to have followed me here from Italy. And I'm not going to ask you questions, I'm not going to ask you anything. Know why, Martin? Because you won't answer me, not until you're damned well ready to.'

His smile, this time, was knowing and aware. She had never carved faces, not human faces, and the artist in her was amazed by how many shadings, how many subtle overtones, could be put into a single upward curve of the lips.

'Quite right, I wouldn't. You're very patient, Emily, an excellent virtue. More people should cultivate it.'

He stood, in a single movement of grace and fluidity; under the black fabric, she saw thigh muscles ripple and clenched her hands in her lap. He dropped some money on the table, reached out and helped her to her feet. His grip was strong without emphasis, transmitting more of that odd heat through her system. The touch was brief. Like a lover long accustomed, he draped one arm around her shoulders.

So this is what Judy means. What did she say about it, all of it, not just physical sex but the whole nine yards? This must be what she meant.

This first real contact between them went beyond electricity. It seemed to Emily like a linking of nerves, so badly did she want more of it, so integral to her core of living was her need to press the length of her body against him. The long slender fingers rested lightly against her upper arm, and she felt their warmth through the jersey sleeve. They walked together, in communal rhythm, and she felt his steady breathing beside her.

Her own breath was not steady at all. She stole a glance up at the long mobile face, and for a bleak moment she hated him. How could she be in such need, such turmoil, and how could he force her to hide it by being so calm?

To this, as to everything else, Emily had no answer. The dark feeling died and was replaced with calm, and a sense of inevitability. What did it matter, after all? However he had come, whoever he was, it was right that they should be walking together. She had been waiting for this a long time, perhaps for her whole life.

He led, and she followed; they walked the length of the Cours Saleya, under the stone arch, and down toward the Promenade. They had reached the sweep of pavement that overlooked the beach before Emily realized where they were.

The air was soft, a miraculous agglomeration of salt and gentleness. It was absurd that the mere existence of night air could make her want to cry. Emily pondered this briefly, aware that she had fallen into a kind of calm, of acceptance. She had never been so easy with anyone in her life.

He glanced down at her. God, she thought, he really was tall. Six four, six five? He had a trick, too, of making her feel delicate; despite her sturdier bones and solid height, there was something about him that made him seem stronger than she was. Emily, unaccustomed to this, knew that with anyone else she would have felt annoyed, possibly even threatened, to the point of asserting herself.

But there was no need, not with Martin. Her reaction did not reflect any sense that he saw her as a lesser thing, in need of protection. He was simply complete, at home within himself; that comfort, that completeness, lent him this presence.

'Tired?'

His voice was light and musical. She knew the voice, it was totally familiar to her. How many years had she been hearing it, unidentified, at the back of her mind? Emily suddenly thought of Judy, of her singing voice. Me too, she thought. Me too, girl friend. I've got one, too.

'No. I ought to be tired, but I'm not.' She looked up at him, from the shelter of his encircling arm. 'Is this your doing, my being wide awake? I mean, is it one of your magical tricks? Do you do it with mirrors?'

He laughed down at her. 'No, with chemicals. Would you like me to tell you something, one thing at least? Or would you prefer me steeped in mystery, leaving clues for you to solve me with?'

Emily's lips curled into an answering smile. 'Oh, no. I'm not nearly as young as all that. Give me a clue, by all means. I can hardly wait.'

'Right.' He tightened his hold on her, his eyes as dark as the hour itself. There was no reading what lay behind them, and nothing to be read from his voice, either; the light cheerful music never altered. 'Here we go. It's just this: I'm here, I was in Italy and England and Paris, because you called me.'

There was a moment's silence, as Emily digested this. She stared up into his face, then out across the Baie des Anges, thinking, puzzling. Finally she said, very slowly, 'I called you?'

'Give the little lady a coconut. You called me.'

How could he be so light, so teasing, over such a huge and momentous statement? She brought her gaze back to his face, studying him. 'How did I call you?'

'With need. And that's all I'm going to tell you, at least for tonight. You're getting chilled; we'd better go somewhere warmer.'

He was right, of course. The night air that bore the sea

within it was seeping imperceptibly through her clothing and marking the flesh beneath. 'Where should we go?'

'I'll take you home. You're not as awake as you think you are, and you mustn't burn your candle at both ends. Did you like your flowers?'

'The orchids. Of course I did, they're my favourites.' She fell into step beside him; he had removed his arm and walked with his hands jammed into his pockets. 'But of course you knew that, didn't you? And of course you're not going to tell me how you knew that, or how you knew where to find me, or how you got into a locked apartment.'

He laughed. 'I'm a magician, remember? Walnuts and apples and bright golden rings. It's my job, Emily my Emily, or part of it.'

They reached the Rue Desboutins, stopping before the front door of her building, and Emily took a long breath. I'm out of my depth, she thought desperately. I've got no wiles, no precedent, no interior feminine language to speak to him with. How do I handle this?

Ask him upstairs, that's all. It's simple.

Well, it was worth a try. Anyway, Emmy Deer was right; when in doubt, keep it simple and direct. 'Are you coming upstairs with me?'

'Not tonight. As I said, you need to sleep.' He tilted her head, looking very birdlike. 'Come up to the Tour Bellanda tomorrow, when you get up. I'll be there, waiting for you. Goodnight, sweet Emily. Sleep deep.'

He leaned over, kissed her full on the mouth, and was gone into the night.

Keep it simple, keep it direct.

By the next morning, the weather had turned warm.

She had slept solidly, as she had not once slept in childhood, without moving and without dreaming. When she woke, her entire body was renewed. She made herself coffee, took a shower, rummaged through her drawers for something light to wear. She sang as she prepared for the day, carolling happy and off-key, a Breton folk song about a fisherman bidding a fond farewell to his children before going off to sea.

She saw him on the Bellanda observation platform when she was half-way down Rue des Ponchettes. Even at this distance he was unmistakable. Holding up a hand, signalling him to wait, she stuck her head through the front door of the Galerie Solferino.

Alain's relief at seeing her made her wonder, until she remembered her grief and sickness at their last encounter. She smiled at him.

'*Bonjour*, Alain. I just popped in to say hello, and to tell you I was feeling much better.'

'Better? You look radiant.' He came to the door and gave her a quick hug. 'You look as if someone has made long sweet love to you, or given you something you have always wanted, or something like that.'

'Neither and both of the above. Forgive me, I'm not trying to be enigmatic. I just can't explain.' There was joy and laughter in her voice, and she heard them with pleasure. Alain, nonplussed, blinked at her. Was this the tired woman he had worked so closely with, the woman who had looked so different, so withdrawn, so old? He studied her face carefully, trying to find where the difference lay.

'You need not explain. I am just very happy to see you so well rested. Can I buy you lunch?'

'Thanks, Alain, but not today. I have to – I'm meeting a friend.'

'Ah.' There it was, then, the change in her. 'The Englishman with the smile. You will be busy. Drop in and see me, if you get the chance. After all, I will have some money for you shortly.'

'Money? Oh, from the showing. Later, whenever, not now. I can't think about money now. Anyway, I'm late.'

'A woman, an American, who cannot think about money? Emily, *ma chère*, you are either unique or in love!'

She laughed, blew him a kiss and disappeared. On a impulse, he stuck his head outside and stared after her, watching her hurrying, almost running, towards Tour Bellanda.

Emily, unaware of his scrutiny, made her way into the tower. Martin met her at the top, holding his hands out. In the sunlight, he was less unearthly and more physically present. The sunlight glinted on his black hair, and his eyes were as happy as his smile.

'Good morning, Emily my Emily.'

He had called her that last night, warming her, making her feel like a teenager. Did he know the effect of the phrase on her? Probably, she thought, and put her hands into his. 'Good morning, Martin.'

'Did you sleep? Yes, I can see you did. You look like life. It's a beautiful day. Come and look at the mosaics, and the bay, and the hills.'

He released her hands, drawing her arm through his. They strolled the tower, Martin in happy silence, Emily paying little attention to anything beyond her own sense of wellbeing. Eventually, having looked at the mosaics and the view without Emily's noticing anything at all, they made their way down into the street.

It was shady there, cooler, and a light breeze ruffled their hair. Martin stretched his neck to the west, sniffing at the air.

'I want some grapes,' he said unexpectedly. 'There's a

marvellous open-air fruit market on the Cours Saleya, and it should be open for another half-hour. Let's go get grapes, shall we? Or perhaps an apple?'

'Definitely.' If he had suggested swimming to Africa, Emily would have made the same reply. 'And some more coffee for me. And maybe an omelette, or some *tartine.*'

'Onward, onward.' He took her hand, laughing, and pulled her towards the Cours Saleya.

They wandered through the stalls for a blissful time, among the ripe fruits, the enormous soft garlic, the bunches of fresh lavender tied in red string. Martin bought a pound of grapes, green and sweet, and ate some; Emily selected an enormous apple and munched as they walked. She was happier than she had ever been in her life.

They found themselves in the winding alleys of Old Nice. Here the streets were twisted and curved, cluttered by women who did their shopping with string bags. Cats sat in doorways and washed themselves, and groups of children not yet old enough for school kicked a red ball and shouted at one another. There were shops, too, selling everything that could be bought: sausages hanging from hooks, great wheels of cheese, loaves of bread bigger than Emily had ever seen.

Martin stopped in front of a *confiserie*, so suddenly that Emily, at his heels, cannoned into him.

'Perfect,' he said. 'Wait.'

He disappeared inside. Emily, jostled by passing people, watched him dreamily through the glass. He peered, he pointed; the young girl behind the counter, obviously taken with him, flirted with verve and experience. When he emerged with a small bag in one hand, Emily was biting back laughter.

He glanced down at her, his eyebrows raised. 'Will you tell me what's funny?'

'You have an admirer.' She jerked her head toward the

confiserie, where the girl, her brief opportunity gone for nothing, was glaring sullenly back at her. My God, she thought, the child's jealous. Of me! To the best of her knowledge, no one had ever been jealous of her before, and the knowledge was amusing. 'The lady was fluttering her lashes, tossing her head, leaning forward to offer you the best possible view of her, um, endowments. And the gentleman was so very unresponsive! Sorry, Martin, I just couldn't help finding it funny.'

'Why not? It's a kind of theatre, after all.' He opened the bag and offered Emily a perfect chocolate robin's egg, white chocolate spattered with milk chocolate. 'Here. Be a small quick dinosaur, eat an egg. Laugh all you want, Emily my Emily. Life is comic theatre or tragic theatre, and comic theatre at least is funny. Why shouldn't you laugh?'

They turned right and found themselves between the walls of deep-windowed buildings, at the foot of a street that was one long staircase. Emily shot a look around. There was no one around them; they were completely alone on the curving stairs.

And she wanted to kiss him, she wanted to kiss him more than anything in the world.

Judy's letter came into her mind, and her own actions in Paris. Why shouldn't I, she wondered, why not? It's me, I'm me and I can do what I want. I'm a big girl. In fact, if Judy's right, I'm big enough to be menopausal . . .

Suppose someone comes along? Supposing some old lady, some Mme Delange, sees you doing that?

But this was France, damn it, where love was the cornerstone of civilization. Suppose someone does come along? What's so wrong with kissing? Am I embarrassed by the very thought?

'Shall I juggle for you? Toss chocolate eggs in the air?'

His voice pushed the thoughts back, but not her need. 'Or would you rather I kissed you?'

Shocked by the accuracy with which he had once again read her mind, she stared up at him. There was laughter in his face, a new kind of laughter; it had something both dark and bright moving through it. She felt her own face darken, swelling with blood, and wordlessly lifted her face to his.

The kiss was long, and perfect, and Emily ceased to care whether they were seen or not. Fifty Madame Delanges could have stood shrieking at her, and she would not have noticed, or cared. The press of mouth against mouth was water in the heat of the afternoon, cool water that somehow became flame in her blood. His breath was warm and sweet; it tasted of grapes, with the faint tang of chocolate behind it.

She knew a momentary resistance, abandoned it, and willingly allowed herself to be drawn into that flame. It was painless, after all. At some point her hands moved from her side, one coming to rest against his stomach, the other against the back of his neck. Both of his arms had somehow snaked themselves around her waist and lay, crossed and passive, at the small of her back.

Here's a poem you forgot. Some hold the world will end with fire, some with ice; from what I've tasted of desire, I hold with those who favour fire . . .

Emmy Deer's words penetrated the fog, and Emily drew back slowly. She became aware that he had straightened his back, and was tossing his head to ease the tension in his spine. His eyes, seen through the distorting red haze that misted her own, were somehow clearer and less guarded. His hands still lay against her, and her own had not moved. Passive yet assertive, defeated yet triumphant, she let him rest where they were.

'It's a good thing you're tall, my lovely one.' The curving smile was back. 'Otherwise I'd need a neck-brace.'

She laughed, throwing her head back with sheer joy in this moment of time, her face turned up towards the light. 'I'll rub your neck, Martin, never fear. I don't know who or what you are, but God, it's good to feel you here!'

These last words were wrenched from her. He stepped back, dropping his hands at last. 'I promised you I'd juggle for you, didn't I?'

'Actually, no. You offered, not promised. Why, do you want to?'

'Not in the least. To tell you the truth, I'd rather dance.' He bowed to her, the kind of bow she associated with the England of the nineteenth century; it was stately, and courtly, and completely irresistible. 'Will you come dance with me?'

'What, here? Now?'

'Tonight. I know a place to dance, the perfect place to dance, and I want to take you there.' He glanced down at his wrist. 'I have some things to do this afternoon, but I want to spend the evening dancing with you. Will you?'

'You bet I will.' The black dress, she thought rapidly, that little black thing I got at Chez Madeleine; those black wedgies with the gold strips, and my leather jacket, and the little antique beaded purse. Leave the hair alone, keep it simple, direct . . . 'What time?'

'Dinner first, I think, and we'll go from there. I'll be outside your building at eight. And now I must go.'

They ate a light dinner at an Italian restaurant near the port, and drove out of Nice in Martin's car.

He had led her to this vehicle directly after dinner. No lingering over coffee tonight; there was something new about Martin, anticipation blending with urgency, and

Emily followed his lead. Her own blood was behaving erratically, seeming to stop and start, pulsing out of rhythm.

The car was an Alfa Romeo, a small blue sports coupé with a faded cloth roof. The night was warm, and fine. Martin, after holding open the door for her and seeing her settled, elegantly folded his long body into the driver's seat and put the roof down, letting the wind in around them. It slipped through Emily's clothing like a ghost. Liking the feel of it, she shrugged off her jacket and let it fall away.

The dress beneath was black velvet, cut like a slip, the barest hug of fabric against hip and breast and belly; it was held up by two pencil-thin straps, both of which kept slipping off Emily's shoulders. For some reason, she found this disconcerting, and her quick pulls at the straps to put them back where they belonged were surreptitious.

Martin, driving with instinctive ease, put the car on the road that led toward Switzerland.

For the first half-hour, the ride was silent. They passed through a small town, built into the side of a towering cliff; Emily saw dark shapes along the road, realized they were geese, and smiled to herself. The night moved around them, stars wheeling across a sky built of fragments and stresses. Clouds that were thin damp breaths wove briefly together; these parted, seemingly without regret, moments later.

The road grew almost imperceptibly rougher as they left the traffic of the main road behind them, and the car climbed steadily. In the dim light from the dashboard, Martin's face was serene, and his mouth was creased into a Mona Lisa smile.

Emily, oddly languorous, slid her eyes to regard his profile. 'I thought we were going dancing.'

'You thought correctly. Dance we shall.'

She smoothed her lap, her fingers trailing the taut black velvet. She had never worn a dress this fitted; for all its formal design, it was equally suited to the Ritz Hotel or to a bedroom. Trust the French, she thought a trifle hysterically. But was it the influence of France, the all-pervasive reality called *l'amour*, that had led her to wear nothing beneath her velvet but a pair of silk briefs?

She became aware that her feet, unused to formal shoes, had fallen asleep. To cross one's legs would be nice, but would it be too obvious a gesture, provocative, construed perhaps as an invitation? No, that was stupid. After this afternoon, in fact, it was ridiculous. Why was she suddenly feeling so shy of him?

It suddenly occurred to her that she had spent whole portions of her adult life worrying about what people would think, think of her mind and her motives, about the trivialities of self. To cross or not to cross? No, leave them be. 'I'm glad we're going to dance, after all. Where, by the way? On Venus?'

The passionless, enigmatic smile turned into an open-mouthed expression of genuine amusement. Emily saw it from the corner of her eye, saw what it did to his face and, without thought, crossed her legs.

His voice was happy. 'In a way. Don't worry, Emily my Emily. The ballroom is entirely suitable, and I consider the band to be the best in the world. By the way, I applaud your taste. That's a dress made for a man's undoing.'

As if in acknowledgement of the compliment, one thin strap abruptly slid from her shoulder. Perhaps she was trembling. She jerked it up again, furtively. 'Martin, the road . . .'

'I see it.' He turned the wheel to the left, taking the car up the narrow fork that had sprung up before them. Where in hell are we going, she wondered dreamily, are we actually going to Switzerland to dance? Well, there was supposedly a casino up there, and Switzerland was not far away, just over those towering purple hills. She had her wallet in the little beaded bag, and passport was in it. If it was Switzerland he wanted, Switzerland let it be.

They had left all traces of urban France behind them. The only illumination came from above them, where the moon was a static silvered disc; on the distant hillsides, Emily saw faint lights. Windows? Windows indeed, so there were houses here, then, but so very far away. Farms, perhaps. Were there people in the houses, she wondered, moving around inside, hearing the distant hum of the motor, reaching for . . .

'We're here.'

Emily blinked, feeling the engine shudder and die. They were parked in a cul-de-sac. Across the narrow road there was nothing but seemingly impenetrable hedgerows, stretching into infinity; beside the car was a lich-gate, opening on to a large field. The road – did it even exist during the daylight hours? – curved knowingly over the hill and away, satisfied to continue on without them.

'I said, we're here. Wake up, my lovely one.'

Martin had gotten out and come around to her side of the car, moving with an odd, light step that was almost a dance in itself. Now he opened her door with a gesture of heartbreaking grace, waiting courteously as she gathered her wits and stepped, bemused and quiescent, on to the grass. His hand fell lightly, almost impersonally, on to her arm and lay there. The gesture was not possessive. Like the night itself, it merely awaited her pleasure.

She lifted her eyes to his face, feeling her skirts rub along her thighs. She heard the hush of the velvet, and the sound was somehow very much in place in this amazing night. 'This is your ballroom?'

'And welcome to it.' Martin swept grandly with his free hand. 'Would you care to dance, madame? Trip the light fantastic? Tread a stately measure or two? Or would you rather halloo my name to the reverberate hills?'

Emily looked beyond him to the weathered wooden gate, to the gently rolling pasturage beyond it, to the distant woods on the high ground that lay to the north-east, towards Switzerland. Laughter bubbled up inside her, astonishing her, lightening her mind and her spirit alike. She slid her hand into his and pulled him toward the gate.

He actually lifted her over it, disdaining the rusty latch. She felt the muscles of his arms against her legs, her bare back, and wondered that a man so slender could carry her as if she weighed no more than a sheaf of wheat. So sure was his step, so well did he seem to know this place, that Emily suddenly understood that he had been here before, perhaps to dance, perhaps for something else.

What were you expecting, fool, an innocent? The Holy Virgin Martin, pure and chaste until you summoned him from the world of light, or something? St Martin-in-the-Fields, maybe, the one that big church in London is named for? That's stupid, really, stupid. Now stop sulking and get real.

Another woman. Whom had he brought here before her? Had they circled together in the same grass? Had she worn black velvet, too, that other night dancer?

Her mood darkened, and although she had said nothing, Martin seemed to understand. He was still carrying her, and possibly she had tensed in his hold.

'I own this, in a way,' he said softly. 'You might say it's been mine for a long time, a very long time. So I've been here many times before, I know every blade of grass and every patch of softer ground. Shall I put you down now? Would you rather walk?'

'It doesn't matter.' He had read her mind again, just as

he had done on that peculiar night at Avignon, and on those empty stairs this morning. So he was a mind-reader, as well as magician. And she had, after all, spoken truly; everything had abruptly ceased to matter. The summer wind laughed against her shoulders, she was intensely aware of the rustle of her dress, and the moonlight was friendly.

She thought, briefly, of the poetry anthology, back at her apartment, of the tiny stone Pan, guardian and incubus. Why did she keep forgetting which poet had written about wasting sweetness on the summer air?

'Gray, Thomas. The *Elegy*. And it's desert air, not summer air, Emily darling.'

More mind-reading. Somehow, it had ceased to so much as surprise her. She became aware of her bare arm, draped across the vital pulse in Martin's neck, and felt an upsurge of something so potent, so alien, that her legs went buttery. Hiding it, pushing it away from her, she chuckled. My God, she thought, I hope he isn't reading my mind right now. My head had begun the dance without me. Is this what being drunk is like? Because, if it is, then I apologize to you, Kirstin Lindstrom Moon. If this is being drunk, let flow the red wine, let John Barleycorn rise again . . .

'What's funny?' They had come a long way into the field; the distant lights that were the eyes of scattered alpine cottages had shifted, looking straight at them. He set her down, his hands sliding down her bare arms and coming to rest lightly on her wrists, holding her, possessing her without threat. 'Share the joke with me.' He added, very softly indeed, 'Share everything with me.'

'Do you really need to ask? I thought you were clairvoyant. If you really want to know, my name is what's funny. My name, and your name, and this whole situation. St Martin-in-the-Fields, dancing with the Moon. Dancing *under* the moon, and me with bare shoulders. Have you got any moon-tan lotion? I'm going to get a moonburn.'

'Of course you are.' He looked intensely pleased, as if she had pronounced the answer to some unspoken riddle. The high strong cheekbones jutted into shadow as he smiled. 'That's one of the reasons I brought you here.'

'*One* of the reasons?' She sucked in breath, realizing how sweet the air tasted; asphodel, new grass, a white scattering of alyssum carpeting the distance. And what was that fainter scent? Lilac, lavender? 'Are there more reasons? Martin, I *like* it here.'

'How could you not? Listen.' He released her left wrist, and laid a finger across her lips. 'Listen closely. Do you hear the music?'

She obeyed him, quieting, opening her ears to the night. At first there was nothing, and then there was. It came at her from all sides, music so beautiful and so strong that she swallowed hard, her hands opening and closing convulsively, becoming a piece of the night herself in her fancy shoes and her black velvet.

'Birdsong,' he said softly. 'Nightjars and owls, sweetest Emily. Crickets. A sparrow or two, a frog. Moths on the wing – do you hear humming? That's the wind in the grass.' He lifted his head skyward, yearning, scenting the season. She thought that she had never been so physically aware of another human being; it was almost pain. 'The wind and it's singing your name. You made all these things, didn't you, out of wood? The birds, the moth, the flying things with the wind beneath them? They're all here, waiting for you. That was the other reason.'

Here it comes, lady. Here it is at last.

Emily began to weep. The tears held wonder, and joy,

and a kind of anger. It was the anger of the child within, discovering something lovely but too long withheld. *How long has this been going on?*

'Dance with me, Emily.' He stepped back from her and bowed, the black frock coat moving like a river across him before settling back into its tight fit across his shoulders. He sank to one knee, an arm held out before him, his legs casting impossibly long shadows in the freshly mown grass. 'A night made for movement, and such incredible music. Come and dance with me.'

Emily had not danced in twenty years, but she went without hesitation. There was magic thick on the ground in this place, perhaps left there by Martin's smile, and her feet would find it. He rose and she stepped into his arms, raising her chin and arching her back to accommodate the curve of his palm. One hand came to rest on his shoulder.

She looked up at him through a cool mist of tears, and saw his face happy and remote, as wild as the hills themselves. As the moon crested the horizon, they circled, slowly at first and then faster, whirling into something that was more a galliard than a waltz. The birdsong swelling into triumph, lacing the wind, enriching it. The grass beneath their feet was damp with the hour, and as they came to rest in a patch of nacreous moonlight, the moisture was a million pieces of shattered silver. For long moments they faced each other, the pose holding into for ever, turning the hour.

The singing had stopped. The crickets had grown quiet, waiting, watching them.

And Martin stood, his breathing not even disturbed by whatever it was that had taken hold of Emily and pulled the restraining mask away. Emmy Deer, that despised angry child, was talking now, needling and urgent, nagging at her.

Do it. You need to begin things. That's what has to happen. Don't play passive, don't wait. This is something new, out of your ken, and it needs a new Emily. Why do you always get scared, damn you? Why do you always have to deny yourself? Just do it.

He watched her, the Mona Lisa smile once again in place. Although she had said nothing, and he had said nothing, he nodded in total agreement. Collaborating with the little nagging bitch resident in her head. Mind-reader. They were as closely synced, as perfectly attuned, as they had been that morning.

Still she did nothing, grappling with herself. Change brings pain, she thought, what about pain? What about that? I don't want to get hurt. I'm tired of getting hurt.

This is no more than the last hold on your old version of self-protective sanity, and you know it. Pain goes away. Who cares about pain? Do it. Do it. Just do it.

Easy for you to say, she thought clearly.

Martin said nothing, but the smile twitched. He ran a long finger down her bare arm and cocked his head. Easy to say, but easier, always easier, to say nothing at all.

From what I've tasted of desire . . . do it!

She slipped the black velvet straps off her shoulders and shrugged free of them. Her hands moved behind her, and the long zipper slid down as easily and noiselessly as if it had been oiled. Trust the French, the bloody French, she thought madly. Martin watched her, making no move toward her and saying nothing of encouragement or disapproval.

Then the wicked, perfect, carefully chosen dress was a black patch against the grass. Out of it, triumphant and shameless as a Botticelli painting, rose Emily, new Emily, awake Emily, Emily alive at last. She stood, accustoming herself to the feel of the night against her bare skin, understanding that she was warm and that her shivering came from another place.

She lifted her arms above her and moved them, one time only. Her elbows were crooked, her hands fluttered limply; it was the motion of a bird taking wing.

Martin stepped forward and pulled her into his arms, down into the darkness of his grassy dance floor, where the heart of light lived.

In the distant heights away toward Switzerland, the cottage windows impassively watched the endless, inevitable coupling in the open field. The windows saw everything, and nothing.

The dew was silken against her back, and Martin was an all-encompassing blanket above her. He kept the cold out, he let the night in. She thought once, dizzily, Judy was right and I was wrong. I've never felt like this. Has anyone ever felt like this or does everyone feel like this? Is it only me who's been deprived, and have I been depriving myself? But she was drowning, madly going down over and over in a deep dark sea, and she gave no more of herself to that question.

Sometime shortly before the morning broke, watching the sky turn rosy gold over the pale flesh of Martin's shoulder, Emily heard a different, fresher song in the air. After a few moments of contemplation, she realized that this new marvel was the sound of her body laughing.

CHAPTER THIRTEEN

My soul is all but out of me, – let fall
No burning leaf; prithee, let no bird call.

(from 'God's World')

In the days that followed that all-night dance, Emily saw more of southern France than she had seen of England, Greece and Italy put together.

Almost all of Emily's time during that period was spent in Martin's company. They drove to Monaco and Aix and Villefranche-sur-Mer in the Alfa Romeo, with the top down; they crossed the border into Italy in Emily's car, which behaved erratically enough to ruin her afternoon. They ate slow, languid seafood dinners at Antibes and Miramar, and watched spectacular sunsets over the Mediterranean, standing on the beach with their arms linked.

They made love, too, at all hours. Martin slept the night away in Emily's bed and Emily, sleeping better than she had ever done before, curled against him like a kitten.

Martin took her shopping in the local markets, and one glorious day was spent on the water off Juan-les-Pins, on a small but elegant sloop which Martin, quite casually, told her was his own. Emily, who had thought herself reclusive to the edge of misanthropy, was bemused to find this constant presence in her life not merely pleasurable, but necessary.

Her body took on a whole new reality, sometimes

disconcerting but always enjoyable. Nerve endings she hadn't even known she possessed reacted like an unbroken horse to the lightest touch. She began to look better in what she wore, her clothing becoming items of intense interest and self-scrutiny.

Under the new passion for being alive that drove her, her physical appearance began a mysterious alchemy of its own. Heaviness and loose flesh became sculptor's dreams, her tendons and muscles toning themselves into lovely, powerful curves, while the few parts of her that had always been poor, too thin, suddenly filled out. Catching sight of herself in the long bathroom mirror one morning after a shower, Emily jumped at a subtly beautiful stranger, in perfect physical shape and shining with health, that looked back at her.

Possibly as a result of this new awareness and pleasure in her own body, she knew within herself a rising awareness of Martin's body, as well. She came to know it, understand it, with the obsessive attention and passion she had once given to the wood that fed her creativity. Fingertips that had once stroked the fine grain of white pine and rubbed in the soft dust of redwood moved down a finely muscled back, and traced the tiny lines that bracketed a curving mouth. She massaged him, turning her palms against the skin, using all the strength of her arms and revelling in the feel of her own shoulders complaining at this usage.

If Martin found this lust and attention obsessive, he said nothing of it. Rather, he encouraged her, pulling his shirt over his head with a slow, impossibly sensual motion whenever he read the look on her face that meant her hands wanted him.

Everything was strange, she thought, very strange indeed. This undirected thought, pointless and meaningless within itself, sat lazily in her mind as she lay beside him on a beautiful beach at Cannes. Out of nowhere, the balmy spring weather had turned unseasonably hot; although it was not yet May, by ten in the morning the thermometer registered temperatures in the mid-seventies, and by mid-afternoon the air felt almost tropical.

Emily had been raised in a hot climate, and had always found herself more energetic in the heat than at any other time. Cold, in fact, made her sleepy. But this warmth was enervating, fight for energy though she would, and after a week of it she found herself wanting to sleep in the sun.

So the ever-helpful Madeleine provided her with a gorgeous bathing suit, a one-piece sheath of glittering grey, and after one glorious day spent wandering through the antiquities of Frejus, followed by an exhausting drive home, Emily had announced to Martin her intention to recoup her vital force on the legendary beaches of Cannes.

She made her announcement while watching Martin rub a salmon steak with fresh garlic. He was not only a juggler and a magician and a mind-reader; he had astonished Emily by proving that he was also an excellent cook. Now he sprinkled the fish with fresh local herbs, placed it on a buttered pan beside a second steak similarly prepared, and slid the pan beneath the broiler of Emily's oven. 'A day of somnolence basking at La Croissette? Now, that's what I call a really lovely idea. You shall sleep in the sun like a lioness, Emily my Emily, and your skin will turn a golden coppery colour. Shall I come too? And will we have some salad with this fish?'

The following day found them stretched out on mats on La Croissette, Emily lying on her stomach and Martin on his back. Unlike the beaches at Nice, where the sharp irregular pebbles made walking barefoot an uncomfortable ordeal, Cannes boasted smooth pale sand. The sea was warmer here, too, friendlier, and easier to swim in.

'What's puzzling you, my Emily?'

Martin's voice roused her from her blissful lethargy. She opened her eyes, feeling them water in self-defence against the strength of the sun even behind her dark glasses, and swivelled her gaze sideways to regard him. He was not wearing a bathing suit; he wore loose white cotton pants and a plain black T-shirt, and like everything he wore, these suited him perfectly.

'Oh, I don't know. Everything's strange. My life is strange, the fact that I'm here is strange, the place itself is strange. I'm strange, that's for sure. And you're even stranger. World-class strange, in fact.'

His face, always impossible to read, remained an expression of courteous attention. Something, perhaps a flicker of resentment, pierced her lazy abstraction, and her voice took on a sharper edge. 'Know something, Martin? I've been sweeping along, just sort of being. When you're enjoying yourself, you don't think; you just *do*. Well, I've got a confession to make. I'm getting tired of strangeness.'

This powerful declaration finished incongruously, on a cavernous yawn. Goodness, but she felt sleepy. Was there some special quality in the Mediterranean sun that leached all the energy out of the human body, or was it something else? Did Martin, perhaps, possess some vampire quality, drinking energy instead of blood, feeding on her, emptying her of some essential thing?

He rolled over on one elbow, studying her. He was smiling, a faint smile this time, and his eyes were wide open; this potent sun, so bright that it made everything in Emily's range of vision seem slightly out of focus, seemed not to affect him at all.

'Strange, strange.' His voice was light, and very clear against the background hush of the sea. 'That's needless repetition, nothing more. Everybody's strange, sweet, everything and everybody, and I for one wouldn't have it any other way. Strangeness must be. Isn't that what makes life bearable?' The smile stayed in place, his head cocked slightly to one side. 'So you're getting tired of it? Well, I can hardly blame you for that. Poor darling, spending time in company with a mystery. But you haven't asked me any questions, you know. You've only hinted.'

Feeling herself to be at some obscure disadvantage, Emily shifted her body and faced him. She was suddenly and irrationally angry. 'Of course I've hinted. I wouldn't be human if I wasn't curious, and I'm definitely human, even if you're not. I mean, you appeared in my life like one of your own illusions, and I've allowed you to pretty much set up camp. And I don't know a single damned thing about you, except that you're damned good at—' Appalled at what she had been about to say, she bit off the words.

Of course Martin knew, he always did. He laughed out loud, a simple crack of pleasure. 'Thank you, dear lady, for what you were going to say and thought better of. Are you merely unwilling to feed my masculine ego, or are you still suffering silly qualms about the hair-trigger responses of the most astonishing body I've ever come across?'

Under its fine coating of sunscreen, Emily's face turned scarlet. 'OK, *touché*, no comment. But I refuse to allow you to change the subject on me. The fact remains that I don't know where you live, or what you do, or how you're able to spend all this time with me. I know that I trust you, that I need you, but I don't know why. I may love you, Martin, or maybe I'm just obsessed, but to tell you the brutal, honest truth, I'm not even sure I actually *like* you!'

This forthright speech, designed to drive the average male into a flurry of defensiveness, did no more than make him nod at her. 'Ah. The thinking woman steps into the spotlight at last. Well, I knew she was in there somewhere. If you're going to be, um, brutally honest, then why not do it? Stop hinting, and ask away.'

Emily felt a little surge of fury, strengthening her, giving her a jolt of much-needed courage. Was he saying, in effect, that her questions would not drive him from her side? Good. So be it; she would ask.

'You're damned right I'll ask. What about your family, and your friends, and the rest of your life? I mean, who *are* you, the Prince of Darkness or something? Last night, take last night. You cook this superb dinner, we make love, I fall asleep. I wake up and there's a full change of clothing that wasn't there the night before, all neatly folded on a kitchen chair. Where the hell did they come from, Martin? Did you wave your hands in the air, say a magic word and conjure the stuff out of thin air? And you have the nerve to tease me for being curious! Jesus, I don't deserve to be teased. If anything, I deserve an award for my discretion and – and forbearance!'

Martin waved at a passing waiter; this section of the beach was the property of the Grand Hotel, and came complete with a beachfront restaurant. The waiter took the order for two bottles of mineral water and hurried away. When he had gone, Martin reached a hand out to touch Emily's cheek. She thought briefly about slapping the hand away, but his face halted her. For once, the smile was gone, and he was completely serious.

'I wasn't teasing you, you know. I haven't told you anything about myself because you don't need to know or even want to, not yet. And trust me, Emily, you aren't ready to hear it. When the time comes, I will tell you. But if you want to ask me questions about yourself, I might be able to answer those.'

Now, there's an invitation you can't refuse. St Martin-in-the-Fields, he who knows all. But keep it simple, keep it direct. And for God's sake, don't think too much about it. Just ask, before he changes his mind.

The question jumped out at once, as if it had been sitting on the edge of her conscious mind. 'OK, magic man, I'm asking. Is my father still alive?'

'No.' He looked steadily at her, some sympathy in the dark eyes. She found the look disturbing, for sympathy was not something normally found in that detached, impersonal face. 'He died six years ago, of a massive stroke. That was in Cheyenne, Wyoming; he'd been working on the roads there. He collapsed and was dead before any of the road workers could even get to him. He felt no pain at all.' He added, very gently, 'I'm sorry.'

For a moment, Emily had no words. That Martin should know this was impossible, but the impossibility, for some reason, was no more than incidental beside the sudden grief she felt. So John Moon was dead, that silent and enigmatic poet-warrior-accountant? Daddy, she thought, Daddy, oh damn.

'You never knew him,' Martin said quietly. 'Or maybe you knew him much better than you thought you did. It's not just memories, you know. There's always more than memories.'

Bizarre as these words were, Emily didn't doubt for an instant that Martin had spoken the truth. She opened her mouth and closed it again, knowing that he would say nothing as to how he knew. But that it was no more than the simple truth was beyond question.

'Yes. Yes, there are always more than memories. After all, you can't trust memories, can you? Of anything in all the world, they're the easiest thing to change.' Her throat had gone very dry, and she greeted the waiter, returning with Martin's order of mineral water, with relief. 'OK, fine, I never knew him. Maybe no one did; he wasn't an easy man to know. But we went to Alamogordo, he and I, when I was young. We went to Three Rivers, to see the petroglyphs, and he told me something that has sat on my shoulder ever since. Was he telling the truth, my father? Did I really have a brother? Was there another child, a boy named Bear Dancer Moon, and did he really die before I was born?'

Martin was silent. He stayed silent so long that Emily forgot her water, forgot her surroundings, and simply kept breathlessly still, staring at him. He was frowning slightly, looking down at the hot dry sand, and the frown did strange things to his face; it gave him a look that was severe, unsettling, even more unearthly than the wild upward curve of his lips.

'I'm sorry,' he said finally. 'Sorry to be taking so long to answer, I mean. But that's a tricky question. How do you define being alive? Bear Dancer was alive in your father's mind, certainly. He was alive in your mother's womb, too. And he did die, not of Foetal Alcohol Syndrome, but because of your mother's drinking bouts. What was that you said, about memories being easy to change?'

The warmth of the sun was as it had been, that day at Three Rivers, and as she had felt the ghost of it, standing in the snow at Stonehenge. The dog barked faintly, children laughed in the distance, and the hum of the insects that she carved but that never landed on her skin or did her any harm gave the superheated air a tonal edge. Odd, how clear that picture was in her mind, and odder still that she could see her mother, after a short mild labour, her small pale face wearing the habitual, meaningless smile that was a parody of Martin's, being given the news that the child, born almost three months too soon, was dead in the womb itself . . .

She set the mineral water down, careful and slow. Her voice matched her gestures; it was deliberate, calm, very meticulous. She was amazed at her own bitterness. 'He was born dead, stillborn. That's what you mean, isn't it? He never really lived at all. My father made the rest in his mind. He named the child, gave it a personality, wove a fantasy around it. And then he used that fantasy as a stick to beat himself with, to beat my mother with . . .'

'Not a fantasy. You, of all people, should know that.' Martin spoke more sharply than was usual for him and Emily, her eyes glazed behind the sunglasses, tried to focus on a face which kept shifting in shape and texture. 'He was a Indian, a Cherokee. He knew things, things that came from his blood and his bone. He knew them, well, rather in the way I know them. He knew what the boy would have been, that's all.' Astonishingly, he sounded defensive. 'You can't call that fantasy.'

A girl walked past them, not three feet away. She was dark, exquisite, and she wore only the bottom half of a bikini. Her breasts were full and beautiful, turning male heads the length of the beach. Martin did not so much as glance her way. His eyes were on Emily's face, expressive but shuttered, trying to convey something to her.

And she knew, or believed she knew, what it was. John Moon had known things, had he? Well, Emily knew that much, she had always known it. Had he known the boy child as it developed, from an amorphous speck of protoplasm to a fully formed baby, with its father's dark skin and strong features? Had they spoken, the thick-set man whose ancestors had worshipped the power of dreams and the tiny creature with its mother-of-pearl nails and heavy-lidded, unopened eyes? Had they communicated in the language of those dreams, their genes, their shared racial memories? What magic of knowledge had passed between them, father and son?

She took off the dark glasses and set them down beside her. The picture, which should have been terrible, was both beautiful and moving. It had happened that way, yes, it had, the communication between spirit and spirit, before the accumulated poisons in Kirstin's system had been fed in all their deadly potency to the unborn child through the placental fluid, weakening it, killing it . . .

'You can't call that fantasy,' Martin repeated softly. 'Or can you?'

'I don't know.' Emily reached into her purse and pulled out a crumpled cigarette, lighting it with fingers that trembled slightly. The anger had seeped out of her, leaving only numbness in its wake. 'I don't know anything right now, except what you tell me.' She met his eyes straightly. 'But for what you have told me, thank you. I needed to know.'

'Of course you did. And for the moment, I think you know enough.' He stretched his neck and kissed her, a full lingering kiss. 'Now sleep in the sun, Emily my Emily, like the jungle cat you truly are. That's what you said you wanted to do.'

Emily, deeply unconscious with Martin beside her, had fallen into the shadowland of dream.

She was a child again, not yet ten, spawled out on the living-room floor. This was not Albuquerque, they had not yet gone there. This was the ramshackle little house in Flagstaff, a weathered A-frame with a hammock suspended from the ceiling. The rug was a leftover from the early fifties, a period when interior decoration was supposed to be sleek and futuristic and succeeded only in being graceless. It was shaggy, lime green and completely hideous.

The child Emily lay on the ugly rug, responding to the summer heat in baggy shorts and a sleeveless blouse. She did her homework, humming a little under her breath. In the kitchen behind her, someone moved around.

It was not Kirstin, not John Moon. They had gone out in a hurry, Kirstin staggering and giving a faint cry, John running out to the neighbours, asking to use their phone. He had returned with the old man next door; Emily had been told to stay here, to do her homework, to behave herself and not cause the neighbour, who had offered to stay with her while her parents went to the emergency room, any trouble.

He was not really old, barely fifty, but to a young child he had seemed ancient. Lost in the mists of sleep, Emily shifted her head uneasily on the pillow and tried to remember his face. His name, if she had ever known it, was beyond her recall. What came back to her sleeping awareness, thirty years later, were porcine eyes and a quivering mass of chins. He'd had a smile, too, a stretch of thin lips exposing teeth too even and regular to be anything but false . . .

His dream-shadow fell over her, over the ruled notebook paper that was covered with spelling questions. She had looked up to find him bending over her, the smile firmly in place. There was something wrong in the smile, a source of fear and disgust as potent as a bad smell, the smell of something that is a wrong thing from its source.

His face glistened and sweated. As she watched him, fascinated as a rabbit caught in a car's headlights, one hand reached down to the fly of his trousers, while the other reached for her, touching her as she had not been touched before, and then his hands and his mouth were all over her, sliding inside her loose clothing as he . . .

Wake up, Emily thought concretely, wake up wake up. This is a dream. But she slept on, her body still while her mind screamed. She felt again his abuse of her, abuse that had been verbal as well as sexual, the breathless, hoarse obscenities that had poured from those thin stretched lips and penetrated her as completely as his body had done. He had dirtied, soiled her to the edge of madness; he had drooled on her face, saliva running in beads down his shapeless chin.

The dream was merciless in its clarity. She saw herself curled up against the sofa, fumbling with her buttons, whimpering and destroyed. He stared at her, smiling, blank, waiting for her to speak.

She said nothing, staring at him in the silence of incomprehension and dread. As if enraged by her lack of words, he picked up the big brass ashtray from the coffee table and hurled it, so close that she felt the wind of its passing. It was an action designed not to harm, but to impress; it said, very clearly, that while he had not hurt her with it, he could have had he so chosen.

The ashtray struck the wall beyond her with a crash, echoing, falling, the noise of it blending with the sound of people's voices from outside, Kirstin and John stepping out of the car, Kirstin just back from the news that her kidneys and liver that had put up with so much alcoholic abuse over the years of her life had rebelled at last, as Emily herself jumped to her feet like a deer and fled for the safety of her own room, away from . . .

'Emily?'

She opened her eyes immediately, opened them into sound and sensation and a hand on her bare shoulder. So near was the dream, so fully alive in her eye, that she cried out and shrank away, flailing with a single uncoordinated gesture. Then she was awake, completely awake, and the echoing crash and confused voices of her dream were still there. The voice and touch that had woken her were Martin's.

'What . . .' She sat up, shivering and wrapping her arms around herself. God, she thought, God, God, that wasn't a dream. It was a memory. It happened and I forgot about it, blocked it out for thirty years . . .

She began to shudder, her breath coming harshly and painfully. She reached wildly for the bedside lamp, disoriented and frightened of the darkness. There had been too much darkness, too much denial, in her life. At this moment, she could stand no more of it. 'Martin? What?'

He was out of bed, pulling his clothes on. 'Your neighbour, the old woman across the hall. I think she's had an accident.'

Emily lifted a hand to her brow, and was surprised to discover it dry; her naked body felt filthy, clammy. 'Who? You mean old Delange?'

'There's something going on. People in the hallway.' He was quite right, something was happening. There were voices, a hushed whispering; there was a long whining noise, too, the voice of a hot wind mounting toward a storm outside. She got out of bed, her legs weak. The bedside clock showed not quite five. She reached for a cigarette and lit it. The familiar dark tang of it, the tiny plume of smoke, was comforting and steadied her. 'Go see, will you? I'll get something on.'

The voices that whispered in the hallway were clearer now, and Emily heard sounds of purposeful activity. She tied her bathrobe and followed Martin out into the hall.

It was full of people, tenants from the building, Martin, a few that Emily didn't recognize. Marie-France, herself in an old terrycloth robe, turned to meet her. '*Bonsoir*, Emily. I am sorry to have woken you, but . . .'

'Has something happened to Delange?'

'She is dead.' A man, swarthy and handsome, detached himself from the group around the door. He draped an arm around Marie-France's strong shoulders, and spoke sombrely, in English with a strong Italian accent. 'I have just spoken with the doctor. He thinks she had a stroke. The crash that woke Elyse, in the apartment below, was because Mme Delange fell out of her bed.'

Marie-France ran a hand through her hair, making it stand up in a disorderly crest. '*Bon dieu*, what comes next, I wonder? Emily, I think you have not yet met Emilio. Emily Moon-Bourne, Emilio, and this is my husband, Emily.'

'A pleasure.' He gave his wife a quick, reassuring hug. 'They have sent to the mortuary, for a stretcher and an ambulance; they will be here very shortly. Do not let this upset you, Marie-France. She was an old, old woman, after all, and it was her time for dying.'

Not a very pleasant old woman either, Emily thought, in fact a stunted, mean old bitch. She kept this thought to herself. While having no use at all for the usual conventions attendant on death, she understood that the others would be shocked by the sentiment. She looked around for Martin, but her attention was distracted by the opening of the downstairs door. A moment later, the tiny lift whirred into life.

Mme Delange left the building, in which she had spent so many years syping on her neighbours, on a stretcher. They had covered her face, but only partly, and Emily saw with horror that the old woman's eyes had collapsed into a wink; while the left eye was flaccid and shut, the right was open, fixed on eternity.

No more spying, then. There would be no more muttering, no more sharp wicked glances, no more turning the comings and goings of the rest of her limited, claustrophobic world into the stuff of her own life.

No more living vicariously, you mean. But why should you sneer at that? What in hell have you been doing, all these years?

Emily, shivering, nodded to the bystanders in the hall and went quickly back into her apartment.

At the kitchen stove, Martin was brewing coffee. There was something intensely comforting about the sight of him, engaged in this homely occupation. The rich smell of freshly ground beans lifted Emily's heart for a moment, long enough for her to manage a tremulous smile at Martin's lifted eyebrow, long enough to answer his unspoken concern.

Outside, in the streets, the wind whistled and moaned in a pitch that sounded uncomfortably like a human child. It seemed to be getting louder by the minute. Light flashed against the shutters, putting bright streaks against the opposite wall, uneven lines of brightness that were like natural shadow puppets run amok. In the distance, out toward Africa, thunder rumbled. On an impulse, Emily went to the balcony and threw the shutters wide. She was usually afraid of lightning; tonight, with its oddity and alarms and dead breathing phantoms, she yearned toward it.

'It's going to storm in a moment.' Martin came to stand beside her, pressing a cup of coffee into her hands, wrapping her fingers carefully around it. His voice was very soft. 'A beautiful wild storm. The clouds over the lighthouse at Villefranche will be changing colours, rose and blue, and there are white-caps out to sea. Birds will come and roost on your balcony rail, trying to stay dry and waiting out the rain. The paths through the hills will be covered in a deadfall of new leaves. It's strange, but it's natural, after all, death and pain and memory. All natural. Trip no further, pretty sweeting. Don't worry about the old woman, Emily. Journey's end in lovers' meeting, after all.'

She began to cry, silently at first, tears seeping out from the corners of her eyes and gathering in the corners of her mouth, salting her coffee. The tears became sobs, primal cries of an atavistic terror that replied to death, to the horrifying memory that had come so unfairly back to her, to the very softness of Martin's voice. She tried to stifle these sobs, unable to bear the sound of them in her own ears. Too much, too much; everything in the world was hovering about her head, and she understood none of it. The grief swelled, threatening to swamp her.

Martin put his coffee down, and removed Emily's cup from fingers that had begun to quiver. His arms went around her, strongly, tightly; the embrace seemed less meant as comfort than as support. He was as strange as everything else, stranger in fact, but she put her face against his shoulder and sobbed into it, sobbed for John Moon and old Delange and the despoiling of the lost and hungry child inside herself, until she was sick and empty and had no more tears to spare.

CHAPTER FOURTEEN

Immerse the dream.
Drench the kiss.
Dip the song in the stream.

(from 'Lethe')

Emily dreamed, as she had not dreamed since her earliest childhood, and every dream was a memory. Every morning on awakening, she wondered what was happening to her. The wonder was rhetorical, and sometimes ironic. After a bad night, it was tinged with something like despair.

Through adolescence and all down the barren years of marriage, Emily's dreams had been laboratory-standard fragments. Never complete, never in colour, they had been no more than bits and pieces of abstract symbols, with no substance left to examine when day broke. Since the night of old Delange's death, that had all changed. Pieces of her life long since left to gather dust in some unidentifiable emotional storage facility suddenly came to the surface, clamouring, merciless, demanding her attention.

Along with the dreams came a sudden upsurge in Emmy Deer's vituperative presence in her mind. Here, too, there was a measurable change; though the small voice spoke more often, it said less. What would once have been a full thought now came as a sharp barb, and every barb seemed meant to plant bitter thorns in Emily's heart. If she refused to examine a dream, if she shied away from the pain of understanding, Emmy Deer would force that dream into mental and emotional prominence. She painted it, enhancing its terrors and exaggerating its impact.

Awake or asleep, there was no escape from this hall of mirrors. A storm door had been opened in Emily's mind; Emmy Deer had her foot planted firmly in it, keeping Emily from slamming it shut. The pictures of her life came pouring through. It was amazing to Emily just how much of her life she had forgotten, salted away, refused to see because seeing hurt so badly.

Although these dreams were vivid and clear, they were not all bad. For every incidence of John Moon ignoring his daughter's existence, of Kirstin withholding some touch of feeling so desperately needed by her only child, there was a corresponding moment of sunlight in the young Emily's hair, or of her fingers shaping clay into a triumphant bird's wing. The dreams that encompassed these small pleasures, however, were fleeting at best, leaving Emily aching with a sense of loss, and of time passing unappreciated. The darker dreams, with their vivid pain, came slow and clear.

Sometimes she woke in the dead hours, opening her eyes into darkness with some incident stamped firmly against the night. She would lay in bed, still and quiescent, taking a weird species of comfort from Martin's light, even breathing beside her, forcing herself to look at whatever memory had flashed across the movie screen of her sleeping mind. They paraded before her, people long dead and houses that had never been homes, waltzing or strutting in an endless panoply, accompanied in every instance by the emotionally starving waif that was the child Emily.

Emily was unused to this exercise, and at first she found it almost too painful to bear. But she had no choice. It had taken no time at all to accept a harsh discovery; if she pushed the past away, the same dream would return until she dealt with it, playing and replaying the same badly made horror movie across her psyche. If the only other option meant watching that movie over and over again, it was better to see and examine the first time. And the study, with its miserable probing of old scars and newer wounds, brought at least one small blessing in its train; it kept Emmy Deer at bay.

If Martin was aware of this new thing in Emily's life, and she had no doubt that he was, he said nothing. His detachment held firm. At first, she accepted this lack of reaction as part of his essential mystery, merely another enigmatic facet of the magic man. Gradually, however, it began to irritate her.

Then say something, you little coward. What's the matter, are you scared that if you open your mouth and get on his case, he's going to disappear? Did Aunt Maud's daily column say something about never nagging your man, or something? God, you're a moral coward. It's disgusting.

'Shut up.'

'Why? I didn't say anything.'

Emily jerked her head around. They were sitting in the orchestra pit of the Theatre Acropolis, waiting for the curtain to rise on an English-language production of *Othello*. The piece, which had premiered in Marseille to rave reviews, was reported to be visually gorgeous, full of period costumes and authentic medieval music. The theatre was full, every seat was taken, but no one looked at her; if she had indeed spoken aloud, only Martin had heard.

'Sorry.' She realized, with a shock, that she had

never mentioned Emmy Deer to Martin. What words were possible in a crowded theatre? 'I was – talking to myself.'

'Oh, I see. Your interior voice. They can be damnably intrusive, can't they?' As the house lights dimmed, she saw the open-mouthed smile. 'Ah, here we go. Show time.'

At that moment, as Roderigo and Iago took the stage and the opening lines of the play filled the gallery, something in Emily snapped. It was a jagged break, almost audible in her own mind, and it was beyond repair. She turned her head away from the timeless smile, the profile that melted her into new shapes, and felt herself fill with this new and dangerous thing.

It began as a tiny astonished ball of light, and grew rapidly into something both dangerous and all-consuming. Martin's comment, that single flash of intuition, had filled her cup; now it overflowed, drowning her in a sense of frustration that threatened to become pure rage. As the exquisite language rolled into the hushed theatre, as Desdemona sank into the spider's web of jealousy and manipulation that would suffocate her at the end of the inevitable tragedy, Emily's rage swelled and grew.

> . . . I would I might entreat your honour
> to scan this thing no further; leave it to time . . .

It wasn't fair. She had suffered and grown, she had travelled half the world to find something in herself that, for nearly forty years, she had been afraid of facing. She looked into mirrors now, and saw a stranger there; she, who had always thought of herself as being in control of her life, had been forced by an incontinent husband and her own need to survive to the realization that she controlled nothing at all.

'Tis destiny unshunnable, like death . . .

And here was this man, this smiling charming mystery, and he knew more about her than she could ever hope to know about herself. What right had he, what damned right? How dared he come waltzing into her world and her arms and her spirit, knowing everything and telling nothing, making her feel like a fool, dependent upon the generosity of a few small scraps of knowledge, hoping he would toss them her way like a man feeding pigeons in the park?

It is the cause, it is the cause, my soul . . .

Shakespeare had it right, as usual. Christ, he had probably been another Martin, another damned archangel with an all-seeing eye and a bottomless well of knowledge to jerk less favoured mortals around with. Emily clenched her fingers into claws, forcing her hands together in her lap, revelling fiercely in her own nails rasping against her skin.

Let me not name it you, you chaste stars . . .

Through the beautiful words and the heat of her own anger, she was aware of Emmy Deer, trying to speak. So deep was Emily's feeling, so strong, that she was able to push that voice out of herself, gag it, force it into a temporary oblivion.

Put out the light, and then put out the light . . .

They hurt, the words and the bitter comprehension, and she writhed inwardly under the lash of self-realization that held only the loathing of honesty. She had put out her light, spent her days in darkness; half her life was gone, and she had wasted it. Now another light had come on and it was bright, too bright. It blinded her, casting unrecognizable shadows, keeping her from knowing what she needed to know, what she had remade herself in an effort to find.

Put out the light . . .

It was the end, the last straw. What had begun with a silly quiz in a woman's magazine would end tonight. All her life, she had run away; Emmy Deer had called her a coward, and Emily had stopped her ears against a truth too horrifying to hear.

But the ears were open now, and never could be closed again. The gears that had been grinding so slowly since an overturned barbecue on Independence Day clicked, tumbled, took on the shape of an entirely new machine. She had indulged herself in the feminist rhetoric so dear to her generation, she had let her voice ring clear and proud in her acknowledgement of the feminine principal. Lies, all lies. All the while, she had been hating her own womanhood. The realization made her burn with shame.

And Martin knew, damn him, damn him to hell. He knew things he had no way of knowing, and no right to know; things about her, about *her*.

> If I quench thee, thou flaming minister . . .

And he wouldn't tell her.

> I can again thy former light restore . . .
> And then put out the . . .

She would have it out with him. Two hours had passed in the flutter of an eyelash, the play was minutes from ending, and that ending would bring others in its wake. She had taken enough, and she was unwilling to take any more. What was her life, after all? All that pain and all that running, forcing herself into a brand of courage as unnatural as the stinger on her ugliest creation, and what had it brought her? Dreams that were unrealized realities, a voice in her head that never let her be, half-truths masquerading as self-awareness, cloaking themselves in ignorance.

No more. After tonight, there would be no more of it.

The curtain came down, the players linking hands, bowing again and again to the echoes of thunderous applause. Emily did not applaud.

Put out the light, and then . . . and then . . .

Breathing hard through her nostrils, she turned her head to the smile, the mystery, that would open their secret doors to her, like it or not.

The seat beside her was empty.

The house lights came up. All around her, the theatre patrons stood and moved. Some stretched their legs, some discussed the play; random conversations in French and English floated around Emily's head, stray words and opinions that meant nothing. She remained in her seat, her head twisted, her eyes fixed on emptiness.

There was no reality in all the universe but this one. Martin was gone.

Clumsily, she reached out and touched the seat beside her. It was as cold and smooth as if no one had sat there since the day the first curtain had gone up in the Theatre Acropolis.

'Madame?'

She straightened her neck with a painful jerk. It was not Martin; this was an usher, a middle-aged man, who looked at her with concern. *Je suis mal*, she thought wildly,

I am ill, ill, I am dizzy and broken and sick unto death . . .

She got to her feet. Without a word or a look, she stumbled past him, out of the theatre and into the warm spring night.

The walk home was an endless nightmare. She passed the port, the boats and the twinkling lights and the couples out for their evening stroll. The wild cats washed themselves and watched her passage as she turned the corner by the War Memorial. She saw nothing, heard nothing. Martin was gone, gone like her youth and the summer and her own understanding.

I know not where is that Promethean heat that can thy light relume . . .

Othello's words, in Emmy Deer's small voice, washed over her, stung, and ebbed away. There were tears on Emily's face, tears born of panic and terror, but she was unaware of them. She passed the glass front of a hotel, and avoided its reflective surface. No amount of looking in mirrors would help with this huge, throbbing sense of loss. Martin was gone, and Emily knew nothing beyond his going.

Maybe he's back at the apartment. Maybe . . .

There was no sympathy in Emmy Deer's comment, it was merely a statement of possibility, but Emily began to run. She hurried down the Rue des Ponchettes, feeling a cramp start up under one breast, pressing a hand hard against the outraged muscle and quickening her pace. She passed the street musicians and the late diners, enjoying the last warmth of the evening on the Cours Saleya. Two blocks to go, one block.

Emmy Deer was right. He might be back at the flat, waiting for her, waiting to tell her what she needed to know, why he had left her alone with herself in the dark theatre, why he had frightened her so . . .

Into the building, breathless, the pain in her side flaring. A whimper of pain, melting into frustration when she realized that the lift she hated to use was all the way at the top. Was that a good sign? Did it mean he had used it, was waiting for her?

She took the stairs two at a time, not caring about the noise of her feet sending pounding, intrusive echoes to the roof and beyond.

A struggle with her key, a quick unthinking glance at Delange's door before she remembered that the old witch would never peer at her again. The click of the latch. Inside at last, slamming the door behind her.

She knew immediately that he was not here. The apartment was in darkness, but even had every light been blazing, Emily would have felt the emptiness; the familiar rooms had a new feel, terrible and lonely, as if a warm fire that burned here had gone out, leaving cold ashes behind.

'Martin?' Fingers in which the nerve endings seemed to have atrophied groped for the wall switch beside the door. She clicked the lights, watching the room come softly into definition. The white pants, the black shirt, these had been strewn across the foot of the bed. They were gone now.

She said his name, not loudly, but with a terrible finality. 'Martin, oh please. This can't be happening, it isn't fair, oh please, please. Martin? *Martin!*'

Silence answered her, deep and final. Whatever had been here, whatever essential thing that Martin had put into the air of the place they had shared, it was here no longer. He had taken himself, his smile and enigma and all the answers to Emily's questions, and gone. The light was indeed out.

Emily pressed against the apartment door. Her eyes went from the bed, surely the emptiest bed that had ever been, to the chairs and the cooking implements and the bathroom. He had permeated every inch of this place, of her life, with a quality that was almost a scent. To have it go this way was brutal, humiliating, a rape in itself. Emily could not lay on that bed, sit on those chairs, touch those spoons and plates. They were no longer hers; they had become a mockery.

In a gesture that would have seemed comical to an unenlightened observer, she slid slowly to the floor. She sat there, mindless, unable to move, supporting her back against the base of the door.

The first grey light of sunrise found her still sitting there. In all that time she had not moved, or thought, or done anything at all. In the face of this obscene stripping away of her life, there was nothing to be done. Gradually, as the grey became gold and brightened into morning, she pulled herself to her feet, changed her clothes and went out into the street.

'Pardon, monsieur. Pouvez-vous m'aider?'

The harbour master at Juan-les-Pins was a retired sea captain. He looked the part, almost too perfectly, being big and brawny and lined; his faded blue eyes, embedded in their bluish networks of wrinkles, spoke of years pickling under a hot foreign sun. His hands were gnarled, his hair bleached white and sparse, his shoulders massively muscled.

My God, Emily thought distractedly, another damned Hollywood stereotype. As if Mme Delange hadn't been enough, they had hired a sailor right out of Central Casting. He was sitting with his feet propped up on the edge of his desk, avidly reading a magazine, but he closed it and rose to his feet as Emily poked her head through the door of the small shack. She thought briefly, distractedly, about how she must appear to him, her hair uncombed, the skin below her eyes puffy and bruised-looking. He spoke kindly.

'Good afternoon, madame.'

Despite her flawless French, he had picked her as an American with her first word. Two days ago, this might have irritated her. Today, it didn't matter. Nothing mattered. Between shock and exhaustion, Emily was having trouble breathing; using her native tongue could only lessen the rigours of the situation.

'I'm sorry to disturb you, but I was hoping you could help me. I'm trying to find a friend of mine, and I – I believe he docks his sloop here. We went sailing here, about ten days ago.'

'Ah.' Hollywood-perfect sailor type or no, the harbour master was still French. The monosyllable expressed perfect comprehension laced with a vague sexual overtone, and it brought a faint warm colour to Emily's cheek. Observing this, he smiled suddenly, and with the smile his entire face changed; the lifted eyebrow, speaking so eloquently of innuendo, became a sympathetic twinkle.

'His name is Martin, Martin Ferrier.' Emily rushed through this explanation, not caring, wanting only to know. 'He's an Englishman, very tall and slender, dark hair. He said the boat was his. Do you know him?'

The blank look, the unmistakable puzzlement and lack of recognition as he mouthed Martin's name, told their own story. There were tears waiting, pressing against her eyes with a terrible insistence. She pushed them back, as she had been pushing them back since the realization that he was indeed gone had sunk completely in. The old sailor shook his head at her.

'I do not know this name, madame, nor anyone like who you describe. Do you know perhaps the name of the sloop? If you tell me, I can see if . . .'

'I don't know the name of the boat. I never even thought to look.' There was no use in scanning the harbour, either; she wouldn't recognize the damned thing if it jumped the pier and fell on her. Only a lover of boats can tell one small white craft from another. She hadn't noticed the boat, or the name of the boat, or even the waves, white and cobalt, that had broken over the prow. She had only seen Martin.

Oh, God, she thought wearily, I can't take this. I can't. She was Desdemona again, Desdemona in sneakers and jeans, shorn of her naïvety and her fancy dress, exhausted beyond measure. Too old to be Juliet, too cynical to be Cordelia; there was only the Moor's tragic wife left to play. Commend me to my lord, Emily thought bleakly; wasn't there something, too, about plucking a rose, and watching it wither? 'Thanks anyway. I'm sorry I bothered you.'

'*De rien*, madame.'

Another failure, another option checked and cancelled. He was not at the Tour Bellanda, on the Cours Saleya, at the café table under the sedate front of Sainte Reparate, he was not on the stairs where they had first kissed. She had driven to Frejus, and found no hint of him there; she had walked the beach at Villefranche-sur-Mer, and found sand and sea and happy couples whose very existence prompted, for a bleak moment, a surge of hatred and resentment.

Once before, through a long night in Avignon, she had hunted him. She would not return to Avignon, for he would not be there, not now. That first hunt had been an act of instinct. This new situation, however, she handled with an iron logic that seemed completely inexpressive of her obsessive panic.

She prowled the streets of Nice, checked the underground garages, and here found a new horror to flavour her grief; every second car seemed to be a blue Alfa Romeo with a faded cloth top, and none of them was the one she wanted.

In a moment of desperation, she had even called around to various hotels in Cannes, mentioning the names of the famous director and his attendant cast from the Hotel Crillon, remembering what she could of the movie to be filmed. No one had heard of Martin Ferrier; no one knew what she was talking about.

Emily stood beside her car, willing her tired body into motion. There were dark clouds on the horizon, and a choppy ragged edge to the horizon itself. Later it would rain, storming as it had stormed once before. That time he had held her, saying nothing, offering the support of his presence, keeping her warm. She had wept into his shoulder, tears that cleansed as they scalded.

Emily gritted her teeth. She was not going to cry, not here, not now, not at all. This much pride, at least, she would cling to. She would not weep for him, and nothing and no one could make her. Perhaps the place in the spirit where tears were made was damaged beyond repair. Perhaps she would never cry again.

She got behind the wheel of the Citroën and headed towards Nice. There were restaurants along the sea road, places where they had stopped to eat. She could look in those; it was a slim chance, but better than nothing.

The roar of a car horn blaring into her ear nearly sent the Citroën into the next lane. She cried out, slowing down and glancing through the passenger window at the Lancia that she nearly grazed. The driver gave her a furious look and a universally recognizable gesture. She glanced away as the Lancia shot by, ostentatiously gathering speed as it went, the driver and his vehicle scorning her.

Another complication, a small worthless reality, intruding at a time when she had no attention to spare. She was going to have to have the stupid car fixed. What in hell was wrong with the damned thing? Her driving was not at fault; the car had drifted, the front tyres bearing sharply to the right. She glanced at her hands on the wheel and saw that the car was pointed straight as an arrow. Tomorrow, or the day after that, she would have to find a garage and have the problem corrected. Not today. There was no time to deal with it, not now.

She stopped at three different restaurants, places where she and Martin had sat outdoors, he drinking wine while she sipped coffee, the two of them sharing a vast plate of prawns, taking turns dipping the shellfish into a hot spicy sauce that caught at the back of her throat. Nothing. No sign of him. Again the tears rose behind her eyes, and again she forced them away, denying the cheap, easy relief they offered. She drove back to Nice, put the car away and went slowly upstairs to the apartment that, since a moment of self-realization and a gorgeous performance of *Othello*, had become a hell to her. She saw a ghost of herself reflected on the glass doors of the balcony, and quickly turned her eyes away.

Mirror, mirror on the wall. Poorest Emily.

Emmy Deer, Emily thought savagely, I hate you. She knew, perfectly well, that in forty-eight hours, more than Martin himself had gone from her life. He had taken with him not only her peace of mind but also that new Emily, the beautiful stranger, the dancer of the mysterious moonlit ballroom, north and away toward Switzerland.

He was not Othello, he was Pygmalion. He had breathed life into her and then blown out that spark. Her hair had gone lank, her skin stretched and puffy, and all the glow had gone out of her. Madeleine's wonderful clothes, which had looked so well on her, now hung awkward and unbecoming. She dreaded catching her own eye in a reflective surface, knowing that she had never looked plainer, stranger, more lost.

'Emily? Are you there?'

The voice was Marie-France's. How long had she been knocking on the apartment door, while her crazed, bereft tenant sat there hating herself? Emily got to her feet and dragged open the door.

'Some mail for you. Letters, I think. One of them I found on your doorstep.'

Emily put a hand out for the papers, seeing them through a red mist. Some instinct that had not flickered in her since a languid wave from the balcony of the Hotel Crillon had begun to work once more. Hope and glowing, the merest ember, waiting for an excuse to spontaneously combust. She smiled at Marie-France, closed the door behind her, and sat down. Slowly, carefully, she went through her mail.

A thick manila envelope with an English postmark; news from Judy, no doubt. Some reviews of the Galerie Solferino show, clipped to a brief friendly note from Alain Verchereux. An American Express statement, a bank statement. At the very bottom, a plain white envelope that had never seen a stamp. It had her name on it, only her name. She knew the writing.

The ears were very far down now. Emily slit the envelope open and shook the contents out on the table.

It was a card, a single piece of rough, cream-coloured paper. Someone had drawn on it, charming pictures, lively and entrancing. There were mountains, blue and distant; there was a road that wound off into infinity, north and away towards Switzerland. The moon sat on the peaks, pale and yellow and somehow watery. A pair of tiny figures, their fingertips touching, danced on the hillside.

Words ran across the bottom of the page, words in the hand she knew so well. Four words only, an endearment never before offered, not by Martin, not by Emmy Deer, not by John Moon in his one and only moment of showing his love.

'Your choice, Emily darling.'

CHAPTER FIFTEEN

Childhood is the kingdom where nobody dies.
Nobody that matters, that is.

(from 'Childhood is the Kingdom Where Nobody Dies')

The sky, vast and angry in the scarlet fancy dress that betokens a coming storm, was shuddering into darkness as Emily turned the Citroën into the first foothills of the French Alps.

Find the field find the field find it . . .

The day had been warm, as warm as all the days had been since her meeting with Martin Ferrier. Tonight, however, all the warmth seemed to have been leached out of the world, and the last pitiful remnant of heat was held in the urgency of Emmy Deer's voice, echoing madly, insisting, again and again.

The twilight had been thick as ether, dense and damp, and even in the stifling enclosure of the parking garage Emily had seemed to feel rain threatening against her cheeks. Once outdoors, her skin felt clammy and chilled, the humidity almost solid in its strength. Through its rolled-up windows, the Citroën was invaded by the darkness of night; even the chaos of her thoughts, the firmness of her resolve, could not entirely mute the hysterical high-pitched whine of rising wind.

Find it find it find . . .

Her actions, from the moment of taking the card from

Marie-France's hand, had been a weird mixture of atavism and rationality. Left brain and right brain had temporarily merged, in a bizarre marriage in which balance was entirely missing. Logic had governed her physical preparations. It had sent her out to the nearest gas station to put air in the tyres and fill the tank; logic, too, had forced her mind to pinpoint on what few solid facts her memories held of that first and only drive to Martin's mysterious place.

At this point, logic deserted her in favour of atavism. She knew, had known immediately and beyond rational argument, that the small square of paper held the answers she needed. It was a talisman, her talisman and his, as much so as a sketch of the magic man on a long-destroyed paper napkin.

It was perfect and proper that this should be so. All their dealings together but one had been on the single plane: her space, her time and his terms. That once, that one night only, he had invited her into what her oddly working mind now understood to be the heart of his mystery. Searching for him in the realm of the real was useless, she knew that now. If Martin was to be found, Martin whom she had somehow appointed the guardian of her life, he would be found in his own place, a soft field of fresh-cut grass and asphodel, peppered with sweet alyssum, waiting under the moonlight for her arrival.

Logic, too, held back when it came to her clothing. She dressed as she had done that one night before, in the black velvet dress which still showed a faint streaky stain where it had fallen in the wet grass. She was bare beneath it except for the silk briefs, covered above only by her leather jacket thrown over it all. Though the weather was very different, she had changed nothing. Something of another time, a hot vital day at Three Rivers, had ridden her shoulders like a beloved ghost: the stones, ancient carved petroglyphs never changing, a field of talismans that belonged to her and her alone.

Go, find, no waiting none, no, go find . . .

She didn't know where she was going. That stood at the core of her sense of chaos; she had only the vaguest idea of the physical realities, the mechanical necessities, of locating that starlit place where she and Martin had first danced, first communicated, first loved. She had paid little heed to the drive itself, that magical night in the hills; it was the same situation as the sloop replayed all over again. She had seen nothing but Martin, his hands on the wheel, his long profile in the dim lights from the dashboard, his open-mouthed smile with its Mona Lisa inscrutability.

A half-hour spent alternating between Martin's hand-drawn little card and intensively studying her road maps had been unrevealing, and after a while she had put the maps away and stopped using reason entirely. Reason, the kind that makes lists and discusses pros and cons, would not serve her here, and she had an uneasy feeling that Emmy Deer, behind the driving repetitive words of command, was sneering at her. All Emily could rely on was a general sense of direction and her own instincts. And her instincts, those familiar and always trustworthy companions, had most unfairly become strangers, fading in, fading out, unreliable.

Find find go hurry find . . .

Emily reached the western turn-off for Marseille and hesitated, impatient and despairing, trying to still the urgency. All right, she thought concretely, enough. Stop this, get a grip. She clenched her fists on the steering wheel, forcing herself to calmness.

It wasn't west, it couldn't be west. Martin's ballroom had been off toward the Swiss border, and the Swiss border lay to the north-east. She peered at the green road signs, finding one announcing a split on to a road called the A202. The urgency flared and receded. The A202. That was familiar, surely?

Unexpectedly the sign faded, taking the Citroën and the moment itself with it. She had a brief moment of dizziness, a sudden wrench of past and present mixing, ghosts and shadows invading the car and taking on flesh. It was clear, and accurate, as clear and as accurate as those memories that had become dreams, taking over her life these past weeks.

That night, that magical night, laid itself across the present like a colour transparency. She felt the cool leather of the Alfa's upholstery against her thighs, more real than the angry sky outside. Once again, she watched Martin covertly from the corner of her vision, glanced hastily away lest he should discover how she watched him, turned her flushed face toward the world slipping past. And there it was, after all; a green road sign, framed for a moment by her own confusion and childish embarrassment. A202, Geneva, Grenoble. That was it.

The past receded, losing definition as it faded. Emily shook off a moment of nauseating vertigo, and a weakness that sapped all her strength. With a soft exhalation of breath, she swung the car to her right, following the road she had travelled once before.

The sense of need was urgent, huge, a rhythmic downbeat like a pulse; this was a kind of hunger, demanding to be fed. The little card, with its rudimentary map and dancing happy figures, sat in her lap, and it seemed to radiate her own violent sense of wanting up at her. She drove well, steadily, the part of her conscious mind that had been rationally trained to handle a vehicle never allowing itself to be distracted from the road which narrowed and, after a while, began a steady climb upward.

The sky was almost completely dark now. The Citroën,

with its full tank of gas and newly inflated tyres, was behaving well; it hugged the road, neither drifting nor slipping. A few drops of rain splattered against the windshield and Emily turned the wipers on. Off to her right and far below, she heard the distant sound of running water, where a railway line ran along the edge of a small river. As the rain smeared the dust on the glass, the vague night-darkened shapes along the roadside took on clarity and she saw that she had reached a town: St Martin-du-Var.

St Martin, St Martin. She felt the past again, felt it climb into the car with her, and immediately pulled the car off the road. Through the inner violence that shaped her present moment in time, the images came sharply. She would not court the obvious danger of driving when the road before her was not the road her body travelled on. That much reason, at least, she still possessed.

The Citroën became a familiar café, the Bistro Marcel with its tiny tables and soft lights, where she had first confronted him.

Under the shadow of the child saint Reparata. His voice, filling the Citroën and her head, drowned out even Emmy Deer. *I am neither Catholic nor hagiologist; I just like to study the competition.*

And then his hand resting so lightly and impersonally on hers, the smile that captured and enslaved and somehow reflected. So much gained and lost, such sweetness wasted on the summer – no, the *desert* – air.

Go come back go find seek seek find find find . . .

The transition between vivid past and cloudy present was becoming easier. This time Emily barely felt the change, the small shock that, all through this inexplicable day, had brought nausea and dizziness in its train. Even Emmy Deer's intrusion brought no physical wrench with it. Emily blinked the past back to dormancy, and glanced out the window at the hill town of St Martin-du-Var. During the daylight hours, it was probably picturesque. She saw a few small houses, their lighted windows faint squares, shuttered against the coming storm. In a garden on the hillside above her, a goat grazed uneasily, its ears pricking at nature, with all its threats and surprises. All this was real, and of the moment. It was time to move on.

The car's interior was cold now, the feeling of damp growing more pervasive by the moment. Emily shuddered, zipping her leather jacket and turning on the heater, touching the card in her lap with the tip of a chilled finger for comfort and reassurance. Then, cautiously, she pulled back on to the road north.

It began to rain in earnest, a steady hum of water that sheeted across the windshield. Yet there was no violence in the rain, and little danger; it was not a storm after all, but merely a steady downpour. The keening sound had died and this rain was devoid of wind, and unaccompanied by unpleasant side effects.

Emily kept her eyes on the road, looking for the fork to the left that she herself had pointed out to him that night. She was grateful for the lack of traffic on the road. Once or twice cars passed her heading south, but she seemed to be the only person going north tonight. And the road itself, while wet and occasionally edged by sheer drops into the valleys below, was in the same excellent condition she had noticed on her drive from Paris.

Emily?

The car swerved, her hands reacting in surprise to this new thing in her head. Emmy Deer, she thought, is that you? The singsong was somehow different, holding an unfamiliar note. Was that actually tenderness, warmth, she was hearing?

I'm hungry, Emily. I'm hungry, I'm starving. Can't you

bring yourself to acknowledge me? Can't you stop hating me, resenting me, at least long enough to give me what I need?

'I've always acknowledged you. How could I not? You're me, aren't you?'

She spoke aloud, hearing the words fall flat and cold. She meant them, and yet she knew they were untrue. It was only since Rome, since dinner with Dolores Aguilar in a small trattoria, that she had come to admit that Emmy Deer was anything other than a kink in her own mind, a flaw of sanity, a failing. Thirty-eight years, Emily thought, all of them dysfunctional, all of them spent pressing both hands against her ears, trying to stop that little voice with its unpalatable truths.

It wasn't my voice you were trying to suppress, Emily. It was my existence. Once, just once in your life, stop trying to con yourself that hiding means safety, because the fact is that it doesn't mean anything of the sort. Thirty-eight years, Emily, half a damned lifetime spent cowering away from yourself, because that's what I am. I'm your memories. I'm a mirror into your own past, your own soul. And you didn't like mirrors, did you? You've never liked mirrors. Particularly not when you looked into them and saw a hungry little brat who never grew up, who's been dying of malnutrition from lack of acknowledgement and the withholding of love . . .

'Stop it! Damn you, shut up! Can't you see, this isn't the time or the place? I can't deal with it now, I can't!'

Emmy Deer spoke softly and implacably.

This is the place, Emily. This is the time. It's now or never, in fact. You've guessed all along what Martin was for, haven't you? Somewhere in the pit of your stomach, where me and all the rest of those trapped starving things live, you knew what you needed. A hand that would turn your face to the glass, a smile you couldn't escape from, that would hold you in place and make you look, make you see. You conjured him up. You made him, pulled him out of the air, out of yourself, out of your dreams and needs and memories. The Magic Man, what a joke. It ought to be the Magic Woman. You performed as neat a piece of witchcraft as anything dreamed of by Cotton Mather. Two hundred years ago, they would have burned you at the stake for it.

'It isn't true,' Emily whispered. 'You're saying, dear God in heaven you're me so *I'm* saying, that Martin isn't real. You're saying I *made* him. Which is impossible, which is lunacy. So you're crazy, which means I'm crazy. Because how could that be true?'

Remember the face on the napkin? Kirstin's reaction? You drew what you needed, and what you needed was a beautiful supernatural man, a demigod, someone who could love you enough to force you into looking your own life in the eye. And what a demigod! All beauty, all sensuality, and absolutely no judging you. You're an artist, after all, and you're a woman, even though you've been secretly hating that fact damned near for ever. No wonder Kirstin called you a whore. She was wrong, actually, but at least she was honest. Your mother knew, Emily. She knew, even if you didn't.

'Oh God, God.' Not only Kirstin, either, it wasn't only her mother who had known. The olive-skinned actor who had shared the street stage at Herculaneum with Martin, he had known too. And it was the very fact of his knowing, not what he had known, that had brought the red shame burning into Emily's face.

And then put out the light. There was something in the clear voice that had never been there before. It was tolerant, sorry, and yet almost amused; this was how a parent might speak to a well-loved and intelligent child who had wilfully done something stupid. *Waste your sweetness, quench your flaming minister, and don't forget that damned light when you're all done denying yourself, and me, right out of existence. Thirty-eight years in an emotional vacuum, Emily. Do you want thirty-eight more? Because that's exactly what's going to happen if you turn your back on yourself now, if you turn your back on me.*

The words, with no malice but the malice of truth, hit like fists. They brought pictures with them, pictures she had always seen but had never been willing to interpret: a torn shirt and torn body, an ashtray hitting the wall beside her head, a terrified silence preserved in terror. A wild rocky gorge full of carved stones, Dodie's swollen stomach and bruised-looking face as one marriage ended and another began. Her defeated mother staring from the eyes of a Greek peasant woman. They were clear now, the tap open and running. No matter what happened from here, she could never shut them away again.

Martin, who knew it all. He knew her past, her present; he knew things about herself, solid facts like John Moon's death and his wish-tainted twisting of her brother's life and death. She had not questioned how he knew, and she had not questioned him. Emmy Deer had spoken only the truth, and that meant one thing and one thing only. The only way he could have known these things was through Emily herself. She had created him, invoked him, just as her invisible twin had said.

A face on a napkin. She was a teenager again, a girl touched by only two masculine influences in her life. One of them, bestial and brutal, had tried to destroy her; the other, the father she loved so much, had been genetically and emotionally incapable of sharing or showing his feelings for her. And so she had drawn a face, a face that was the physical antithesis of the man she hated, a face that held all the mystery of the father she adored.

Kirstin had known, of course she had known. Through the dense alcoholic haze in which she wrapped her life, she had seen her daughter drawing a picture, she had taken that picture up, and she had seen Emily's need and John Moon too in the cheekbones, the smile, the wild untouched freedom that was like the starlight on Martin's field. It was no physical resemblance that had led her to label her daughter a whore, but the guilt and recognition of desire, of witchery, of unrecognized need that she and her husband had been forever unable to fill.

The midlife crisis, that's what Judy had called it. She said, what, that you were on the young side for it but that things had happened, shocks, and they had opened you up to the big changes, made you vulnerable. Ask yourself the questions now, and cushion the shocks that come later. She said that to you. Remember?

'I remember.' Emily spoke softly, quietly, and then paused; she was almost expecting a spoken answer. 'Haven't I been asking myself, forcing myself to look?'

Some questions, yes. It's true, you have. It's like I said before, like you said before, using me as your voice and your conscience: Martin was created to force you, a kind of passive-aggressive demon love cum spur. But there's one question that you haven't asked, that nobody thought to ask you. So ask yourself now, Emily. You've carved a thousand flying things, things that flutter and hover, things that sting as badly as I do. Yet I'm the only thing that ever stung you. All your life, you've been immune. Mosquitoes landed on you and took off again without a touch; remember when you fell asleep in the park and you woke up and there was a hornet crawling on your face? How you brushed it off lightly, how it flew away, how you weren't even afraid?

'But that was in another country . . .'

And, besides, the wench is dead? Well, yes and no. That's my point, your point. You've never been afraid of stinging things. So why were you so terrified of the wasps, at Heathrow, outside your London window? Why did you choose to exorcise Gary by imprisoning him in a wasp's shell? Why?

'I don't know.' She was numb now, beyond sense and feeling. Her driving was purely mechanical, and she had forgotten to watch the road for the forking bumpy twist that led to Martin. St Martin-in-the-Fields, she thought dully, thirty-eight years. God, dear God, what had happened to her? What had she been, and what had she done to herself?

From what I've tasted of desire I hold with those who favour fire fire fire fire . . . look out!

For a confused moment, Emily thought the wind had risen again. The car was full of a high steady hum, a hum that was not coming from beneath the hood. A second went by, an eternity, before she realized that this new sound was not the wind. It was loud, angry, all compact of menace. And it came from beside her, from the air itself, mere inches off her right ear.

Look out look out look . . .

Slowly, keeping her head still, she swivelled her eyes to the right. The hum grew louder as her vision expanded to include what hung in the air and a familiar curve of hill just ahead, with a fork in the road.

A small tubular body, striped black and yellow. Wings that were aerodynamically as perfect as a hummingbird's. A stinger that projected out from the creature, a stinger too long to be normal.

Outside, across the white line, lay a blackness which could cover solid mountain or bottomless void. To the right, a bare minute in the future, lay the twist in the highway that led to Martin's field.

She began to whimper. The tiny high-pitched breaths that were forcing themselves from her throat were familiar, they were known to her as everything was now known to her. She had whimpered like this during that long-ago rape; she had whimpered like this the night old Delange had gone so gracelessly to her own future, when the night had taken on the life of storm and Martin had held her against his shoulder, breathing into her hair.

She eased the pressure of her foot on the gas pedal, and knew a blind moment of gratitude when the car slowed. The universe had become sound, that single infuriated droning in her right ear. She was dimly aware that she had never been so frightened, had not even realized that this kind of fear existed. Martin, she thought, Martin, Mother, Daddy, please please.

Queens have died young and fair . . .

'No.' It was a tiny whisper, but the chitinous tube reacted to it, darting at her face, backing off again, taking up its stationary position of threat. The car was barely moving now, and she was almost level with the turn she had tried so hard to find. If she could make that turn, bring herself intact to that lich-gate over which Martin had lifted her, she would be safe.

It will not last the night . . .

She had made her choice, faced it; she understood what she was now, and what she wanted. All she had to do was to escape this stinging chimera, this ghost, that had somehow worked its way free from the mists of her past denials and mistakes, and manifested itself in a closed car.

Wasting its sweetness, wasting, wasting . . .

Something dropped from her face and fell on the lap of the black velvet dress; sweat, a small puddle of it. Slowly, carefully, she shifted her hands on the wheel. Her foot dropped back to the accelerator, giving the car the necessary gas to get it up the hill.

And then put out the . . .

The wasp drew back and up. Its body arched, the

dangerous lower half thrusting forward. In a motion too fast for the human eye to follow, it dropped.

The stinger went in just below her right ear, sinking into the soft fleshy part of the neck where nerves are clustered and vital arteries carry blood and signals of life to the brain. The world became pain, blood and fire exploding in her body. Both hands came off the wheel, flailing uselessly, trying to kill the agony in her neck that was spreading to her face, swelling her eyes shut, killing her in its turn. Her feet, separated from the rest of her body, their muscles no longer commanded by her brain, remained where they were, one on the floor and the other immovably on the gas pedal.

The Citroën, its faulty steering moving it to the right, ran off the fork in the road. At nearly seventy miles an hour, it hit the curve, turned over on its hood and slid.

It slid across the road, across the white line, into the blackness on the western edge that was, after all, not a mountain but a deep, deep valley. For a moment, suspended in time and space, it hung there, caught on the guard rail. Then it toppled slowly, falling end over end, moving with a horrifying slowness that was like a dance.

There were boulders all the way down, sharp wicked protrusions like shark's teeth, snatching at anything that passed. At the bottom were more rocks, and railroad tracks, and a spur of the river. The Citroën, a smashed and flattened heap of overheated metal, landed on its wheels. By that time, of course, there was very little left of the car and it no longer mattered.

On the distant hills above Martin's ballroom, the windows of the farmhouses off toward Switzerland twinkled, uncaring, through the long wet night.

Epilogue

In some moist and Heavenly place
We will set it out to grow.

(from 'The Blue-Flag in the Bog')

Light, a pale diffused brilliance that was the colour of a fresh and beautiful morning after a bad night.

Emily opened her eyes slowly into that brightness, and found them fixed on several things at once.

There were clouds, the streaky cirrus kind that looked as though they had been laid across the blue backdrop of the sky with the feathered edges of a painter's brush. There was the road, hundreds of feet above, a thin crest of land that bristled with stopped cars and tiny people looking down. At the periphery of her vision was a tangled mass of metal; it lay in a thin pool of broken glass.

And directly above her, smiling, his hand cool against her brow, was Martin.

'Good morning, Emily my Emily.'

Some hold the world will end with fire . . .

Her mind was beginning to work. Everything was slow, languid; pictures danced just beyond her memory and refused to clarify themselves. Something had happened, she remembered that much. She had been driving, driving the Citroën through the rain and darkness, looking for . . .

'You went over the edge, poor darling. A few scary

moments for you. I'm so sorry.' He bent and kissed her, a swift generous kiss that held more of himself than she had yet been offered. 'But you're all right now, really. It's all right.'

'Over the edge.' She made no move to get up. Her body felt as strange and different as her mind; it seemed lighter, less intrusive. And there was a peculiar place beyond her eyes, a new emptiness that was almost painful.

Some hold with ice . . .

A tiny wreath of mist drifted across her face, across Martin's hand. As if the mist had been a written cue, something presented itself to her.

'There was a wasp in the car. It stung me. I remember that.' The memory, though clear, seemed remote and oddly unreal. Emily moved at last, bringing a hand up to the side of her neck. It was smooth, untouched. 'Didn't it sting me?'

'Yes.' Martin had been sitting beside her. Now he lay down, stretching out to his full length, slipping one arm under her shoulders. She automatically lifted her head to accommodate that arm and snuggled against him. Everything was strange, very strange; little things kept coming back and she kept looking at them. They were things that should have horrified her, yet they did not. Nothing seemed to matter.

From far above them came the distant wailing of a siren. A police car, Emily thought dreamily, or an ambulance. What the hell is going on here? And why don't I care?

'Those people up there,' she said tentatively. 'They're going to think we're crazy, lying out here, snuggling in the wet grass.' She had been rolling, turning. Surely she had done that, her hands thrown up to shield her burning face, the entire universe going round and round. Or had it been her going round and round? 'They will, Martin.'

'They can't see us.' He spoke simply, happily. 'They can't see us at all, not you, not me. They see the car, of course, what's left of the car. That's why they've all stopped up there.'

The wet grass should have been cold against her, it should be soaking through the velvet. She should have been shivering with cold, there should be bones broken, teeth missing, pain beyond endurance. She had gone over the cliff, she had been stung and the car had crashed into a bottomless well of darkness. She felt nothing at all, beyond the physical reality of Martin beside her; he alone was real. This time, she knew the reason.

'I died, didn't I? I died in the car.'

'Don't worry about it, Emily my Emily.' Martin got to his feet, took her hands in his, pulled her upright. He kissed her and the kiss was real, warm, she could feel it more intensely than she had ever felt anything before.

From what I've tasted of desire . . .

I died, she thought wonderingly. I was worried about a midlife crisis, a kind of death. And instead I actually did die. And it feels great.

She burst out laughing.

'Come along.' He dropped his arm across her shoulders, the old familiar gesture. His hand was warm, and real, and his smile, the electricity of her existence, hid nothing. Fire, she thought, fire. 'Let's move on, shall we? You don't really want to be here when they pull you out of the wreckage, do you? Altogether too grim, my lovely one.'

'You're damned right I don't.' They began to walk north, up the length of the valley, away from what remained of the Citroën. There was activity on the ridge, what looked like a fire engine, several uniformed figures uncoiling ropes and beginning to make their way down the hillside. Something was nagging at her, an unresolved question; it was ironic, she thought, very nearly funny, that she could ask him anything in the world right now, all those questions he had the answers to. He would tell her if she asked, and she no longer wanted to; she only had one question. 'Martin, will you tell me one thing?'

'Of course I will.' The black frock coat brushed against the velvet of her dress. 'I'll tell you anything you like. Ask me anything.'

'What is this funny little space behind my eyes? It's like, I don't know, a bowl that used to hold flowers, and now the flowers have been taken out. Is that because I'm dead?'

He stopped, turning her to face him. 'Is it right here?' He stooped, laid his fingers lightly above the bridge of her nose. 'Is it right here, that empty bowl, right where I'm touching?'

'You know it is. Is it because I'm dead, Martin, St Martin, St Martin of the Fields? Is it?'

'St Martin-*in*-the-Fields, and the answer is no. The empty space is where Emmy Deer used to live. She's gone, Emily my Emily; she's what really died last night. Now, what shall we do today, tonight, for ever? Shall we walk and walk, knowing that we won't ever tire of it, or shall we go up this impossible hill and climb over the lich-gate and dance in the grass?'

Back in the real world, Emily thought, life was going on. People, Judy Waite and Marie-France and Gina Wade back in her California office, they would all be going about their business. Eventually, they would learn what had happened, and they would react, grieving or horrified or uncertain, each in their own way. Gary and his consort would hear of it. Perhaps her death would rate a mention in the San Francisco papers; perhaps a young waitress would read of it, glancing involuntarily at the glass-encased wasp on her wall, cold for a moment without knowing why.

She looked steadily into Martin's face. She could read it now, recognize it. Its mystery, after all, was her own.

'Your choice, Emily darling,' he said.

Deborah Grabien
Plainsong £4.99

'Things have been fairly quiet these two thousand years, and now it's all happening at once,' said Gad the cat . . .

A fable for the millennium.

After the mysterious plague, pregnant Julia believes herself the only survivor. She lives out lazy, empty days in a green and pleasant countryside.

Until one sunny afternoon she meets the child Dilly and her little sister, Gad the cat and the four ravens – companions, protectors and guides as the new life approaches . . .

'Full of marvels . . . both witty and wise, always engrossing, and often profound'
KATHERINE KERR

'This beautifully written fable set in England in the near future . . . makes the fantastic seem possible'
PUBLISHERS NEWS